IT'S ONLY A CLOCKWORK MOON

BILLY O'SHEA

It's only a
CLOCKWORK
MOON

BLACK SWAN

ISBN 9788799642618

Lyrics from the following songs are quoted in this book:
The Holy Ground (trad.)
Aba Daba Honeymoon by Arthur Fields and Walter Donovan
The Laughing Policeman by Charles Penrose
It's Only A Paper Moon by Harold Arlen, E. Y. Harburg and Billy Rose

The author has made all reasonable efforts to trace all
rights holders to any copyrighted material used in this book.
In cases where these efforts have not been successful, the
author welcomes communications from copyright holders,
so that the appropriate acknowledgements can be made in
future editions, and to settle other permission matters.

Front cover illustration:
Andrey Dorozhko (www.andreydrz.com)

Originally published in Denmark by
Black Swan, Copenhagen (www.blackswan.dk)

For Christopher, Catriona and Ciara

'In the beginning was the word. And the word was: Begin.'

- Marginal note in illuminated copy of programming code, prob. monastic, 22nd century.

*Extract from The Life of Saint Michael, Kilkiernan manus.
A.2303, date unknown*

A pilgrim once came to Saint Michael and asked him if all machines were of the devil. And the Saint answered him thus: 'The machines that eat of the fruits of the air and of human labour are of the angels, and these you may use as you will. But of the machines that eat of the fruits of the earth, and that burn the stones and blacken the fair fields, these you shall not touch with a bargepole, for these are of the demons that dwell beneath the ground, and of no manner of such machines shall you profit, neither of their motion nor of their products. And neither shall you suffer your poor and your slaves to go beneath the ground to dig and to mine the fruits of the earth for these machines.'

Added beneath, in a different hand:
And the pilgrim further asked if it would be alright to mine such fruits of the earth as are used for trade and decoration, and Saint Michael replied that that would be quite all right, provided that the profits were given to the true Anglian Church for the protection of the miners against evil.

CHAPTER ONE

There are advantages to not looking like a monk when you are in a drinking establishment, and Christopher Xavier Mc-Murphy looked nothing at all like one. On the contrary, with a stocky build and blue-tattooed arms showing beneath his black leather jerkin, he looked like he belonged right there in the tavern. His dark hair had grown out, leaving no trace of a tonsure, though he sometimes unthinkingly swept a hand across his head just to make sure.

When he ordered a mug of beer the barman sized him up with a glance and answered him in Alban. Cheek of the man, thought Brother Christopher. This was an Anglian town, or was meant to be. He surely ought to be able to buy a beer in the Lord's language. Still, at least it must mean he didn't look suspicious.

'*Tapadh leat*,' he thanked the barman grumpily when the beer came. Then he continued in Anglian. 'A friend of mine will be coming in shortly. We have some business to attend to. Will you have one yourself?'

He pushed a silver coin across the counter. The barman pocketed it.

'Blind and deaf, me,' he said.

Brother Christopher took his beer back to his corner table.

The courier was late. Christopher did not want to risk taking his typically monkish timepiece out of his pocket, but it must be surely be half an hour past the arranged time. He had chosen the tavern carefully – not so central as to be busy at this hour of the afternoon, nor so peripheral that a stranger would stand out among the locals. A little light entered through stained-glass windows, giving the place an oddly chapel-like air. The few other customers present seemed to be engaged in their own very private business.

The door opened, admitting a slice of sunlight that revealed a galaxy of dust motes in the air. But it was only a barefoot peasant woman selling flowers, and the barman shooed her out.

I will give him until I hear the nones of St Kevin's, thought Brother Christopher, but no longer.

Shortly afterwards the door opened again and a small, slender, red-haired young man entered. He was wearing a long cloak despite the warm weather, and looked nervously back and forth among the faces.

Brother Christopher stood up, smiled, and extended his hand in the traditional Anglian greeting.

'What is it? Is there trouble?' he asked quietly, still smiling, as he grasped the other man's hand.

'Trouble? No…'

'Then calm down, man. You look like a ferret in a greyhound pen. I'll get you a beer.'

'Actually, I don't…' began the man, then caught Christopher's glance. He sat down.

Brother Christopher returned from the bar with a mug of porter and placed it in front of the stranger.

'So – you're Adam, I take it? How was your journey?' he asked cheerily. The man looked confused.

'The journey? It went well. By barge downriver to Thorgrimstown, and thence on horseback to…'

'And the roads?' interrupted Christopher. 'Dry, I hope?'

It was high summer, and it had not rained for a week.

'Yes, they were…quite dry,' answered the man.

'Good, good,' said Brother Christopher. 'But your burden looks heavy, my friend. Why not put it down?'

'My burden?'

With his eyes, Christopher indicated the sheaf of papers protruding from beneath the man's cloak.

'Just put it on the table in front of you,' said Brother Christopher, still smiling.

The young man looked around him almost theatrically as he

brought out the papers. Christopher resisted the urge to cast his eyes up to heaven.

'Excellent! Thank you!' he said, taking the documents and putting them into his leather satchel.

'Now let us drink up like old pals. When we leave, we will say goodbye outside. Then you go to the left, and I will go to the right. You have your transport arranged?'

The red-haired man nodded.

'I have a man and horses at St Thomas Gate.'

'Good man.'

Christopher smiled and raised his beer. As he did so, he glanced over towards the bar. The barman was nowhere to be seen. Christopher drained the mug, got up, and walked across the room.

'Barkeep! We're dry!'

No-one appeared from the back room. Christopher craned his neck to look inside. The room was empty. He swung around and strode rapidly back to the table.

'Get up! We must go! Now!'

Christopher pulled the bewildered man to his feet and bundled him through a back door and out into the urine-smelling back yard. There was a door in the side wall, but it was bolted and padlocked.

'Here – I'll give you a leg up.'

The other man uncertainly placed a sandaled foot into the cupped hands of the monk, who gave a powerful heave and launched him up onto the top of the wall, where he clung, his cloak flapping around him. The back door opened and the barman shouted out after them.

'You! Hey, you!'

Christopher hopped up onto a beer barrel and dragged himself and his leather satchel up onto the top of the wall, then jumped down on the other side.

'Come on, quick!'

The red-haired man let out a yelp as he hit the ground. A

group of four or five Guards appeared at the corner of the street and began to run towards them. One of them began blowing a whistle.

'This way!'

The red-haired man was limping and could not keep up. Christopher ran back to him and dragged him into a side alley, then down another. The 'kettles' started up, as the local people of Garrystown began banging bin lids and buckets with hammers and fire tongs – though whether to warn the neighbourhood, or the fleeing men, or just in celebration of a little afternoon entertainment, it was impossible to say. It was traditional.

The narrow alley led to a row of respectable but run-down-looking town houses in a short street leading down towards the river. Their front doors gave directly onto the road. Christopher hammered a staccato on one of them.

The red door opened on a chain. A dark-haired woman in her thirties, dressed in startlingly fine clothes, looked out.

'We're closed,' she said.

'Hello, Sissie.'

She glanced at his face in surprise.

'Is it you, Chrissie Mac?'

'It is. Can we come in? We're in a spot of bother.'

The woman hesitated. The whistles and banging were loud all around them. She unhooked the chain.

'I'm going to regret this, amn't I?'

'You won't, Sissie.'

'Cecilia to you, chief.'

She led them down a narrow hall and into a dark back kitchen. The iron range was lit. Christopher helped the young man into a chair.

'So? What are you after doing now?' asked Sissie.

'Notton. They didn't like the cut of me, is all.' Christopher relaxed easily into the dialect of his home streets.

'Sure who would, the mug of you! You'll have some tea?'

Without waiting for an answer she began to fill a kettle with water from the pail.

'I thought you'd joined the teds?' she remarked over her shoulder.

'I did, Sissie.'

'So what's this? A day off?'

'You might say that.'

She looked at them, the kettle in her hand.

'Well, it's no business of mine. You'll be wanting to lay low, I suppose?'

'Just till the morning.'

'You'll have to pay our usual rates. I can't let a room go for nothing.'

'I will Sissie, and more. Sure you're taking a risk.'

She put the kettle on the range.

'I'm not doing it for you, Chrissie.' She pointed at one of the tattoos on his arm. 'She was a good woman, God rest her.'

She walked over to a row of keys hanging from the wall and took one down.

'Room twelve, first landing, on the left. I'll bring you up the tea and a bite to eat.'

'God bless you, Sissie. You're a decent woman.'

'Go on away with ye.'

The house smelled of musty damp and perfume. A few portraits hung in the hall in a futile attempt at respectability. The red-haired man had to more or less hop up the narrow stairs, supported by Christopher. Room twelve was at the back of the house, and was bare except for a double bed and a small bedside table.

The clanging noise outside had died away. Christopher helped his companion over to the bed, where he sat staring forlornly at the floor.

'So – what do they call you?' asked Christopher.

'Adam.'

'I mean your real name.'

'It's...Joe.'

'Holy Joe?'

The other man looked blank.

'Never mind. I'm Brother Christopher. Have you done this sort of thing before?'

Joe shook his head.

'First time.'

'Thought it might be. How bad is the ankle?'

'I can't put my weight on it.'

'I have a donkey tethered a mile out the Carrarine road. If you can get that far, it can carry you the rest of the way to the Rock.'

Joe looked appalled.

'I can't go to the Rock! I have to get back to Kilkiernan!'

'You can't go back through the city now, man! A red-haired man with a limp? They'd pick you up in a minute. And then they'd give you the thumbscrew, and you'd tell them everything. You'll have to come with me.'

There was a knock on the door and Sissie entered, carrying a tray with a teapot and chipped teacups, and a plate of triangular sandwiches of ham and lettuce.

'Stay in here and don't come out,' she said. 'We get all sorts in here. Guards, too. So don't show yourselves. There's a pot under the bed.'

She walked over to the window and opened it.

'You know your way across the roofs, if I remember rightly?' she asked with a sardonic smile.

'I do. But I'd hardly be able to go that way with my friend. His foot's hurt.'

She nodded.

'Then make sure you go out the door early, before anyone's about. You can pay me now. I won't be around in the morning.'

Christopher took a purse out of his satchel and placed three silver coins in her hand. She kept her palm out.

'Silver's not what it was, Chrissie. Your lads have paid too many bills with it. It's gold people are looking for these days.'

Christopher grimaced and handed over another two coins.

'Danger money, so,' he said. 'And I'll say a prayer for you.'

'You will of course. Sleep well.'

When she was gone, Christopher poured out the tea.

'What bills?' asked Joe suspiciously.

Christopher laughed.

'The monks of St Michael aren't big customers here, if that's what you're thinking. We buy all our materials from the city. Nails, sailcloth, ropes. Everything except timber. We have silver enough from the mine to pay for it. But the prices keep going up.'

'Inflation?'

'Greed. They know we have nowhere else to go. But they'll be laughing on the other side of their faces one of these days when the Albans take over.'

He took a sandwich from the tray and sat down on the bed beside the other man.

'Right. Let's see what delights Kilkiernan has for us this time.'

Christopher opened his satchel and carefully took out the sheaf of papers, examining the documents one at a time. He used a small magnifying glass to examine the details.

'We don't need all this decoration,' he said. 'I mean, it's beautifully done, but these are blueprints and codes, not sacred texts.'

'The bishop says the copies are made for the glory of God, not man,' said Joe.

'The bishop of Kilkiernan is an unworldly man. But what God needs right now are weapons, and the sooner, the better. Any gun designs in here?'

'The bishop says we are to stop killing people.'

Christopher glanced sharply across at the other man.

'He does, does he? And how does he propose we defend ourselves?'

'The bishop says it is killing people that has brought the

curse of the Albans upon us. He says we should obey the Bible and not kill.'

'Seriously? Not even the Albans?'

Joe shook his head.

'We should pray for them.' He gave a shrug to indicate that the policy was nothing to do with him.

'He'd agree with our abbot, so. God save us all from idealists,' muttered Christopher through a mouthful of sandwich. He drew out another document, and snorted in amusement.

'And just what in hell is this supposed to be?'

Joe cringed at the profanity.

'It's a boat. A new type of boat.'

'It looks like a fish! Where are the sails?'

'It has rotary sails – here and here. They can be retracted into the hull when the boat is submerged.'

'Submerged!'

'It's designed to go beneath the water – for when you need to escape.'

Christopher studied the design.

'Joe, let me tell you something. Before I joined the teds I used to be a sailor. A fisherman. Take it from me, this yoke is pure mad. It'll never work. Where did it come from?'

'It's based on a design by one of the ancients. A monk called Holland.'

'From Holland? That explains a lot.'

Joe shook his head.

'No, he was from round here. But the design has been adapted a lot.'

'Is this Brother Anselm's work again?'

Joe shook his head.

'Not this time.'

'Well, it has the mark of his lunacy,' said Christopher. 'Listen, when you get back to Kilkiernan, tell them we need fighting machines, gun designs, explosives recipes, not contrivances like this.'

'The Bishop said we must become fishers of men. All men.'

'In *this*?'

'I've no notion. You'll have to ask your abbot. He was the one who ordered it.'

Brother Christopher stared at the drawing of the bizarre craft. Whatever this was about, he hoped it did not involve him. But he was the only real sailor on the Rock.

CHAPTER TWO

The farmer looks around my little basement shop at the timepieces. His old leather boots are dragging mud across the red-tiled floor.

'You are a clockmaker?' he asks.

No, I am a cheesemaker, you oaf. I just collect clocks as a hobby.

'Indeed I am, sir. What can I do for you?'

He jerks a thumb towards the door.

'It's out on the cart.'

He doesn't want to bring it in – it might be a waste of effort, after all. So we go outside onto the street to inspect the device. Wrapped in old newspaper on the back of a cart is a long pendulum clock in a fine wooden case. Guckstad mechanism, I would guess. Probably about a century old. But it has seen better days.

'Can you fix that?'

'I don't know, it depends on what's wrong with it. It might just need adjustment, or it might need the whole works replacing.'

I still don't speak Northlandish very well. It comes out half Kantish. I have developed the habit of speaking slowly, in case people have trouble understanding my accent. Some people think that means I am slow of mind, too. Come to that, some people have trouble understanding that we are no longer at war.

'What will it cost?'

I hesitate. He is my first customer this week.

'I can fix it for half a sovereign. In advance.'

The parts alone might cost me more than that. But if I am lucky, it will just need freshening up.

'Done.'

Between us we manhandle the clock out of the cart and

down the steps into the shop. He laboriously counts out fifty pennies onto the counter, and leaves without another word.

I get out my tools and open up the back of the clock to take a look at its workings. Marieke comes out from the back room.

'Customer?'

'Mm. For half a sovereign.'

'That won't pay the rent.'

'No. But it will buy us food today.'

The clock must have been standing by the farmer's fireplace – the gears are coated in a fine layer of soot. That is probably all that is wrong with it. I should take the works apart and soak them in alcohol. No, not for half a sovereign. Brown soap and a good scrub, then. I go into the back room to put the kettle on the stove, then take a cloth and go back out to clean the mud off the floor. It reminds me of the day, up at her father's house, when Marieke showed me how to clean and polish my boots.

'You can't tell me people don't polish their boots in Kantarborg, Karl! Did you never do it at home?'

'The servants did it.'

She cocked her head and gave me an ironic smile as though I was joking, but when I didn't smile back her eyes widened and she brought her hand up to her mouth.

'You had servants?'

I nodded. And then she laughed that broad, open laugh of hers, wiping away the tears with her sleeve. I didn't know women could laugh like that before I came to Sandviken.

Marieke doesn't ask me much about my life before. I thought at first she was being discreet, until I realised that my old life is utterly irrelevant here. Sandviken may be almost within sight of Kantarborg, just across the water, but this is not just a different country – it's a different world. *Fine ways buy no beans*, they say here. They have their own league table of prestige, and a man with no local roots doesn't even figure on it, whoever he might once have been.

She's not laughing today, though. In fact, she is looking a bit tired. I hope she is not sick. Or, God help us, with child.

We don't want children yet – not when I am in hock and the work is scarce. But there are ways to avoid fecundity. On our wedding night, Marieke was at first shocked, then amazed, then enthusiastic. Eventually, laughing, I had to plead with her to be still, for fear that old Svensson upstairs would think someone was being murdered down here. It was Erika's teaching, of course. Marieke has never asked me where I learned these things. I suppose she thinks that since I studied engineering in the big city, I must know everything.

Now she puts on her coat, takes the farmer's coins, and heads off to the market to buy vegetables. There is a plot of land at the back of our house, much overgrown, but it belongs to Svensson and he won't let us touch it. It offends Marieke's Lowlander heart to see good planting soil going to waste, but there is nothing we can do.

It is a dull day and a little rain spatters against the shop panes. There probably won't be any more customers today.

Marieke was puzzled by me when we met – is puzzled still. Every day I seem to do something that amuses her. Up at her father's house, before we were married, I heard the sisters giggling in the kitchen. My Northlandish was not good then, but I could catch the gist of it: *He keeps a handkerchief up his sleeve, like a fine lady. He washes his hands before he eats.* But if I was wearing my silken Kantarborg jacket, Marieke would always suggest that we took a walk through town. If I asked her why, she'd just smile. It was old, that jacket, and nothing special, mind you.

Hendrik wasn't much impressed at first with the man his daughter was seeing – this Kantarborgan with his high-born ways and not a penny to his name. But he warmed to me when I fixed his great-grandfather's clock on the square. Hendrik is a carpenter and clog-maker, and a man gains his respect if he has a skill. He helped us with the shop when we were setting up. 'One less shoe shop in town,' he said with pleasure. 'I'll have the last laugh yet on cobbler Svensson.'

I had asked the town council for permission to repair the clock, partly, I admit, in the hope of currying favour with Marieke's family – and of course to advertise my skills to the town in general. But partly also because it was simply such a beautiful mechanism: fine, ancient and alien. And an automaton, as well: on the hour, a solemn tune would play, a wooden door would open, and a parade of aristocratic men and women in strange clothing would emerge, bowing and dancing. It was quite entrancing to watch, especially for the local children.

I was proud of my work when I got the clock working again, but Marieke seemed unimpressed. I was a little peeved at this at first, until I realised that it was part of the Northland ethos. You must always disparage your own efforts, and never praise anyone else, even if you are proud of them. Especially if you are proud of them. They are suspicious of flattery. They have a saying: Fear three things above all; hunger, cold and the praise of strangers. Well, I am learning.

'I suppose you don't have much experience of such things around here,' I said huffily.

'I have something like that up at the house. I'll show it to you.'

It turned out to be a sewing-box that had belonged to her mother. Outwardly it was just an ordinary cabinet, but when you opened it a tune played, and a small figure of a dancing girl sprang up and twirled around. A simple contrivance, but rather charming.

'I used to love it when I was a little girl. It is all I have left of my mother.'

'How old is it?'

'Very old. It came with my family from the Lowlands.'

'Perhaps you should get it valued.'

'No! No-one must see this.'

With that she quickly packed it away again. It was special to her, very private. And somehow I knew at that moment that she would consent to marry me.

Things went well for me here at first. Everyone wanted their clocks fixed after the 'the Long Quiet', as they called it. (I thought at first that referred to the absence of clocks ticking. I was very naive back then.) And I soon learned the tradesman's tricks. Never do a job too fast, they'll wonder what they're paying you for. These are country people, they don't throw their money around. Always keep a piece overnight, even if you can see that all it needs is oiling. Well, I do come from a merchant's family after all. Perhaps there is more of my father in me than I knew.

Though on the other hand, perhaps not enough, because there was rarely a week any more when the sums added up. Before I came here time had abandoned this town – in more ways than one – but now time is restored, and you can hear the chiming of bells at night from the houses all along the canal front. The two-faced liar on the square lies no more. Plenty of clockmakers can make a living in the city, but Sandviken is no Kantarborg. I did my best to put a brave face on it in front of Marieke, but things were much worse than even she suspected.

On Sundays Marieke attends chapel with her family, while I go to the Cat and Crown. The Cat has become something of a Sunday club for the local merchants and shopkeepers – the chamber of commerce, they call it ironically. The pipe smoke hangs heavy in the air as they discuss the ways of the world – by which, of course, they meant Sandviken. Men in black suits that went out of fashion twenty years ago. Self-satisfied, canny, expansive on any subject but themselves. The pharmacist never pays for his drinks. It wasn't until I sampled the schnapps that I realised why.

The peaceable first impression I received of the town was of course an illusion. There had been conflicts and strife here, just like everywhere else; families against families, going back generations, even before the Schisms. And beyond the feuds, there are the skirmishes and the stories: Who cheated whom on that land deal, who turned their back on whom outside church this morning, whose wife gets free bread at the baker's every Saturday. In its own way, it's almost as bad as being at court.

There are rumours about me, too, of course – the favourite theory being that I was in the rebellion and am hiding out here. I let them talk, and change the subject if Kantarborg comes up. For them, that confirms I am a rebel. They like that; they are all rebels around here. Against the king or the bailiff or the nobles, whoever is in power or claims to be the law. If I were to say that I used to be a counsellor in the royal court, a confidante of the Young King, they would only smile at me pityingly, the way they smile at Pétur Jansson when he claims King Magnus was his real father. So I am a rebel in hiding, and a clockmaker by trade. That is good – it gives them a box to put me in. Nothing disturbs country people so much as not knowing where to put somebody.

It was on a Sunday morning in the Cat that I made my big mistake. I was off my guard, relaxing with a beer. I was trying to make it last a long time, and perhaps the stranger noticed that. Or, more likely, the whole thing had been planned well in advance. At any rate, he came and sat down at my table.

'Was that a Kantarborgan accent I heard? Delighted to meet you! Hapgaard is the name. But look, let me buy you a beer, I'm dying to talk to someone in Kantish for a change. I've been in this country a month and I've hardly been able to have a single decent conversation.'

I missed my native language too, so the company was not unwelcome. The stranger was engaging, amusing and very talkative. He wore a smart dark suit and had an excellent Gudsberg timepiece in his vest pocket, which I admired. He was fascinated when he heard that I was a clockmaker.

'You repaired the clock in the square? Really? The one with the automata? Why, that's marvellous! You must be a very talented man.'

He bought me that beer, and then another, against my protestations. By midday we had become fast friends, and he insisted on buying me lunch. I asked him what his line of work was, and he told me he was involved in providing help to small businesses.

'You simply would not believe how many skilled artisans are being forced out of business because they cannot get the right short-term financing to tide them through the hard times. It's disgraceful. They go to the banks, and the banks turn them away. But these craftspeople are the lifeblood of our economy! Without them, the whole shooting gallery collapses! And then what will we all do?'

He stabbed at his lunch plate with his fork for emphasis. It had been quite some time since I had last tasted meat.

When I talked about my own problems in the clock-making trade, he listened with great sympathy.

'No! And he never came back to pay you! But that's disgraceful! Mind you, what would you expect of the farmers around here? I have heard the same story time and time again. But tell me, a man with your talents, why don't you do more work for the nobility? They have the money, and I'm sure they have plenty of clocks to be repaired.'

I explained that the clocks belonging to the local gentry were, like their owners, of antique and delicate disposition, and would require much more sophisticated tools than those I had at my disposal.

'Well, look; I hope you don't think I'm speaking out of turn here, but this is exactly the kind of problem I deal with every day. You are stuck in a downward spiral; customers who pay too little, and the work slowly drying up. You need to raise your sights a bit, get well-paying jobs, so that you can also put a little bit aside to promote your skills and the reputation of your business. That's how to get into an upward spiral. There's plenty of good work available for a man with skills. But of course you must first of all invest in new tools, that's essential.'

'But how can I do that? I don't make enough to pay the rent, let alone make investments.'

'Well, I can see you are a gentleman, so obviously you are not someone who likes to be in debt, but every businessman needs to borrow, you know. You mustn't be afraid of it. It's the only way out of a situation like yours. I mean, to do high-quality work at high volume, you would need, what? A good staking and jewelling set, some diamond saws, pin vices, a microscope...'

He seemed remarkably well-informed about clockmakers' tools. I was impressed.

'Then, once you have the right tools, you start getting the quality jobs in, and within a year you will be one of the most respected merchants in town. The nobles will be fighting for space in your order book. And you will no longer need to make a beer last an hour.'

Well, you've guessed it: the deal was done, and a thousand Northlandish sovereigns were handed to me in a large sack one night by a burly man I had never seen before, and who seemed to be of a rather less genial disposition than Hapgaard. To tell the truth, I was beginning to feel somewhat nervous about the whole affair, but felt that I would have to go through with it now. As recommended, I used most of the money to buy the best tools available, and spent what was left on advertising in the local newspapers.

Weeks went by. I received a few more jobs than usual, but nothing like enough to keep up the interest payments, which were hefty. The local nobles turned out to be even more parsimonious than the farmers, and many of them had fallen on hard times since the enforced union of our two countries. What's more, while the farmers would come to me, the nobility expected their artisans to come to them. Not having a horse of my own, I ended up spending far too much money on hired carriages, and the result was often a net loss. Some of the gentry were apologetic about the low prices they were prepared to pay, and hinted that there would be much more work for me in future. There never was.

Eventually, of course, I fell behind with the payments, and the threatening letters began to arrive. I hid them from Marieke. They were unsigned, but clearly not written by the erudite Hapgaard. '*If you don't belive we wud do this you are a ful,*' said one. '*We no you have a wife. Think of her and find the money.*'

I was a fool all right, and ten times a fool. I needed no loan shark to tell me that. Fear three things above all…

As I work on the farmer's clock, Marieke returns from the market with potatoes, carrots, leeks. The season has been good, and vegetables cheap and abundant – but prices will be rising soon as the days grew shorter.

'There is a carriage on the square,' she says as she passes me.

There are always carriages on the square, what is she talking about? I make a note to ask her about it later. For now, I concentrate on cleaning the clock.

It was nearly closing time when I saw a shadow coming down the shop steps. 'Those look like women's shoes', I thought to myself – and my heart quickened.

I knew him the moment he came in, though he was wearing a hooded cloak, with a scarf pulled up over his mouth. And from that moment on, I can't quite explain it, but all I felt was a white rage. Not because of anything that had happened in the past, but simply because he would seek me out here. In my shop. In front of my wife. In this town.

He removed the scarf, though not the hood.

'Good afternoon,' he said in Northlandish. He had grown a beard, but the brown eyes were unmistakeable.

'Why the masquerade?' I asked in Kantish. I didn't even bother with Anglian.

'It is for your own protection,' he muttered, sticking to Northlandish.

'I have a clock I would like you to look at,' he said, a little more loudly, placing a carriage clock on the counter.

'This?' I picked it up. It was an unremarkable machine,

though decorated in the ornate style of the court.

'Yes, but there is also another device I need built. It is rather unusual, and you are the only person I can turn to.'

'I regret to say that I am somewhat booked up for the foreseeable future, *sir*.'

That stung him. Anger flashed in his eyes.

'Have a care, Clockmaker!'

'It is for your own protection, *sir*,' I replied.

He looked at me a moment, then he smiled.

'Karl, you and I have a long history together. Can we not at least be civil? You have a wife now, I hear. No children yet? Maybe times are a little hard in the clock-making trade. The carriage clock just needs a new spring, I think. Perhaps you would allow me to pay you a small advance.'

It's an odd thing, but I think it was because of the velvet purse that I took it. When he put it on the counter, I remember thinking, *Marieke would like that little bag.* I picked it up.

'I would have to leave here, I take it?' I asked.

'For a while.'

'I want time to think about it.'

He smiled.

'Of course, of course. I will collect the clock in a week's time. And perhaps by then you will have made up your mind on the other matter.'

I nodded. He turned and walked out the door and up the steps. Outside, a couple of other men stepped out of the shadows and accompanied him down the street. I watched them go.

Marieke came out of the back room.

'Another customer?'

'Yes. A man from Kantarborg.'

I opened the purse and poured the coins out onto the counter. Marieke gasped.

'*Verdomme*, Karl! That's a whole month's income!'

I picked up a couple of the coins. Some bore Queen Gudrun's face – the rest were shiny and freshly-minted, with the profiles of the Young King and Ingeborg, his Northlander queen.

She looked at me.

'Was it someone you knew?'

I nodded.

'Is he dangerous?'

'Yes.'

After dinner, I took out my set square and compass as usual, while Marieke read to me from the newspaper. Lowlander women are educated. They have their own school here and pay tithes to their chapel for its upkeep. The older generation keep up the language, too – though so discreetly that at first I thought it was a language of murmurs. Marieke and her sisters can understand it, but to each other they speak only Northlandish. Physically they differ little from the Northlanders, so it may be that in a generation or two they will be indistinguishable, and only their surnames will remain to tell of their origin.

(At least, so it seemed to me. I voiced this thought to Marieke one evening as we sat by the stove, but she shook her head. She spoke in a low voice, even though we were quite alone.

'I will tell you what my father said: "You are not a North-lander until you can speak your mind without being told to go back where you came from." That's what he learned in the Schisms.'

'But he was born here!'

'It makes no difference.'

She leaned over to poke the fire.

'They believe in blood.'

It was the first time I had ever heard her refer to the North-landers as 'they'. It shocked me a little.)

Marieke read the headlines. Things were not going well in the North. The tribes were angry about the iron mines in their territories, which they said were desecrating their sacred sites. They had joined forces with the Häkonite rebels and had taken control of large areas. Queen Gudrun was claiming the rebels were being armed by the Ursans…The tip of my pencil snapped. Marieke looked up. It was not like me to swear.

'Karl?'

'War again! Why must everything always end in war!'

I got up angrily and went to find a knife to sharpen my pencil. She looked at me, but said nothing. She's no fool, but what could I tell her? Anything I could say might put her in danger.

I lay awake a long time that night. It's odd how one's life can suddenly become complicated – from one moment to the next, almost. Damn the man! It seemed I would have to accept. What choice did I have? But his offers were never simple, and never without danger. I just hoped it did not involve going underground again.

Exactly a week later, a hooded figure came down the steps again. But he had grown taller in the meantime. He entered the shop, threw back the hood, and laughed. It was Johansson.

'Expecting someone else, were you?'

Beneath the cloak he was wearing his naval uniform. I cannot deny it – I was pleased to see him. I shook his hand warmly. Marieke came out to see who it was.

'Marieke, this is Lieutenant Johansson. We knew each other at university.'

'Captain, now. I have my own command - *Ariadne*. But call me Kaare, madam, please.'

Marieke looked the tall young officer up and down, took his hand, and, to my irritation, curtsied.

'You must stay for dinner, sir.'

'I was hoping you would ask. I brought something.'

He produced a bottle and handed it to Marieke, who looked at it wonderingly. Around here they drink only beer and schnapps. It is entirely possible that she had never in her life seen a bottle of wine before.

Over dinner, Johansson regaled us with tales of his life at sea, of lucky escapes and near misses, and of humorous situations he had found himself in. Being a Northlander by birth, he of course spoke the language perfectly. Marieke was charmed. Women generally are charmed by Johansson. Eventually, no doubt sensing that he and I needed to talk, she declared that she was exhausted and retired behind the curtain to the bed.

Johansson and I switched to Kantish.

'I suppose he wants an answer?'

'Indeed so. And the sooner, the better.'

'Kaare, we need the money. You can see that. But what does he want from me?'

'I honestly don't know. But I do know that whatever it is, only you can do it. Otherwise he wouldn't have come calling here in person. He took a real risk for you, you know, coming here like that.'

'He wants me for some grand scheme of his, I'm in no doubt of that. When he needs people, he always presents it as a great favour to them.'

'But if you need the money, then he *is* doing you a favour, isn't he?'

I was silent a moment.

'If I have to go away, I want her provided for,' I said, nodding at the curtain.

'Of course. He mentioned that you were making around sixteen sovereigns a month. He suggested half that for your wife. Plus whatever he pays you, naturally.'

'He's done his research. I hardly know myself nowadays what I will earn in a month.'

'He has his researchers.'

And you are his spymaster, I thought. *What have you been poking around in?*

We fell silent for a moment. The stove crackled with the last of the wood.

'Is she still in Sythorn?' I asked.

'Who?'

'You know who.'

I could see he was about to lie, then thought better of it and nodded.

'I want her released.'

Johansson sucked in a breath through his teeth.

'Karl, she was sent there by the court physician. It's a medical condition. There is no appeal.'

'Then call it a miracle cure. I want her out of there.'

'She's a dangerous woman.'

'She is not dangerous. She was duped by the enemies of the King. An injustice was done to her, and I was mixed up in it. I want that put right.'

He frowned into the dying embers of the stove.

'You drive a hard bargain, Karl.'

'Well, I am a merchant now, you know. So tell him it's take it or leave it.'

Johansson sighed.

'You've changed, haven't you?'

I looked at him.

'Yes, Kaare. I have.'

'I will tell him. But he will not be pleased. If she causes trouble, he will likely hold you responsible. And I must tell you, the King's ways have hardened since the rebellion.'

We sat for a while in silence.

'Don't you ever miss it?' he asked eventually.

I could well imagine how this place must look to him.

'It was not by accident that I came here, Kaare,' I said sharply.

He nodded.

'How do my brothers fare?' I asked.

'Jonas disappeared along with some of the other plotters. We suspect they are fled abroad. I don't know what happened to your other brother. William, was it? There's still a lot of confusion and chaos in the city, many people are displaced. It will take a while for things to settle down again.'

He got up to return to his guesthouse. I fetched the repaired carriage clock from a drawer and wrapped it in paper for him.

'And De Martinus?' I asked.

He gave a snort of laughter.

'On a clear day, you could probably wave to him from here.'

He smiled at my puzzled expression as he pulled on his cloak.

'His head is on a spike above Island Gate.'

Marieke was awake when I crawled into bed. She asked me what Johansson had wanted.

'He wants me to go away for a while. To do some work. I will earn good money if I accept.'

She was silent a few moments.

'Then you must do what you think best, Karl. I will be all right here.'

'But will you be safe?' I asked.

'I have learned to protect myself, Karl. But I can go to my family. I will be quite safe there. What about you? Johansson – Is he a man you can trust?'

I thought about that.

'I don't know. What did you think of him?'

'He's very handsome. But he's rather full of himself, isn't he? A real sailor type.'

Maybe she meant it, maybe she was just trying to reassure me. She would do that.

She smiled at me and ran her tongue over her lips.

I smiled back.

CHAPTER THREE

'How much fecking further?'

Joe was becoming less holy by the mile.

'We just have to get across the mountains. After that it's downhill all the way to the coast.'

'And how long is that going to take?'

'A couple of days, tops.'

'A couple of *days*?'

'If you don't want to come along, you can always get off that donkey and hop your way back to Kilkiernan.'

The red-haired man made no reply, but gathered his cloak about himself. Surely he can't be cold on a day like this, thought Christopher. The weather had been sweltering for weeks, and although they could feel the beginnings of the mountain breeze as they ascended the track, it failed to take more than the edge off the heat.

'Relax, Joe,' said Christopher. 'It's a beautiful day. Sure aren't you travelling in style? Sit back, take in the view.'

Joe stared moodily back down the mountainside at the distant river estuary, as the donkey jerked and stumbled its way up the track.

'Why can't we just take the road?'

'Because we wouldn't get more than a mile. The Guards would have us at the next checkpoint.'

You save a man from ending up in an interrogation chamber, you'd think he might be a bit more grateful. The midges were out in force today. Christopher waved them away irritably.

'That was quite a fuss they made about two fellows in a tavern. Wouldn't you think now they'd have bigger fish to fry?'

Silence. He tried again.

'I suppose we must have been unlucky. Group of Guards like

that, they don't usually hang around on street corners, do they?'

'I didn't say nothing to no-one!'

'I'm not saying you did, now. I'm just saying it's odd, that's all. See lad, we're on a war footing here, we have to be suspicious all the time. Are you quite sure you weren't followed to the tavern?'

'How could I possibly be sure of that!'

Right answer, Joe, thought Christopher.

After a while, the track brought them to a small ford across a stream. Christopher tethered the donkey and took a soot-blackened pot and a bag of oats from the saddle-bag.

'I'm going to boil us up some porridge,' he said. 'You keep an eye out.'

The twigs and leaves were bone dry and the fire caught quickly in the sparks from the tinder-box. Christopher had only one wooden bowl and a spoon, so they passed it back and forth as they ate. The porridge tasted of wood smoke.

'So how did you get into this line of work?' asked Christopher. 'You're not a monk.'

'My father's a butcher. The monastery is one of his customers.'

'Oh, so you're the butcher's boy? Makes sense I suppose. Used to carrying the messages, are you?'

Joe bristled.

'A monk would never get through. The Guards in Garrystown know them all.'

And if someone was planning on giving the game away, thought Christopher, *they wouldn't want it to be one of their own that got caught.*

'What about you?' asked Joe. 'You don't look much like a monk.'

'That's why I'm doing this job. I've been running this route for a while. But I think it's getting too hot for me now below in Garrystown.'

'What will happen to me at the Rock?'

'They'll probably send you off in a coracle.'

'What's that?'

'One-man balloon. It's what they do with the monks who don't behave themselves. Pack them off to the missions on the four winds, let God send them where he will.'

Joe looked appalled.

'Ah, I'm only messing with you,' said Christopher. 'They'll send you back by boat when your foot has mended.'

'Do they really send the monks away like that?'

'They take the Good Book seriously, Joe. "Go out into all the world and preach the gospel to all creation". They beatify them first, though. Seeing as they're not likely to be seen again.'

'They what?'

'They make them happy.'[1]

'How do they do that?'

'They put them in a cave for forty days and nights with nothing but holy mushrooms to eat.'

'And that makes them happy?'

'Let's just say, I've seen fellas come out giggling like idiots.'

'I bet.'

Christopher spat out a husk.

'They're meant to have a vision that tells them which way they're supposed to go. Meanwhile the lads build the coracle and fill the balloon with hydrogen. They give them a grand send-off.'

'Do any of them ever come back?'

'Once in a while. Not many. But you hear stories. Fellas starting monasteries in far-off lands. They say one guy landed on an island, then he had to take off again sharpish when it

1 Beatification, from the Latin *beatus facere*, to make blessed or happy, was originally the first step in the process of canonisation, and could therefore be performed only after the death of the person concerned. However, with the rise of the Anglian Church in the 22nd century, and especially after the monastic reforms introduced by Pope Andreas II, the procedure came to take on a different significance, as a purification rite undergone by monks in advance of some special task. See *Saints and Scholars in the Early Anglian Church*, AP Rutherford (2397), pp. 21–24.

turned to be a whalefish.'

Christopher grinned and handed the bowl back to Joe.

'That's some tall tale,' said Joe scornfully.

'Maybe it is, maybe it isn't. No-one knows what's out there, Joe.'

'Are they going to send you?'

'They might. If I cause any more trouble, like. But I'm a good man for the undercover jobs, so the abbot will probably keep me for now.' Christopher patted the satchel full of documents.

'What do they do with all that stuff out on the Rock, anyway? Do they have, like, workshops where they build things, like at Kilkiernan?'

'Not on the Rock. No room. But we need somewhere to store the documents.'

'Why, if you can't use them for anything?'

Christopher paused and looked down the mountainside.

'Let me put it to you this way, Joe. Do you know why the Dark Ages are called dark?'

'I dunno. Because they were dark?'

Christopher smiled.

'You know, that's what lots of people think. There were lots of clouds all right, after the bombs. And then there was the Long Winter, that must have been pretty dark. But that's not the reason. The reason is that we don't know what went on back then. No-one was writing anything down.'

'Sure they must have written something down. What about the sagas?'

'Most of the sagas were written down long afterwards, when the dust had settled and the machines were all gone. In the Dark Ages they hardly wrote anything, they put it all into the machines, but all that was lost in the Cataclysm. So anything we can find on paper is precious. We copy it to keep it safe. You never know, one day someone might be able to build the electric machines again.'

'I'd like to build machines like that.'

'Would you now?'

'I would. Imagine if you could bring back the Golden Age, when people didn't have to work.'

'People have always had to work, Joe. But maybe it wasn't so hard work, back then. The machines probably did a lot of it – but they burned up all the blackstone to do it. So anyway, that's the reason why we have the great library at Kilkiernan. But now we have to get it all out of harm's way, because Kilkiernan's not safe anymore.'

'The Albans aren't anywhere near us yet.'

'Well, as the bard says, you don't need a weathercock to know which way the wind blows.'

'And the Rock is safe?'

'As safe as anywhere can be. You can't land more than a small boat, and it's too windy for airships to raid.'

'Then why do you need weapons?'

Christopher gave a scornful laugh.

'You sound like our abbot. *Ah, we don't need weapons, Brother, they'll never get up the cliff.* Oh but they will, says I. One day, they will. And anyway, we have to defend the silver mine. If they take that we're sunk.'

The young man looked astonished.

'You have a silver mine on the Rock?'

Christopher laughed.

'Not on the Rock, ya eejit. On the mainland, at Cooley. That's the problem. It's too exposed. 'You can move a city, but not a well', as the saying goes. Or a mine, for that matter. It was church property for centuries before the monks found silver there.'

'I thought monks aren't supposed to go underground?'

'Not beyond sight of daylight. The local people mine it for us. Between that and the brewery, we're the biggest employers in the district. But that's our only source of income, like. It's not like Kilkiernan, we don't have any farmlands.'

'Why not?'

'Wait till you see our land. It's nothing only mountain, bog and rock. We have some sheep, that's about it. We're under the patronage of the McCarthys, so they're supposed to defend us. But that won't last long, if you ask me.'

'I heard it was McCarthys that pushed you off the mainland,' said Joe.

'Not a bit of it. The Rock just looked like the safest spot.'

'They say you're Ignatians.'

'Anyone who has something the McCarthys want will always be Ignatians. And we have the silver mine. But aren't you very well informed now, for a butcher's boy?' said Christopher, scraping out the last of the porridge.

''Twas you said I was a butcher's boy.'

Christopher noted the smile.

In the early evening, the track brought them across a ridge and down into a wide valley. A road meandered across the hill-side below them, where, beneath a clump of trees, a ramshackle two-storey house could be seen. A faded wooden sign announced the name 'O'Hanlon' above the lintel. Christopher led the donkey into the front yard. A dog barked somewhere.

The door was locked. 'They're hardly closed at this hour,' muttered Christopher, knocking. An upstairs window slid up.

'Is that you, Christy?' said a man's voice quietly.

'No, it's flipping Joseph and Mary. Did you not see the donkey? Is there any room at the inn?'

'Hold on, I'll come down.'

The door opened slightly and a bearded man peered out.

'You can't come in, Christy. It's too dangerous.'

'Ah for feck's sake Gerry, we've been on the road all day.'

'We've had the Guards round twice already looking for you. What did you do this time, steal the Alban crown jewels?'

'Is there any chance of a bite to eat at least?'

'Go on down to the byre in the low field. I'll come down to ye.'

The byre was a low stone building with a red corrugated iron roof. It stank of cow shit.

'Fine kip this is,' said Christopher, tethering the donkey to a blackthorn bush. 'I was looking forward to a decent bed before we got back to the Rock.'

'Not much luxury there, I suppose?'

'Not exactly. All the more reason to enjoy some clean sheets while you're on the road.'

The bearded man eventually reappeared with a pot of stew and a couple of bowls.

'Sorry about the accommodation lads. Best I can do.'

'Never mind,' said Christopher. 'Have you the gear?'

'Coming in tomorrow morning early. They had to go around by the back roads, avoid the roadblocks. The Guards have half the force out on the hills. What in the name of all that's holy have you done, Christy?'

'Nothing, I swear to God. Wish I had, now. At least it might be worth all the fuss.'

Brother Christopher smiled as he tucked into the stew.

Bitter is the wind tonight
Combing the white tresses of the sea
I fear no Alban raiders
From the skies on such a night

- Marginal note in illuminated copy of technical manual, monastic, late 24th century.

CHAPTER FOUR

A month later, bearing a letter with the royal seal tucked inside my jacket, I dragged my suitcase down the hill to the harbour and joined the queue at the jetty. The King's offer had not been as much as I had hoped, but it was more than three times what I had been earning lately. (No doubt Johansson had done his research well.) If I was careful with my spending, it would be enough to pay off my debts.

There was a daily steam packet now across the Sound – one of the fruits of the peace. It was not cheap – it took the last of the shiny new sovereigns I had received in my advance – but it was clearly well-used. I stood in the early morning drizzle with Northlander merchants and peasants taking eggs, cheese, chickens and even a pig or two to the market in the big city. It looked as though the citizens of Kantarborg dined rather better now than they did when I lived there.

The crossing was not a smooth one, and the rhythmic throbbing of the engine and sour smell of woodsmoke did not help anyone's stomach. The pigs were squealing, several of the passengers were leaning over the sides, and one old woman could be heard loudly saying her prayers in a voice that rose in intensity every time a wave washed over the gunwales. For myself, I was distracted from the lurching and the spray by my intense curiosity about the workings of the engine, which could be occasionally be glimpsed whenever a crewman opened a hatch to go below. The captain stood on a raised part of the deck at the fore of the vessel and shouted his commands into a speaking-tube, much like those we had had on board the airship *Freya*. I wondered that those below could hear anything through the din of the engine, but then I saw that he also had a kind of lever with a pointer indicator, which must be connected to some similar device in the engine room. Clever. A single chimney – no, *funnel* – amidships coughed out thick black smoke. As the grime rose it looked like ink being poured into water. Man, trying as usual rather ineffectually to write his name upon Nature. Given the amount of wood the thing must consume, it seemed to me that it must be a rather inefficient mode of transport, as well as being noisy and dirty. Perhaps if they could get hold of some blackstone from the north, it might be a better proposition. But with the northern isles lost, that was no doubt going to be difficult. I wondered whether the King had ever instituted his project to create a clockwork seagoing vessel, as he had talked about in the past. Maybe that was what he wanted me for this time.

At the quay in Agaholm, I was surprised and delighted to be greeted by an old friend: the clockwork locomotive, or at any rate its very close cousin, looking very handsome indeed in gleaming red paint and brass. A group of curious onlookers on the platform were examining the engine; I joined them. It looked to be my design, exactly as it had been before, though with its new livery and fittings I could not tell if it was the same machine. A man stated confidently that it was powered by hydraulics. He had read an article about it in the Journal.

My third-class ticket entitled me only to a bench seat in an open-sided carriage at the back, squeezed in among the peasants and their chickens. It was quite different to the luxury I had enjoyed on my previous rail journeys, but I was content, enjoying the sight of the fields and market gardens. It seemed an eminently sensible way of transporting people from the ferry to the city.

But just as I was beginning to relax and enjoy a dream of future civilisation, I was jerked abruptly back to the rather more sinister present. As the towers and spires of Kantarborg drew near, I saw what I at first thought were flagpoles mounted on the city walls. When I realised what they were, I looked away in disgust. Executions had been rare before the rebellion, and the public display of traitors' heads unknown. This did not bode well.

We stopped at Island Gate for clearance, which consisted of one of the King's Men walking along the train and glaring at us suspiciously. I handed him my letter – when he saw the royal seal he handed it back straight away. *If I were a spy*, I thought, *that would be the way to enter.*

The train then rattled its way across a wooden bridge and under the echoing archway in the ramparts, after which it became a street railway, like those I had seen in some of the ancient books, and mingled with the bicycles and oxcarts of Kantarborg. The smell of my home town, at least, was the same as it had always been.

But nothing else was. This was not my Kantarborg; this was a bitter and alien place, and the sight of what had once been familiar streets only made it seem more unreal.

The first thing I saw was ruined buildings everywhere. I had watched the bombardment from across the Sound, but the word in Sandviken was that it was all for show: blanks and pyrotechnics fired to frighten the city into surrender. The King of Kantarborg, they said, would never risk killing his own people. But perhaps his Northlander allies had been less restrained towards their old enemy. Someone, at any rate, had done this, and very little of the destruction had been made good, even now. I saw gutted houses with blackened timbers sticking forth, bare walls, rubble, ragged children gathered around bonfires. Rubbish and graffiti everywhere – on the remains of one wall I saw 'DOWN WITH THE KING' painted in large white letters, and a party of the King's Men just walking past, ignoring it. In my day…but my day, clearly, was gone. My city was gone. It seemed the King had been right about that: you can never go home.

The train stopped at a small platform in the city centre, and the passengers disembarked – they to the markets, I to the royal palace. The bombardment seemed to have done less damage here, or perhaps it had just been repaired faster. Only the scaffolding around the palace tower suggested that not all was as it had been. The palace itself also had many more guards than it used to have, and I had to pass through several checkpoints.

Inside the halls, however, it was as though nothing had changed. The place was as draughty and gloomy as ever. The courtiers hurried to and fro in their silk jackets and scarves. I thought I saw a small group of them glance at me curiously as they passed, then turn away contemptuously. Perhaps it was just nervousness on my part. No-one else had recognised me so far.

I decided I had better stick to the procedures, and so I showed my letter to the porter at the desk, who called a boy to take me to the audience chamber. We walked up the wide, sweeping staircase and along a long corridor in the direction of the King's private apartments. When we got to the appointed room, the boy picked up a handbell that was lying on a small table in the corridor, rang it and announced me. That was new. Before, we just used to knock on the door.

As I entered, the King was standing talking to a group of men. He acknowledged me with a wave, but continued his conversation. I found a chair and sat down – no doubt against royal protocol. Finally the men left, and I stood to offer the King my hand. I did not bow, and he did not offer me one of his brotherly embraces. He looked into my eyes.

'It's good to see you, Karl.'

He sounded as though he meant it. Perhaps he did.

'How was your journey?'

'It was fine, Majesty. I was pleased to see the locomotive again.'

'Marvellous, isn't it? Your design has certainly proved its worth. Actually we have three of them in service now. And more on the way.'

'It was a very smooth ride.'

'Rails of good Northlandish iron, brought down by sea from the mines in the north. We could never have done that before.

And this is just the beginning! I have great plans for this kingdom, Karl, great plans. Come and see.'

The King led me to an antechamber, where a giant model of the city had been laid out on a table.

'The place where you alighted is the terminus now, but soon we will have lines *here* and *here*, to the harbour and the North Gate, and one day they will pass through the East Gate and all the way to Alsina!'

Thirty leagues or more through the wildwoods. As well build a line to the moon, I thought.

'Would that not be somewhat…expensive, Majesty?'

'We must secure the peace first. But then prosperity will return to Kantarborg, you can be sure of it!'

He paused.

'You know, you could have a fine future here as chief engineer of public works, Karl.'

I made no reply to that, but pretended instead to study the model, which, of course, showed no sign of the destruction I had seen earlier that day. The ruined buildings on the south side of the city were here discreetly replaced by fine residential streets.

'What is this, Majesty?' I asked, pointing to what looked like a wooden tower near the North Gate.

'Ah! Now that is where we are currently pursuing our research into the Irrational Layer. We are delving into the unconscious of the city, Karl! And we have found some remarkable things.'

'No monsters, I hope!'

The King laughed.

'No, no monsters. Not so far. But many strange artefacts from the ancient past. I am most anxious to show them to you. I have my own team of archaeologists now, you know. Except that we do not call them that, of course. It makes people nervous. You cannot ban something as a black art for a hundred years and then make it official policy. So we call them knowledge miners.'

'What does the Church have to say about all this delving into the underground? They always held it to be sinful before.'

'They can say what they damn well like. These are new times. I have made myself Defender of the Faith, so I expect no further turbulence from that quarter. I appoint the bishops myself now.'

That was a bold move. But boldness is all, for a king, as he had once told me. Still, I wondered at what cost his survival had been won this time.

'What does the Pope say?'

'There is no Pope. Haven't you heard? Pope Nicholas disappeared from Birmingham some time ago – while you were living here before, if I remember rightly. The cardinals don't know if he's dead or alive, and they can't agree on what to do. So for now, the Church is rudderless. And that is why I must take over here. Every ship needs a captain, otherwise we risk running onto the rocks, don't you know?'

I nodded, as usual, at things I did not know at all.

'You must dine with us this evening at the Rose Castle, Karl, and meet the Queen. I am going there directly. You can ride with me.'

The King's landau was already drawn up outside. For reasons of discretion and protocol, a servant brought me around by a side entrance and showed me to the open carriage, while the King made his grand exit by the main door of the palace. A king should not only rule but be seen to rule, and exits and entrances were important. I had learned that much in my time at court.

As a commoner – the servant quietly instructed me – I should sit opposite the king in the carriage, with my back to the horses. Horses were rare in Kantarborg, and only the King was allowed to have a team of four. When the King was seated we set off down the canal side and across the narrow bridge, with a party of the King's Men riding alongside, sabres drawn. The day was grey but not cold. Some onlookers removed their hats, and a few women curtsied, but the King made no acknowledgement of them and did not wave as I remembered he once used to do.

We passed by the Royal Theatre, which was now a blackened hulk, missing its roof.

'We must have the theatre open again soon. It keeps people's spirits up,' remarked the King.

'The city seems to have suffered considerable damage, sire.'

'Indeed, the rebels did a great deal of harm.'

'The rebels, sire?'

'Yes, they burned down the theatre and a number of other buildings, and tried to blame it on us. Some of them even put on Northlander uniforms. There were some unfortunate incidents.'

'Were there many civilian casualties?'

'Well, the rebels were cowards, you know – they hid behind their women and children. But what else would you expect of such people?'

We turned into the fine, broad street that leads to the Rose Castle. Here the destruction was less obvious, and the houses and shops looked more like the city I had once known. By the entrance to the castle demesne, we paused while the gates to the King's Garden were opened.

The King was about to say something when I heard a sound like a whip being cracked overhead, and one of the horses reared. The King reached out and put his hand on my head.

'Get down!'

The driver shouted out and lashed the reins, and the horses quickly pulled the carriage into the park and down the castle driveway. From my crouched position, I could see the King's Men milling around the gateway behind us.

The King opened the carriage door before it had stopped moving and jumped out, striding furiously along the gravel path. I followed him across the wooden moat bridge and past the sentries, through the main entrance and up the stone spiral staircase. He said nothing until we were safely inside the throne room, but then he gave full vent to his feelings.

'God *damn* them! God *damn* them! I brought them peace, Karl! Peace! And this is their gratitude!'

He pointed out through the window at the city.

'Every second one of them is a rebel! Traitors to their king and country. I should have them all hanged! But they will feel the wrath of their king soon, I can promise you that.'

He stomped out of the room, leaving me alone. I felt curiously calm despite the danger we had experienced; and the King, too, was perhaps less affected by the attempt on his life than by the lack of respect – to put it mildly – that it implied.

Some time passed and the King did not reappear. I examined the fine timepieces in the room, some of which I had worked on in my time at court. Eventually I took off my jacket and walked out into the hall to find the cloakroom. At the other end of the corridor, a lady in a fine long yellow and cream dress was walking towards me, accompanied by a bearded courtier in a splendid black doublet, and two impossibly large dogs.

I recognised her at once, though I had previously seen her only from afar, at her mother's court. I immediately bowed low, and stayed in that position while they approached. One of the dogs sniffed at my head.

'Oh do stand up, Clockmaker!' said the Queen irritably. 'I wish to speak with you.'

I straightened. She was quite small, untypically so for a Northlander, with broad cheekbones, not unlike a peasant woman. But her eyes were sharp, green, intelligent and piercing.

'My husband sends his apologies,' she said. 'He will be with you shortly. He is in quite an agitated state after that incident.'

'Of course, your High…Majesty. It must have been most traumatic for him. And for you, too, of course.'

'It takes more than a musket ball to disturb me, Clockmaker. Where I come from we are perhaps more accustomed to such things. So, who did it? One of your Democracy League friends, perhaps?'

The abrupt question surprised and startled me.

'Majesty, I…I have no idea.'

'Well said, Clockmaker! If you had said you were quite sure it wasn't them, then I really would have been suspicious. You are staying for dinner?'

'His Majesty was kind enough to invite me.'

She paused, eyeing me intently.

'The King is fond of you, Nielsen. God knows why. You are of a reasonable cut, but I perceive none of the brilliance of which your monarch speaks so highly.'

She had her mother's directness. I had never before heard the smooth Northlander tongue spoken as though it were being pierced by steel barbs.

'But I am of royal Northlander blood,' she continued. 'I do things my own way. If I discover that you have had any involvement with the seditionists, the King's friendship will not protect you. I will personally see to it that you are skewered above Island Gate. Without the bother of having you executed first.'

She held up a hand in front of my face, and twisted it.

'I will happily do it with my own hands. Are we clear?'

'Perfectly, Majesty.'

She swept off without another word, with her dogs in train. The courtier gave me a contemptuous smirk and followed her.

Well, I had met the Queen.

Dinner was duck, just as it had been the first time I had visited the Rose Castle. I was beginning to think that duck must be the staple of the royal household; they had, at any rate, a ready supply of the birds in the moat. The Northlander courtier I had encountered, and whose name, I learned, was Arkdur Andersson, was there too, as was Johansson, both keeping up a lively conversation in Northlandish with the Queen. It looked as though Johansson was the Queen's man at court; indeed, he seemed almost over-familiar in his manner, frequently making her laugh raucously. I hoped that he did not contemplate any impropriety, or he might soon be welcoming guests at Island Gate, too. But surely not – Johansson was nothing if not a cautious man, as I well knew. The queen's two enormous dogs – wolfhounds, I had learned from Johansson, who went by the names of Cerberus and Barghest – lay by the fire, eyeing the guests with suspicion.

The King for his part was unusually quiet. As the table was being cleared and the servants brought in liquors and sweetmeats, he took me aside.

'I apologise for my outburst earlier, Karl.'[2]

'Under the circumstances, Majesty, it was perfectly understandable.'

'Life here is becoming intolerable. The people have lost all sense of respect and loyalty. But what do they imagine would happen if I were gone? Would that solve their problems, bring peace and prosperity to this country? I work night and day for them, yet they think me a tyrant.'

'I am sure the people are loyal, sire. Surely the disaffected are few in number?' (My Anglian has always tended to be rather formal – probably all to the good in a royal court.)

The King sighed and turned to the window. He muttered something.

'I beg your pardon, sire?'

'Humpty dumpty sat on a wall,' he said, turning to me. 'It's a children's rhyme. Do you know it?'

'Yes, sire.' I had seen it long ago, in a nursery book. Those were some of the first Anglian words I had ever learned, sitting on *Tanta's* lap.

'It's not just a rhyme,' said the King. 'It's a riddle, too.'

'A riddle, Majesty?'

'Yes, you are supposed to guess what it is. What is it that, when broken, cannot be fixed by all the King's horses and all the King's Men? Well come on, Karl, you're a scientist!'

---

2. For Kantarborgans, raw displays of emotion are considered vulgar. (Cf. Barrison, C., *Culture and Custom in Kantarborg*, pp.18-24.)

'I'm only an engineer, Majesty…and I really have no idea.'

'Well, in the rhyme it's an egg. Break an egg, and no power on earth can mend it. No matter who you are.'

He turned and looked out of the window again.

'So the question is, do I have a humpty dumpty kingdom? If it is broken, can all the King's horses and all the King's Men put it together again?'

CHAPTER FIVE

The sound of a gunshot, much too close, caused Joe to spring up in alarm from the straw where he was sleeping. In his panic he forgot about his sprained ankle, and winced with pain as he stumbled out of the byre.

Outside, Brother Christopher and the inn-keeper were standing in the morning sunlight. The monk was holding a smoking flintlock pistol.

'Morning, Joe,' said Christopher. 'Sorry about that.'

'What the feck are you…? You'll have the Guards on us!'

'Not at all. Just out shooting rabbits, aren't we, Gerry?'

'A fox. I'm sure 'twas a fox,' said the inn-keeper with a grin.

Joe gave an exasperated sigh. He brushed the straw off his clothes.

'That place would leave a stink on you. I'm going to have a wash.'

He limped down the hill towards the stream, his cloak flapping around him.

'Always washing, that fella,' said Christopher, watching him go. 'And never takes the cloak off. What kind of carry-on is that for a young lad?'

'You're taking him to the Rock?'

'If they'll have him.'

'He'll be for the missions, so.'

'Like as not. Don't say nothing to him about that, now. I told him they'd send him back by boat.'

'Not much chance of that, the way things are. How far up the river are they now?'

'Garrystown is pretty much gone. I had to order a pint in Alban, can you believe that?'

The inn-keeper tutted sadly at the iniquity of the world.

'They're even changing the signposts, did you hear that,

Christy? It's not Garrystown any more, it's Baile Gearóid. I'm not codding you, orders of the Jarl. People don't know where they're going anymore.'

'The Lord's language should be good enough for anyone.'

'But you know they say Alban used to be our language, too. Like in our place names and such.'

'Sure of course it was, back in heathen times! But I can tell you as a monk, Gerry, we've copied documents from way back before the Cataclysm, and none of them were in Alban. Anglian has been the language of this country since the monks brought the light of the Lord to our shores. Anyway, Kilkiernan is bound to fall soon. We have to get as much out as we can, while we can.'

'Looks like you'll be needing the gear, so.'

'One way or the other, when the abbot sees sense. Alright, it's good enough. What's the asking price?'

'It's the best. The new formula. Two sacks will cost you a hundred and twenty.'

'Ah, you're joking me! That's nearly twice what it cost last time.'

'You can't keep buying stuff with that silver, Christy. You lads are flooding the market.'

'Maybe we should pay in beer next time?'

The inn-keeper grinned.

'Maybe's you should. You'd need a fine big wagon of beer to pay for two sacks of gunpowder, though.'

'Is that it?' Joe asked as they picked their way down the meandering track, across heather-strewn slopes that swept downwards towards the sea. On the horizon, a number of buildings carved out sharp silhouettes against the evening sky. The wind was fresher now, the sky clouding over, with a hint of rain in the air.

'Not yet,' answered Christopher. 'Not much further, though. Promise.'

'I can't walk any further. I need a rest.' Joe was leaning on the loaded donkey, hopping along beside it in a kind of awkward three-legged race. The donkey occasionally shook him off in protest.

'We'll take a break by the old monastery. I'll unload the donkey there, then you can get back up on him again.'

'What's that tower?' asked Joe as they approached the ruined buildings.

'The round one? Lots of the old monasteries have them. You must have seen them before, surely?'

'Nothing like that in Kilkiernan. It looks like a rocket ship.'

'Ah, so you've seen a rocket ship, but not a round tower? Dear God, the young. And where did you see that?'

'In the old books. Brother Anselm showed me. There's loads of pictures of them. The ancients used to go to the moon in them.'

'Don't believe that old nonsense, boy,' said Christopher. 'I don't think even the ancients could make a round tower fly. They're probably just airship mooring masts like we have today. They had airships back then too, you know.'

'I know. There were pictures of them, too.'

Christopher tethered the donkey beside the tower and loosened the straps on the animal's back, letting the two heavy sacks slide to the ground. Then he disappeared into a roofless stone building and returned with a long wooden ladder.

'Give me a shout if you see anyone.'

There was no doorway into the tower at ground level, but an entrance of some kind could be seen about ten feet up, above the waist-high weeds. Christopher placed the ladder against the tower wall, hoisted one of the sacks onto his back, then climbed up the ladder and disappeared inside. After a few minutes he returned for the second sack.

'Why'd they put the doorway so far off the ground?' called

Joe.

'To stop people being nosey.'

Joe failed to take the hint.

'How much stuff have you got in there?' he asked.

'Enough.'

'Enough for what?'

'Enough for us to defend ourselves when the time comes. I've been collecting it here for a while now. But not a word about this to the abbot, alright? We'll need a slight change in Church policy first. Ah, feck it!'

This last comment was occasioned by a few threateningly heavy drops of summer rain. Christopher hurried to get the second sack onto his back and into the shelter of the tower as the shower became heavier. By the time he returned to Joe, it was becoming a downpour.

'Can we not go in there out of the rain?' shouted Joe above the din.

'And how would you get up the ladder? We can go in under the trees.'

Leading the donkey, the two men sought the shelter of the nearby apple grove that must once have helped to feed the monks of the monastery. But the trees were small and stunted, and offered little protection. The rain battered their exposed heads and began to soak through their clothes. After a while a low growl emanated from the west, then another. The barrage of rain increased still further. Then there was a sudden blinding flash, followed by a peal of thunder.

Christopher dropped the reins of the donkey.

'Ah no, ah *no*, don't feckin' do this to me now!' He began to run in the direction of the tower.

'Do what?' Joe called out.

There was another flash and a deafening thunderclap that sounded as though it were directly overhead. The donkey brayed in fright and galloped off. A flickering light, like a lamp borne by some ghostly monk, appeared in the doorway of the tower. Christopher turned around and ran back towards Joe.

'Get back! Get up the hill! Quick!'

Before they could react, a colossal, gut-punching blast knocked the two men off their feet. The ground rumbled and shook as the round tower, in apparent imitation of the rocket ships of old, gently rose some several yards vertically into the air, before sinking back on itself in a roar of dust and smoke.

When the dust cloud cleared, the tower was gone. Only a heap of stones remained, hissing in the rain.

'Holy crap!' exclaimed Brother Christopher.

'What happened?' asked Joe.

'I think I just beatified myself, Joe. It's the missions for me now, for sure.'

Extract from *The Garrystown Sentinel*

Weapons tests in the mountains?

Several witnesses on the Ivory peninsula have reported seeing an apparent weapons test last Thursday in the vicinity of the townland of Cooley, near the abandoned monastery of the monks of St Michael. Fragments of the device were found as far away as Kileery and Balliferra. The Jarl of North Muhan and Ulla, Alistair McLochlainn, has accused the monks of the Rock of using ancient technology to develop a destructive weapon of extreme power and range:

'There can now be no doubt in anyone's mind that this sect is reviving the Ignatian heresy – the same one that brought calamity to the ancient world with its bombs and rockets,' said the Jarl in a statement. 'If we fail to act now to confront this evil, the whole world may suffer the consequences.'

The monks deny that they have any such weapons.

CHAPTER SIX

'Here? Really?' I looked up in puzzlement at the looming mass of the great astronomical tower in the centre of Kantarborg.

Johansson handed the lantern to me, then took out a large iron key and unlocked the tower door, which gave way to his push with a loud echoing creak. We were in the city centre, but it was after curfew and the streets were deserted.

'There's an apartment near the top. It was the residence of the Astronomer Royal, but he's had a falling-out with the King. His Majesty was not impressed with his predictions. Anyway, the soothsayer has taken himself off to an island in the Sound in a huff, so this place is empty.'

'I wouldn't have thought the King held much truck with astrology,' I said as we walked up the spiral gallery, our footsteps echoing. The last time I had walked here had been to board the royal airship moored at the top. A few years and a lifetime ago.

'You're right there. He doesn't give a hang for astrology. But old Brorsen got on his nerves. He's required to publish an almanac every year, and last year it was full of dire warnings about the state of the realm.'

'And was he right?'

Johansson laughed.

'Well, you be the judge. Things could be better, there's no doubt of that.'

As we approached the top of the tower, Johansson pointed back at the giant astronomical clock that straddled the gangway.

'I think he may want you to take a look at that. It hasn't been going right for a while. Either that, or there's something wrong with the solar system.'

'That's not why I'm here, surely? To fix a clock?'

Johansson made no reply, but gestured to an archway set in the wall near where the spiral ramp became a set of steps leading to the top of the tower. Here he unlocked a discreet, anonymous door.

'Welcome to the stargazer's cave. I think you'll find it to your liking.'

He was right. The apartment, as I could see when Johansson lifted the lantern, was full of brass telescopes and other scientific instruments of great beauty. The windows had stained glass panes with allegorical scenes and representations of the sun and planets. The bookshelves were full of scientific works. Papers with calculations lay discarded all around. Evidently the Astronomer Royal had left in some haste.

'And watch this,' said Johansson, flipping a large black switch.

Yellow light instantly flooded the room, making me shade my eyes.

'Electric light! From the Great Windmill. Just like at the offices of state.'

The light began to flash.

'It comes and goes a bit. But not even the Rose Castle has anything like this.'

The flickering of the electric light was rather disturbing, so Johansson turned it off and brought the lantern instead. Then he found a bottle of the astronomer's wine and placed it on the marble chessboard between two old leather armchairs. I was still woozy after our meal at the Rose Castle. Alcohol was expensive in Sandviken, and I was not accustomed to drinking in such quantities – and certainly not wine, the drink of the nobles.

We sat across from each other in the armchairs, sipping from our glasses. There was something I had on my mind, and I wanted to ask it while I still had a reasonably clear head.

'So, did the King keep his side of the bargain, Kaare?'

'What bargain?'

'Erika Thorne. Has she been released?'

He seemed reluctant to reply.

'Because if she's still in Sythorn, the deal's off. I'll take the first boat back.'

'That would be extremely foolish, Karl. You would be breaking your contract with the King. You know what the consequences would be.'

'Nonetheless.'

He grimaced.

'Yes, all right, she has been released. But you are not to mention it anywhere, or to anyone. And I mean anyone. Least of all the King.'

'Why not, if he has kept his word?'

'Because the King did not release her, Karl.'

'But you just said he did!'

'The King did not release her. I did.'

I stared at him. 'You!'

'The King knows nothing of it. I did not present him with your conditions. I thought it was best. For you, and for her.'

'But do you have that kind of power?'

'If I say I am acting on the King's orders, yes.'

There was a silence. He was walking on very thin ice here, and we both knew it. It was even, potentially, a hanging offence.

'But…surely it will be discovered!' I said at last.

'Not if we are careful. The King has other things on his mind. And if he gets wind of it, we put it down to an administrative error. She was in Sythorn during the rebellion, so she has a solid alibi. As far as the King is concerned, Erika Thorne was just a petty criminal, locked up for defacing library books. Instead of…what she truly was.'

'Which was what?'

'The ringleader, of course. The one who put the whole damn plan into operation.'

'*She* planned the rebellion?'

'Of course she did. Her father is – was – a physician. She had asked him to prepare a report on the King's state of mind. It was all ready for publication. Clear signs of mental infirmity, delirium. The Church and the merchants had already had quite enough of the King and his heretical talk about the past and the underground, and they were itching for an excuse to confine him to the Rose Castle. But De Martinus of the Watch got wind of the scheme, one way or another, and so she ended up in Sythorn on a trumped-up charge of vandalism.'

He paused to refill our glasses. *One way or another?* Last time we had talked of it, he had seemed pretty sure that it was my brother Jonas who had betrayed her.

'De Martinus had his own plans, of course, and he wanted her out of the way. Then when the King escaped he looked like the man of the moment. "Never mind all that democracy nonsense, that's just students' talk. What we need now is law and order." Clever.'

He took a sip from his glass.

'But not quite clever enough to save his head in the end.'

'What proof do you have of any of this?' I asked.

'I can't tell you that.'

'Then how do I know that any of it is true? How do I even know she has been released?'

'You'll just have to take my word for it.'

I put down my glass.

'I can't, Kaare, I'm sorry. I've spent too much time at court. I know how these things are done.'

He smiled. 'By deception, manipulation and lies, you mean?'

I said nothing. Johansson sighed.

'I can't blame you, I suppose. But it was all…'

'For my own good. Yes. I know.'

Johansson looked down and rubbed his fist thoughtfully along the arm of the chair. Then he looked into my eyes.

'If I can prove to you that she is out, will you promise me not to try to contact her? And believe me, I mean that. It would be a very bad idea.'

I hesitated, then nodded.

'You know the market in the square on West Fountain Street? There is a bookstall there. She is there most days, I'm told.'

'Sounds like a bit of a come-down in the world, if she is as important a person as you say.'

'Circumstances have changed for many people, Karl. Her family is gone. The house took a direct hit during the bombard-ment. They were sheltering in the cellar. Her parents, brothers and sisters; all killed. Being locked up in Sythorn saved her life. Ironic, isn't it?'

That took me aback. Johansson leaned over towards me.

So you see, Karl, she would have every reason not to feel very well disposed towards an associate of the King. And she has dangerous friends. So for your own sake, stay away from her.'

I nodded. He sat back in his armchair.

'Between you and me, the invasion was badly handled. Resistance was stiffer than we expected, so we had to apply quite a lot of force. Our Northlander allies, in particular, got a little over-enthusiastic. You've seen the damage.'

'The King said it was the rebels.'

'Yes. Well. There are allegations and counter-allegations. All wars are like that. But the fact is that many people died, and many more were made homeless or destitute. And the King is being blamed for that.'

'That seems rather unfair. He wanted peace for his kingdom.'

'Fair and unfair doesn't come into it, Karl. This is politics.'

We sat for a minute in silence. In the apartment hallway, a clock began to chime midnight, followed a moment later by the town hall clock, outside in the silent city.

CHAPTER SEVEN

'Father Abbot...I didn't expect to see you here.'

Christopher knelt before the small assembly of monks on the quay of Rock Harbour. A narrow black rowing boat bobbed at the bottom of the harbour steps.

'Well, Brother Christopher, you announced your arrival in some style. You might say we could hardly miss it.' The monk who spoke wore white robes, and was small and grey-haired.

'It was an accident, Father...an act of God, you might say.'

'Oh, an act of God, was it? You disobeyed my explicit command, wasted our scarce resources, demolished property of this order that has stood for nearly two thousand years, and handed an excuse to the Albans for their military attentions. And you lost a donkey. So which aspect of this catastrophe do you wish to blame on the Almighty?'

Christopher opened his mouth, looked at the abbot, then closed it again.

'At least you saved some honour from your disgrace by bringing Kilkiernan's secret weapon with you.'

'The design for the underwater vessel, Father? Yes, I have it here...'

'I was referring to your companion.'

'My...you mean *Joe*?'

Joe stepped forward and shook the abbot's hand, bowing slightly.

'Very pleased to meet you, my Lord Abbot. I have heard much good about you.'

'And I about you. Brother Anselm speaks very highly of your talent. But I had hoped we might meet under better circumstances. You realise that certain administrative arrangements will have to be made before we can offer you shelter?'

'I understand that no woman may step onto the Rock, if

that's what you mean. So I am willing to become a man.'

'Wait, hold on a…what's going on here?' said Christopher, struggling to his feet. 'You mean to say you're a *woman*?'

Joe turned and looked at him. And now, without the all-enveloping cloak, Joe suddenly appeared very womanly indeed, albeit a woman with short-cropped red hair. The other monks could barely suppress their smiles. The abbot, however, was unamused.

'According to my sources you spent the night with her in a house of ill repute. Are you telling me you didn't *notice*?'

'Well…it was dark,' said Christopher lamely. A monk giggled and was elbowed into silence. 'And he…she…you never told me!'

'You didn't ask,' said Joe.

'Josephine Caffrey is a very fine artificer. She will be a very welcome addition to our design team, for however long she wishes to stay.'

'But…women can't go onto the Rock!' protested Christopher.

'Indeed not. Which is why we must ask Joe to become a man. Remember: "Whatever ye loose upon earth shall be loosed in heaven".'

'But surely, Father Abbot, there are physical limits…I mean, there are no other women on the Rock.'

'Of course not. They are all men. For administrative purposes, at any rate.'

'For administrative…?' It was all too much for Christopher. His head was spinning.

The abbot took Joe aside and asked her to kneel. Then he blessed her and muttered some prayers. After just two minutes Joe had been transformed in the sight of God from a woman to a man, and returned with a radiant smile.

'Welcome to our community as a lay brother, Joe,' said the abbot. 'You are not bound by our vows, but we would be grateful for your assistance at this difficult time. We have one mission, especially, which is of great importance for the survival of our community, and indeed, the Church itself.'

'My Lord Abbot has my complete loyalty. I will be glad to help in anything he feels is necessary,' said Joe.

The abbot gave Christopher an admonishing look, then the party descended the steps in the harbour wall and climbed aboard the narrow rowing-boat.

'You're for the missions alright,' said Brother Eamonn as he pulled on the oars beside Christopher. 'I heard Himself yelling it in the scriptorium last night.'

'East or west, do you think?' asked Christopher glumly.

'Neither. From what I hear, he has a very special mission just for you. But you'll have to be beatified first.'

'Naturally,' sighed Christopher.

CHAPTER EIGHT

When I woke in the astronomer's lumpy straw bed, the brass bedside clock showed it was past ten in the morning. I had dreamed of Erika. In my dream she was trying to tell me something very important, but she could not speak. Or I could not hear her.

After the previous evening's excesses, my belly felt like a theatre performing the first act of a melodrama. With the villain about to make his entrance. I groaned and rolled out of bed.

The narrow, arched windows in the stone walls admitted but little daylight. There was no food in the apartment, but I boiled a little water on a tealight stove to make some tea, cupping my hands around the mug to warm them. The summer was turning into autumn, and it was cold behind the thick stone walls of the tower. I would have to go out and buy some supplies. No servants here. I had learned to cook a little in Sandviken, but my culinary skills weren't up to much. Johansson had given me another advance on my wages, so I could survive on the snacks from the stallholders for now. I had an appointment with the King for the next day, but on this day I was in theory a free man.

I poked around the apartment a little. One could scarcely conceive of a greater contrast to the Rose Castle. There were no soft furnishings here, and little in the way of luxury, except the scientific instruments and the books. I had never seen so many books in a private home. I pulled down a few and inspected them, but they were mostly academic works in foreign languages, neither Anglian nor Kantish. One of those I opened, however, offered a detailed map of the moon, and some drawings of the other planets, which I examined with interest.

In an otherwise empty cubby-hole, I discovered a ladder leading to a trap-door. This was locked with a padlock, but I opened that easily enough (I am, after all, a horologist) and found that it led up to the observatory on top of the tower. I had often seen the round wooden building up there, but had never been inside it before. It had a domed roof that could be opened up by winding a handle. There were several telescopes here, wonderful brass devices. Lying flat in the centre of the floor was a large concave mirror, as broad in diameter as a man is tall, which seemed to be linked to one of the telescopes, although I could not immediately discern its function.

I had grown fond of observing the astronomical bodies while serving as navigator on board *Freya*, and I looked forward now to exploring the heavens with these even more sensitive instruments. But that would have to wait for the time being.

I climbed back down to the apartment, put on my city coat and made my way down the spiral walkway, my footsteps loud in the curving passage. It felt odd to have the whole tower to myself – I was used to seeing it teeming with the King's Men. But the royal airship was no longer moored overhead, being berthed over at the naval docks, so that was perhaps the reason for the lack of guards.

As a place of residence, the tower felt at one and the same time uncomfortably Spartan and uncomfortably grandiose. I still had a house of my own in the city, in theory, but the legal situation was complex. As a traitor, I had forfeited all my property, and although the regime that had condemned me had now been overthrown, I had not occupied the house for a long time, and according to Johansson a general was now installed in it. Getting it back would require legal action, and, conscious of lawyers' fees, I had decided to let the matter lie for now.

At the bottom of the tower, beside the entrance, was a new doorway that I hadn't noticed before. It was located at the very end of the spiral, and was locked. On the wall beside it, part of the whitewash had been removed to reveal a hand-painted notice. It looked very old, and read, in curling Anglian letters: '*As above, so below*'. I made a mental note to ask Johansson about it.

The noise and light of the city poured in as I opened the tower door. Outside, I was reassured to see that the stalls lining Woolmerchant Street were apparently as busy as they had always been. I bought a herring sandwich – how I had missed them! – and ate it as I wandered along the stalls. I noticed that there seemed to be rather more antiques stalls than there had been before, and that the 'antiques' on sale looked mostly like small domestic trinkets of little intrinsic value.

About half-way down the street, some silver cutlery suddenly caught my eye.

'Half a sovereign for that, friend. Twenty pieces. Most of the set is there. Nice quality.' The stall-holder picked up a knife and handed it to me.

I examined the handle and the initials engraved on it.

'Where did you get this?' I asked in Anglian.

His manner changed at once.

'It's all signed for, sir. Do you know it?'

'It belongs to my family.'

Well, sir, perhaps you've been away and don't know, but many people are selling things now.'

Or looting, I thought.

'I hardly think my family would have sold this.'

'But you aren't the only member of your family, I'll warrant, sir? Because somebody did sell it, and it's all legit. I don't sell no stolen goods here. You don't believe me, go to the Watch.'

William. I had been meaning to visit my elder brother and his family since landing in the city. The silver must have been stolen, it was the only possible explanation. I should inform them at once. Unaccountably, as I walked briskly down the street, I felt tears in my eyes. I brushed them away irritably.

The walk to William's house took me about half an hour. I began to feel uneasy as I approached Foundry Street, seeing more and more buildings that were mere blackened ruins. Then, as I reached the bridge and turned the corner, my worst fears were realised: every house on the south side of the canal had been gutted. A few walls remained, no roofs. The elegant trees that had once lined the canal were all gone – perhaps burned for winter firewood. I walked down the quay and eventually found what must have been the house, though it was hard to be sure. I stood staring uncomprehendingly at the pile of rubble that had once been my childhood home. Nothing but the cellar remained.

A woman stood a short distance away, eyeing me.

'You're one of the family,' she said in Kantish. It was not a question. I turned to her. Her hair was tangled, her clothes dirty. She looked like a beggar.

'He's dead, I'm afraid, sir.'

'What happened here?'

'Airships come over, firing incendiaries. Got the whole street blazing. He got his wife and the little girl out, but then he went back in for his things. That was what did for him. He didn't come out again.'

'Where is he buried?' I asked, struggling to control my voice.

She looked at me as though I were an imbecile.

'Buried, sir? Why, in there somewhere. But it's no use going looking for him. He was burned, so there won't be anything left.'

'What…what about his wife and daughter?'

'She went down the barracks,' she replied, pointing along the canal, 'but I heard she died in the spring pox. I don't know what happened to the child.'

I suddenly felt violently angry. I had dreamed of this street, of canal boats, rain on the water and trees in leaf. Damn them. Damn the whole rag-bag of them, court, king and country!

The old woman turned away from me and began to walk down the steps to the cellar door, which was open.

'Hey!' I shouted, going after her and taking hold of her arm. 'Just a moment! That house is still my family's property. You can't just…'

She turned and looked into my eyes.

'You don't even recognise me, do you?'

She pulled her arm angrily out of my grasp, walked down the steps, and closed the door behind her. Inside, I heard the faint chiming of a clock. My parents' clock. The one I had repaired as a child.

And only then, with a hot flush of shame, did I realise who she was. And she had called me 'sir'! I wanted to hammer on the door and offer a grovelling apology, but I realised it was no use. I hadn't even thought to ask what had happened to the servants. *Tanta*, my old nurse, had seen me quite clearly for what I probably was: a stupid, unthinking, uncaring man of the court.

The 'barracks' turned out to be a fenced compound with long rows of red-painted huts, set up by the King's Men, so a sign informed me, to provide temporary housing for women and children made homeless by the bombardment. (Their menfolk, no doubt, had all been co-opted into the Reserve.) I showed the King's seal at the gate and found the administrator's office after much fruitless wandering about in the compound, during which time I acquired a tail of ragged, giggling children curious to see what the man in the fine clothes was up to. The administrator, a tall, Anglian-speaking woman of my own age, was not unsympathetic but clearly had more pressing problems than locating my niece. She eventually found the ledger entry that confirmed that an Ingrid Nielsen and her young daughter had been admitted shortly after the invasion, and that the mother had died of a fever the following spring. Of the daughter, it said only: 'Received into the care of family member'. There was no address. 'Probably the mother's sister or brother,' she said, closing the book.

So that was that. I did not know Jessica well and had no claim upon her. Ingrid's family could no doubt care for her better than I could.

I walked back into town in sombre mood. Thoughts of the Yule I had celebrated with my brother and his family not so very long ago filled me with an almost unbearable sense of grief.

And why, why did it happen? Long-distance bombardment was one thing, but airships firing incendiaries at civilian homes? This was not war, this was atrocity. What possible purpose could it serve? *A merchant's street*, said a voice in my head. *Suspected anti-royalists. To teach them a lesson.* No, no, it must have been the fog of war. Foreign airship crews, unfamiliar with the area. Some of the militia must have fired at them from the canal side, and they responded. That must be the explanation. *They killed your brother using mechanisms you helped to design.* But I did not know they would be used for that! I was just an engineer, a clockmaker. All I had ever wanted to do was to be useful, to help people. *Ah yes, but it is who are you useful to – that is the question.*

The sight of some small girls playing a familiar clapping game amongst the rubble put me in mind of my niece.

'Skinny Malink fell down the sink...'

Some things never change, even in time of war.

The road back brought me past West Fountain Street. The market was still open, although the afternoon was drawing to a close and some traders were packing up. Now was as good a time as any to find out whether the promise to me had been kept, or whether I had been deceived again. Outwardly, the place looked just as it had done in my student days: the same flower sellers, fruit stalls, fishmongers and fortune-tellers. The same statue of some long-forgotten hero on horseback, dolefully surveying the scene. It was busy, too – even on a grey day with the threat of rain in the air. But here, too, there seemed to be rather more bric-à-brac and personal belongings on sale than there had been before. Candlesticks. Paintings. Clothes. Sets of crockery.

It took me a while to find the bookstall, tucked away as it was in a corner. It was manned by two women. One of them looked like Erika. She had the right height and build. With the first drops of rain as my excuse, I raised the hood of my cape and walked closer, standing among the other browsers. I picked up a book from the stall and pretended to examine it.

It was her. The blond hair was a little longer, her face a little older. But it was Erika, no doubt about it. I felt my heart leap. I should have turned away immediately, but my glance lingered a little too long. She looked up, and I saw the recognition in her eyes. Too late. She smiled.

It was not the response I had been expecting, after Johansson's warning, and it took me completely off guard.

'Does that book interest you, sir?' she asked, without taking her eyes off mine. 'I have some others by the same author.'

She turned away for a moment and rummaged in a wooden crate behind the stall.

'This one, in particular, I think you might find interesting.'

She handed me a slim volume with a red cloth cover. It had no visible title.

'Yes, thank you,' I managed to stammer out. 'I will take them both.'

I handed over half a sovereign and received some coins in change. I was about to turn away when she stopped me.

'One moment, I'll write you a receipt.'

She scribbled something on a scrap of paper and handed it to me. I tucked it into one of the books.

'Thank you.'

As I walked away I opened the first book to see what I had bought. The receipt almost blew away in the breeze. I caught it and looked at it. It said simply: *The Thimble at six.*

CHAPTER NINE

The pelican was a problem. Of all the beasts that the good Lord has given us, thought Father Aloysius exasperatedly, the man had to be visited by a *pelican*. An eagle would have easy: John the Evangelist. A lion: St Mark. A lamb: Christ the Saviour. Even a dragon would have suggested St George and the perils of the underground riches. But a pelican! How did this vexatious monk even know the *name* of such a beast?

The candle was guttering in the draught from the open doorway. Father Aloysius sought in vain beneath his desk for the clever wind-up lantern he had recently received from Kilkiernan, the work of that young artificer. It must be well past the hour of retiring by now. He had almost fallen asleep at vespers. Outside the stone hut, the screams of the seabirds had changed in tone; the night shift had taken over. The noise they made was one more point of complaint in the community. The anchorite rock was not really a suitable place for the finer points of monastic life, and some of the monks had had trouble adjusting after the relative luxury of the mainland.

Father Aloysius rubbed his eyes and closed the heavy, illuminated copy of a volume of the *Encyclopaedia Britannica*, raising a little dust from the desk, and rang the bell for his acolyte. He would have to take the pelican business up with the council of the brethren tomorrow. After a few moments the acolyte appeared in the doorway, looking as though he had been roused from a doze, and helped the abbot out of his chair.

'You are a bird man, are you not, Ignatius?' asked Aloysius, leaning on the young man's arm as they slowly made their way along the pathway between the stone huts. The night air was cold and fresh, pungent with the smell of seabird droppings.

'A what, Father Abbot?'

Aloysius was tired. Anglian did not come easily to him at

such times. He struggled to find the right words.

'You are one who is interested in the birds of the air?'

'Indeed I am, Father. In my youth, especially, I studied them earnestly.'

In your youth, thought Aloysius. *You can't be a day over twenty-five.*

'Ever heard of the pelican?'

'It's a seabird, Father Abbot. Not found in these parts. More down south.'

'It is real, then? Not just allegorical? You're quite sure?'

'Oh, they're real all right. They live in the warmer countries. Great big bills to catch fish in. They are said to…'

'…feed their young on their own blood. Yes, so I've heard. Aquinas mentions it. Odd behaviour for a bird, I would have thought.'

'There are many strange things in nature, Father Abbot.'

'Indeed so, indeed so. Remind me, what was your vision when you were received into the brethren of the beatified?'

'It was of fire, Father. Hence the name.'

'Ah, of course. After St Ignatio the Firebrand. But we are none of us Ignatians here, I hope. Whatever the Albans may claim.'[3]

3 St Ignatio, born Gerald O'Malley of Tarraquin, was a 22nd-century prophet who believed in the power of fire to purge the world of sin, as he claimed the ancients had done. His oft-quoted saying was 'Ye have heard that ye shall be baptised in water. But I say to ye, unless ye also be baptised in fire, ye shall not be cleansed.' According to the *Annals of Kilmaide*, he had cleansed half of Muhan in this manner before being felled by a crusader arrow on his way to burn the library of the monks of Malo. The abbot of Malo was suspected of connivance, even complicity, in his death, but nothing could be proved. Two weeks later, lightning struck the monastery and the library burned down anyway. This was seen as a) proof positive of the abbot's culpability and of the iniquitous content of the works in his library, and b) a sign of divine approval of the martyred Ignatio. What remained of the monastery was then torched by Ignatio's devotees, and the monks were massacred. The cult of Ignatio grew in the following decades, and by popular demand, the prophet was finally canonised in the early 23rd century. His miracles generally manifested themselves in the form of lightning strikes on places that attracted his wrath. The canonisation of St Ignatio coincided with the beginning of the tradition of low, single-

The young man smiled and drew back the leather sheet covering the door to the abbot's cell. He wished Father Aloysius goodnight and a safe rest, as was customary among the monks. Not that a monk ever got more than a few hours' rest at a time. But the abbot had no sooner begun to say his office when Brother Ignatius once again poked his head around the door-cover.

'Father Abbot? I apologise for interrupting. We may have a slight problem.'

In his hands, he held the carcass of a very dead seabird.

The council of the brethren met in special disciplinary session next morning in the island's small scriptorium. The senior brothers of the order sat in a row with the abbot in the centre, glaring at the monk who stood humbly but unbowed before them.

'Brother Christopher, we have endured much from you since you joined this order,' thundered the abbot. 'Many, many malfeasances, for which you have had to do a great deal of penance. But now it seems that you have attempted to cheat this community and the Lord your God, and enter the brotherhood of the beatified by the back door!'

'What back door? Wait, is this about the bird? I can explain that...'

'You are supposed to wait in the cave of trials in *humility* and *patience*, eating only the manna that grows there, for a minimum of forty days and forty nights, until you receive a divine vision. And when it appears, you are supposed to listen to what it says. Not strangle it and devour it!'

'Right, gotcha. You mean the vision wasn't real?'

storey buildings that eventually came to characterise ecclesiastical architecture throughout the Anglian world. Ignatianism is sometimes identified with the cult of fire that swept the world during late ancient times, but this is an anachronism, as St Ignatio was born some time later.

'It *was* real, Brother, that is the problem! It was a real bird, not a holy vision. And you ate it!'

'Well, to tell you the honest truth, Father Abbot, I don't really remember. I might have done. I was out of my box at that stage. Anyway, there's no pelicans this far north, are there?'

'Apparently there are. There were. There was at least one specimen. Before you put an end to its brief existence.' The abbot held up the sorry remains of the bird.

'OK, you've got me bang to rights, Father Abbot. *Mea maxima culpa*, right? I'm sorry I ate the vision.'

'You didn't *have* a vision, Brother! You had dinner!'

'Right, OK. So what can I do about it now?'

'There's only one thing to do about it, Brother. You are going back into the cave. And this time you will stay there until you either have a genuine vision or die in the process!'

'Ah no, Father. I nearly went off my head in there. Can't we say that the pelican was magic, I mean holy? There's no pelicans around here, it must have been sent by God, surely? Get off me, will ya?'

Two burly monks appeared at Christopher's side, and he was led away, still protesting loudly.

'Why do you put up with him, my lord abbot?' asked Brother Geoffrey of the Library, a thin-faced, middle-aged man who, with the privilege of office, was permitted to speak his mind. 'He is hardly suitable material for a man of the cloth.'

'I put him up with him because he is a sailor,' replied the abbot. 'He knows the southern seas and the northern ones. And that is precisely what we need right now.'

CHAPTER TEN

The Thimble was crowded, mostly with students. They were as boisterous as young people always are, but, oddly, the style of their clothing seemed to have reverted to that of my parents' generation; less colour on show, more sensible fabrics. My mother would have approved. Perhaps that is what happens when times grow harder, I thought to myself. Still, at least war was a less likely prospect for them now than it was for me when I was a student. But then again, who could say?

I was sitting in a corner, watching the door. My mug of beer was almost empty; I had drunk it much too quickly. *This is ridiculous*, I told myself. *You have been in battle. You have faced monsters and the underground. And you are nervous at meeting a woman!*

Eventually Erika walked in, wearing a cape and a long grey dress in the prevailing fashion, and smiled cordially, if not quite warmly, at me. I rose to buy her a drink, but she waved the offer away and went to the bar herself, returning with two mugs.

'So Karl, we meet again! Quite a dramatic time we've both had.'

'Yes. Erika, I was so sorry to hear about your family.'

She looked puzzled.

'My family?'

'I heard they were killed in the bombardment.'

'Then you heard wrong. My family is fine, Karl. They live out on Agaholm. They were well away from the fighting, thank God. Who told you they were dead?'

'It was…just something I heard.'

'And your family? Are they safe?'

'My brother William was killed. His wife died afterwards. I don't know where Jonas is.'

She nodded.

'These have been hard times for many people. Almost everyone I know has lost someone.'

She took a sip of her beer and looked around her. (Was she slightly nervous, too, or was I imagining it?)

'Karl, I wanted to say. I know it was not you who betrayed me. I should not have suspected you.'

'It was understandable.'

'Are you still in the employ of the King?'

'I tried to get away from the court, to make a life for myself in the Northlands. But…circumstances drew me back. Lack of money, to be honest.'

'You're married?'

I nodded.

'Three years now. And you?'

'No. I'm seeing someone, though. Perhaps we will marry eventually, when things settle down.'

'It is a difficult time.'

'Difficult is the word, all right.' She glanced away from me, out of the window.

'At least there is peace now,' I ventured.

Her eyes flashed back to mine.

'Peace? Any ruler can make peace if he sells his kingdom to the enemy.'

'But surely it's better than being at war?'

She regarded me for a moment in silence.

'Karl, wake up, look around you. Kantarborg is in ruins. People are begging and desperate. The Sound Dues were the city's only real income, and now they are gone. There would be riots in the streets, except that the people are so worn out and dispirited. This is not peace, this is defeat.'

'But what is to be done?'

'What is to be done? It's obvious what is to be done – we must throw off the people who brought this disaster upon us.'

'Is there no alternative? Conditions are bound to get better eventually.'

'Nothing will change until the King is gone. He is the chief author of all our miseries. Him and all his crew. Before, people just wanted him confined to the Rose Castle. Now they want him dead. The monarchy must go, and Kantarborg must be an independent nation again. That is what is to be done.'

'But what then? Would you just go back to the old ways? To war and piracy?'

'To self-determination and pride, Karl! We don't have to go to war with other nations, that is just the vanity of kings. But we must deal with them as equals, not as serfs.'

I sighed. It all sounded very well, but behind the noble words, all I could see was blood and death. Again. She read my expression and changed the subject.

'So…,' she asked, smiling a little. 'Come on. Who told you my family was dead?'

'It was Captain Johansson. Do you know him?'

'I thought it might be him. How very interesting. What is he up to, I wonder?'

'Everyone at court is playing some game or other. I could never figure it all out. That's why I don't feel I belong there.'

'No, I don't think you do. I think you belong with us.'

I shook my head.

'Erika, I'm an engineer. Great causes…they aren't really my thing.'

'And yet you have rendered valuable service to the King. Could you not be useful to others besides him, for a change?'

'Gladly. But what could I do?'

'Read the book I gave you. That might give you some ideas.'

She knocked back her beer and stood up.

'I have to go now. But we should meet again, Karl, while you are here. I think we might have a lot to talk about.'

I smiled at her – flattered and, I must confess, a little bewildered. I finished my beer slowly and then got up to leave, too – and as I did so, I caught sight of a bearded man in dark clothing, talking to the barkeep. Arkdur Andersson, the Queen's counsellor. Not a man you would normally expect to encounter in a student haunt. He had probably seen me talking to Erika. But what of it? She was a woman I had known in university, and who had been convicted only of a petty crime. In fact, technically, she had not been convicted at all, but like me had been confined to a mental institution. So let him say what he wants, I told myself as I walked back up Woolmerchant Street.

Back in the tower, I poured myself a glass of the astronomer's wine and sat down to read the books I had bought. The one I had picked up at random at Erika's bookstall turned out to be a racy tale of adventure, bordering on the pornographic. How my choice must have amused her! The other book was of course not 'by the same author' at all. It was a slim, anonymous volume entitled *The Necessary Republic*, and was about the evils of monarchy, and how a republic would restore the dignity of mankind through suffrage for all. Or at least, for the merchant class. Reading the litany of catastrophes brought about by kings and queens, it seemed hard to deny the baleful effect that the monarchies seemed to have exerted. Even the King, after all, had once described it to me as a barbaric system of government. But were republics really that much better? The ancient nations that had unleashed the Great Cataclysm on mankind had nearly all been republics of one kind or another, or so I had heard. Perhaps the fault is not in our systems but in ourselves.

And amid these rather doleful speculations I must have dozed off, for I awoke shivering with cold some hours later, still sitting in the armchair with the book in my hand. I got myself off to bed as quickly as I could, for the next day was the day that the King had promised to reveal to me the purpose for which he had brought me to Kantarborg.

CHAPTER ELEVEN

'Brother Chris! Hey boss! You in there?' The voice was barely audible above the crashing of the waves outside the cave.

An emaciated, bearded figure huddled on a bed of twigs and straw at the side of the cave turned his head slowly and regarded the red-haired young intruder with suspicion.

'Are you real?' he demanded.

'Of course I'm real, you eejit. It's Joe.'

The monk pointed a weak forefinger.

'You're not real! You're an artificial.'

'An artificer. Someone who makes things'

'You're only for…'ministrative purposes.'

'Well, right now I need to administer you out of here. Have you had a vision?'

'Vision…loads of visions. Nothing but fecking visions. How many do you want?'

'One will do. Let's go.'

'Water…get me some water, would you, lad?'

Joe crouched and stepped over to the back of the cave, where he found the small stone basin that collected the drinking water from the holy spring. He took the tin mug lying alongside it, filled it and handed it to Christopher, who slurped back the contents.

'For this relief much thanks, Barnardo.'

'You're raving. Shut up and give me your arm. We're taking you up in the basket.'

'Can't…I've only been down a week.'

'You've been down here four weeks this time, chief. The abbot wants to see you. He's worried about you. You've been howling at night.'

Joe took the monk's arm and laid it across his shoulders, and the two figures shuffled slowly towards the mouth of the cave, which opened out in the cliff face about twenty feet above the frothing waves below. A large wickerwork basket hung suspended from a thick rope outside the cave entrance, swaying in the wind. Joe grabbed the rope with his free hand and gave it a tug. A bell from above replied. Then he drew the basket into the cave.

'Right, if my lord would like to enter his carriage.'

'You're not real,' muttered Christopher. 'And that's no carriage.'

'Just get in it, will ya?'

Christopher reluctantly flopped down in the basket. His legs stuck out.

Joe took hold of the rope and jerked it twice. The distant sound of two answering bells could be heard.

'See you on top,' said Joe, and pushed the basket out over the churning sea.

Two days in the infirmary had helped to restore Brother Christopher's physical condition somewhat, but his eyes still bore the look of a man who has seen rather more than he would have wished to do. At the hearing in the scriptorium, he stood slumped slightly to one side, staring into the middle distance. His voice was earnest, but rambling and occasionally indistinct.

'…and I saw a dragon with seven heads, and each head spoke one word, and those words were 'I Am That Which I Will Be'. And the dragon had seven fiddles, and it played seven tunes. And there was a penguin, too, and lo! It danced. And behold, an angel appeared to me, and it was neither a man nor a woman. And the angel said, 'Arise and go with me, for we must go up to the administration.' And the angel took me up to the great heights…'

The abbot, who was sitting with his chin in his hand, exchanged glances with Brother Geoffrey, who was acting as recorder.

'And there I saw an elephant that spouted flames from its trunk. And the elephant had a key that could open a secret door, and the elephant said…'

'We've had that one,' said Brother Geoffrey impatiently.

'What?' said the abbot.

'The elephant and the key. We've had that one already.' He consulted his notes. 'It came between the palace made of ice and the tower that spoke with a voice of thunder.'

'Yes,' said the abbot. 'Brother Christopher, you are repeating yourself. Have you anything more to add?'

Christopher gave no indication of having heard.

'…and the other dove flew north. And there was a mouse that played a golden trumpet…'

'Wait!' said the abbot. 'Stop. Go back. What was that about doves?'

'Doves…yeah…there were doves alright.'

'Yes, doves. What was it that you saw? We didn't catch it.'

'I saw two doves, a male and a female. And the male dove flew west over the ocean, and the female dove flew north.'

The abbot sat back with a sigh of satisfaction.

'That's the one.'

A week later, almost restored to his normal self, Christopher was back in the scriptorium, sitting on a wooden three-legged stool and watching gloomily as Brother Ignatius carried in the abbot's throne. Known as a cathedral, for some reason Christopher could not fathom, this was a folding canvas chair with elaborate scrolled carvings on the wooden parts. The room had been purified with incense, and candles had been lit. No expense was being spared. It made him uneasy.

The abbot kept him waiting there alone for half an hour, but finally appeared and pulled the door skin closed across the doorway behind him. He muttered a few words of prayer, then sat down on the throne.

'Today is a very special day for you, Brother,' he began. 'You are to be received into the brethren of the beatified. So what I say to you today, I say from my chair. Do you know what that means?'

'Yes, Father Abbot. It means you're infallible.'

'Well…that is the popular belief, at any rate. But what it does mean is that I am speaking in my official capacity as your abbot, and whatever I say to you now is something I have thought about very carefully, and about which I have prayed for guidance to the Most High. So it is to be taken seriously. Do you understand?'

'Yes, Father.'

'I will hear your confession first. Have you committed any sins since your last confession?'

'No, Father. I haven't really been able to.'

'No. Well, given your recent record, perhaps we should thank God for that. What about inner sins? Have you been puffed up with pride, have you experienced jealousy, lust, anger?'

'Not really, Father. I've been a bit confused all right.'

'That is only to be expected. Good. I think we can conclude that you are ready.'

The abbot paused, and seemed to look inward for a moment.

'Your vision was of two doves. Do you know what a dove is called in the old Roman language? It is *columba*.'

'Right. I've heard foreign sailors call them that.'

'And that is where St Christopher Columbus got his name.'

'The fella who discovered the Americas?'

'Not at all. It was our own St Brendan who discovered that fabled country. But St Christopher Columbus used Brendan's map and flew an airship there, the *Hindenburg*, to convert the natives. Unfortunately his airship was hit by a native fire arrow, and he was martyred. But that is another story.'

The abbot paused and drew himself up.

'Your name is also Christopher. Were you named for Christopher Columbus?'

'No, Father, it was my given name before I entered the order. After St Christopher, patron saint of travellers, I think.'

'But still a good name for a sailor.'

'I suppose so, Father.'

'It has protected you so far, I think we can agree. I have heard the story of how you entered the order. The Lord must have had some purpose in directing you here.'

'Do you think so, Father?'

'I do. And the purpose for which he brought you here may very well be the task that we are entrusting you with today. Because it is one that is vitally important, not just for this order but for the Church itself. Do you understand?'

Christopher nodded nervously. This was all starting to sound a bit over the top.

'The male dove that you saw in your vision was St Christopher Columbus, who flew west. The female dove flew north. That was you. Today, you receive your new name: you are to be known as Brother Christopher Columba.'

'Columba? Isn't that a woman's name?'

'It is of no consequence.'

'Right, Father.'

'We are sending you on a mission, Brother Columba. But it will not be in a coracle, you will no doubt be relieved to hear. We want you to do what you do best. *And by that I do not mean mendacity, theft, disobedience and the destruction of Church property.* I mean sailing. We want you to sail to the far north, to the edge of the known world, and there accomplish a task of great delicacy.'

'What task is that, Father?'

'I cannot tell you that yet. There is a risk you might be captured and interrogated. You will have sealed orders, to be opened when you reach your destination.'

'But…aboard what vessel, Father? With what crew?'

'As I said, this is a highly unusual mission, so it will require a highly unusual craft.'

The penny dropped for Christopher.

'Ah no, not that yoke!'

The abbot looked at him.

'Perhaps you would prefer a coracle after all?'

Christopher shook his head.

'As for your crew, it will consist of one person only. And it seems the Lord has already picked out a suitable companion.'

'Ah jaze, no..!'

The abbot raised an eyebrow.

'Sorry, Father. Of course, Father.'

'Kneel, and I will give you absolution. And then I will ask you to swear fealty to me and to this mission.'

'I will, Father Abbot, I will of course.'

Christopher knelt. His day, he felt, had just gone from bad to a good deal worse.

CHAPTER TWELVE

'It simply cannot be done, Majesty,' I said as emphatically as I could.

The King, standing by the octagonal table in the library of the Rose Castle, pursed his lips patiently.

'And why not, pray?'

'Because it is completely ins…impractical. It will not work.'

'Ah, but that's what you told me last time! And look what came out of that – the clockwork locomotive!'

'This is different, Majesty.'

'I don't see how. We know the ancients did it. So why not us?'

His gaze returned to the drawings he had spread out on the table. The King was quite a good draughtsman, and his mechanical drawings could look almost convincing – if you knew nothing of basic engineering principles. In the past, he had on several occasions presented me with designs for perpetual motion machines. This time, he had drawn a coiled longitudinal spring in a tube, compressed and restrained by a ratchet arrangement. It looked like a simple spring-loaded gun – until you looked more closely at the 'musket ball' and saw the tiny figure of a man inside. He had also copied some pictures from ancient books, showing what appeared to be tiny huts perched on top of giant flying towers, like the observatory on the Round Tower – although as always with the literature of the Electric Age, it was difficult to know how much was real, and how much merely fable. He pointed to one of them.

'It's strange, they are always portrayed with an exploding base, like fireworks, but that would have burned them up. I think it more likely that they were spring-powered,' said the King. 'Rather like the human cannonball trick at the circus – you have no doubt seen it? He is of course not actually fired out of the cannon by gunpowder, that would blow the poor fellow to pieces. So they use a spring instead, and set off gunpowder at the same time, to maintain the illusion. I have a feeling that's how the ancients did it, too. The fire was probably all for show. Otherwise, it would never have worked with human travellers.'

'That may be so, sire, but I doubt that such a spring could be scaled up to launch a person out into the cosmos.'

'Of course it can. We just make it bigger. I'm sure a man of your talents can come up with something.'

'Majesty, if you will forgive me, I have gained the impression that right now the kingdom is in urgent need of rebuilding and reconstruction. Surely a project such as this could await a more opportune time?'

'Ah, but that's just the thing, Nielsen! You've put your finger on it. Yes, we need rebuilding, we need economic growth, but with what, hmm? Where are our resources?'

He sat down at the table and indicated that I should do the same.

'Look Karl, here is our problem. We urgently need to restore Kantarborg to its former prosperity. For that, we need two things above all: iron and blackstone. A kingdom that has one of these will stand. A kingdom that has both will rule. But a kingdom that has neither will become a vassal state, a mere supplier of labour.'

'But the Northland mines...'

'The mines are gone. They have fallen. Yes, I know you won't read that in the newspapers, but that is what has happened. They were overrun by the Witch and her people. Like a ripe fruit for the plucking.'

'But what use do reindeer herders have for mines, sire?'

'Do not underestimate them! We made that mistake once before. And don't believe all that nonsense you hear about sacred sites – the tribes know very well the value of the mines, and how to use them. Last month, our spies told us that a very large quantity of ready-smelted iron was transported via the railway line to Jernhavn. After that, we lost sight of it. It may have gone to the Ursans. But what was the other side of the bargain, hmm? That is what worries me. The Ursans already have the blackstone mines on the islands of the far north. What will happen if they decide to go into alliance with the rebels? It is not something that bears thinking about. We might see that damned woman on the throne of the Northlands, for one thing. And Kantarborg paying homage to her!'

The King's fears seemed somewhat melodramatically expressed, but then he was better informed than I. And I knew that Ulrika's support stretched well beyond the tribal regions, and included the supporters of the deposed King Häkon, her father. So the scenario he sketched out was perhaps not entirely inconceivable.

'That is the situation,' the King continued. 'We and the Northlanders can make a good fight of it in the north, but if the tribes call in the Ursans, we are finished. So we must ensure that such an alliance is a prospect that neither they nor the Ursans will find attractive.'

'If you will forgive me, Majesty, I still fail to see the connection with this...project.' I indicated the curling sheaves of fantastical drawings on the table between us.

'It's a question of resources,' said the King. 'The blackstone is almost exhausted, since ancient times, and what little there is left in the north is in the hands of the Ursans. And now we have lost the iron mines to the Witch. So where are we to turn?'

He waited. I did not know what to say.

'What is the one country that has lain unexplored since ancient times, with all its resources intact? Well, think about it!'

Geography had never been my strong subject in school.

'Majesty, I have no idea.'

'The *moon*, Karl!'

'The moon, Majesty?!'

'Why not? It is, what, fifty leagues away? A hundred? If it turns out to be full of minerals, it would be very foolish indeed to leave it unexploited.'

'I believe the consensus among astronomers is that it is very much further away than that, sire.'

'Well, if it is further away, we cannot reach it, and no harm will have been done. We might as well try.'

'But even if we managed to catapult some poor wretch there in this device, how would he get back?'

'Ah, well for that he would probably have to rely on the inhabitants of the moon for assistance. I feel sure they must have such devices. If they have not visited us before now, it can only be because they fear us, as the warlike beings that we are. So it is vital to convince them that we come in peace.'

It was not the first time in my long acquaintance with the King that I was led to consider whether his reputation for madness might actually have some substance to it.

'What about the language? How would he communicate with the moon-dwellers?' I asked, wondering why I was bothering to ask rational questions.

'I hardly think that would be a problem. Our historians tell us that Anglian is the oldest of all the languages, the one spoken by Adam and Eve, so the probability is that this will also be the language of the people of the moon.'

'But surely the Anglian language comes from Anglia, sire?'

'From Anglia? Good grief no, where did you get that idea? It's the other way round. Anglia is named after the language. The Anglian language was brought there from the Holy Land by Joseph of Arimathea. Did you not learn all this in school? All the world spoke Anglian until the time of the tower of Babel.'

'But...was it not precisely because mankind tried to reach the heavens at Babel that our speech was confounded by God, sire?' I asked, surprising myself. (Perhaps not all of my schooling had been in vain after all.)

'Well exactly, Nielsen! And since the moon-dwellers have committed no such sin, they have lived in a pristine state from the beginning, and have suffered no such punishment. Ergo, their language must still be Anglian!'

There was method in the King's argument, yet it was madness. There must surely still be some way out of this. I tried another tack.

'With respect, Majesty, I am merely a clockmaker. For a project such as this, surely a physicist would be better suited? Dr Hansen, for example?'

'Hansen is away in the far north, developing weapons for the Northlanders. And anyway, you do yourself an injustice, Karl. You are a skilled horological engineer – and you are the expert when it comes to spring-loaded mechanisms.'

'About that, Majesty...' I laid a hand on the drawings. 'A spring-powered device has its limitations. I know of no spring that would be anything like powerful enough for this purpose. Besides, the acceleration alone would likely kill the unfortunate air mariner.'

'Nonsense, Nielsen! The human cannonball seems to come out of it all right, doesn't he?'

'But...where are we to build such a device?' (I admit it, I was growing desperate now.)

He smiled, as one who had been expecting the question.

'In the very place where I suspect the ancient kings of Kantarborg launched their air mariners into the cosmos. In the astronomical tower in which you currently reside!'

'The tower? In the middle of the city? Surely we could pick some more discreet spot?'

'There is no more discreet place, believe me, Nielsen. Hidden in plain sight, and well protected. The core of the tower is hollow, did you know that? Well, it is. No-one knows why, but I think it is designed for precisely this purpose. The place is dedicated to the exploration of the heavens, after all.'

'Take the drawings with you,' he said, dismissing me and my irritating objections. 'Come back in a week and show me what you have been able to come up with.'

I did as the King asked, but after a week and much calculation, it seemed to me that all I had been able to devise was an unusually elaborate device for executing a man. The core of the tower was indeed hollow, but narrow – no more than a couple of yards in diameter. The most powerful spring we could secrete there – even assuming that we could overcome the engineering problems involved – would not be able to shoot a man in a small projectile more than a thousand feet into the air, at the very most. And a thousand feet was certainly high, but…

'Not even as high as our airships can fly,' mused the King, as I laid my calculations before him.

'Indeed so, Majesty.'

The King paused and looked out of the library window, his hands clasped behind his back. If I had somehow imagined that this news would discourage him from pursuing the project further, I should have known better.

'What about a balloon?' he asked, turning abruptly to me.

'A balloon, Majesty? To the moon?'

'Yes! Why not? We construct a balloon with a very light manned vehicle beneath it, and send it as high as we possibly can.'

'The balloon would surely burst at such altitudes, Majesty.'

'Yes, but this is the clever bit: we use a very large balloon, but we don't inflate it completely. Just halfway. That will leave plenty of room for it to expand in the thin atmosphere. Then it should be able to get all the way to the moon.'

As always with the King, some of his ideas were apt to appear positively sane when compared with some of the others.

'If the moon is as close as you suggest, Majesty, that might be a possible approach.'

'Then we must move with all possible speed, Karl. In my experience, no good idea is ever thought of by just one person in one place. Even a king. If I have been able to speculate on this, then you can be quite sure that the rulers of other kingdoms have done so, too. So it is imperative that we act first and send an ambassador of Kantarborg to the moon, and immediately afterwards enter into trade arrangements with the ruler of that country.'

Since there seemed to be no way out under my contract with the King, I promised him that I would deliver a first draft of the design within a week. The King gave me some drawings that he had made, based on ancient pictures of vehicles that were alleged to have visited the moon, and I spent the next few days studying them. Some of them were quite fantastical and showed vehicles of enormous size, but there was one small, four-legged contrivance that looked as though it could be adapted into a balloon gondola.

It would have to be light, so I designed a version of this to be built in cedar wood, which was light but strong. It would have four legs like the original, and a table-like platform, on top of which was a spherical metal capsule for the cosmos mariner. The main hatch, which would also serve as a window, would be sealed with a rubber gasket and held in place with screw bolts that could be opened from the inside or the outside (in case the poor man was unconscious when he arrived at his destination).

Inside the device, the air mariner would lie on a comfortable chair, made of light basketwork and well upholstered to offer some protection against a possible hard landing. When the air grew thin at high altitudes, he would have to breathe through a mask connected by a tube to a bottle of compressed air, using the device that the physicist Martinsen had invented for underwater divers repairing bridges. The King furthermore insisted that the air mariner should have the following items with him: a Bible, maps of the known world and the moon, drawing pads and paper, a telescope, and a personal message from the King to the lunar denizens. Apart from the usual diplomatic greetings, the message, which would be written in the King's own handwriting and bear his seal, was to contain a proposal for a meeting with the King of the Moon at the latter's earliest convenience, for the purpose of discussing matters of trade and mutual economic benefit.

'We will give him a good welcome here on Earth when he

visits. But first we will have to find an elephant.'

'An elephant?'

'Yes, it's the traditional gift for visiting monarchs. Unfortunately there are none in the Kingdom at present. Unless of course a circus ship calls here, they might sell us one.'

'It might prove a little difficult for the King of the Moon to take an elephant back with him in a balloon, Majesty.'

'Ah yes, good point. Perhaps you could design me a mechanical one, then? A clockwork elephant? That would be just as good.'

'Sire, perhaps we should consider the possibility that there might not be a king of the moon,' I said, hurriedly changing the subject. 'There might not be any inhabitants there at all.'

'Well, if there is no-one there, that is even better, isn't it? We plant a flag and claim the whole thing for Kantarborg.'

There was no answer to that. I went back to my designs.

It was bound to be cold at such high altitudes, so in my first venture into clothing design, I drew a warm, padded suit – not unlike the one the King and I had seen on the body of Himmelson, the founder of the Irdai tribe in the Westlands. This was duly produced by the court tailors – whence the rumour soon circulated that a campaign in the far north was imminent, as we were designing a new winter uniform for cold climes.

I designed a helmet, too – also based on what we could remember of the Himmelson shrine, but as we did not possess the strange, smooth materials of the ancients, we would make it in metal and leather instead, with goggles for the eyepieces. The King insisted that we should write the letters 'CCCP' on top of the helmet, as he had seen this in some of the ancient pictures. (When I asked what they signified, he told me they stood for 'Christopher Columbus, Cosmos Pilot', after the ancient captain of the *Hindenburg*. I was not entirely convinced that he had not made this explanation up on the spot.)

The King was certainly right about one thing, though: it would cost comparatively little for the Kingdom of Kantarborg to build such a balloon, while the potential gains, if by some un-likely chance he was right about the lunar mineral deposits, might be very great, so I managed to persuade myself that the project might at least be worth trying. But although I looked up many old books in the astronomer's lair at the top of the tower, I could find no evidence at all to support the King's contention that the moon was quite close to the Earth, and in fact a great deal that suggested it was very far away indeed. According to the sagas it had taken the ancients three whole days to get to the moon, which at the normal speed of a balloon voyage would suggest that it was almost as far away as Africa. I decided to increase the supplies of food, water and air on board.

CHAPTER THIRTEEN

Christopher watched grimly as the boathouse winch lowered the strange, shark-like craft backwards down the ramp into the water. It came to rest with its deck awash, seawater slapping over its black carapace. As the fruit of a winter's work it was certainly impressive, but also somehow disturbing. It looked ominous down there, like some predator waiting to strike. Several odd, tube-like projections poked upwards from the hull, some of them secured by cables. Joe, now wearing the traditional brown habit of a monk of St Michael, clambered down onto the craft and up into its cockpit.

'Step on board, boss, and I'll show you the ropes. Not that there are many of them.'

Christopher walked down the ramp and stepped gingerly onto the tarred hull, which felt reassuringly firm, despite looking as though it were made of old rags sewn together. The waves sloshed over his sandals.

'Tell me this,' he said. 'If she's this low in the water, the first big wave is going to swamp her, and she'll go down like a stone. How are you going to prevent that?'

'Come up here and I'll show you.'

Christopher carefully stepped over to the side of the cockpit and looked into it.

'The basic structure is like an elongated barrel,' said Joe. 'Staves cut to shape, held in by iron hoops, so she's watertight and able to resist pressure. Then we covered it in pitch and canvas for extra protection. This bit here is known as the conning tower. See that hatch? You keep that bolted shut at all times when you're up here. Everything below decks is kept airtight. That pipe there gives us air below, but there's a valve in it to keep water out. Any wave that comes over the boat will drain out through the scuppers, just like normal bulwarks. If any seawater does get inside, it'll go down into the bilge, and we can pump it out. We've done tests with the hull completely filled with water. She won't sink as long as the buoyancy tanks are full of air. You can steer her from above or below deck with these levers. Now...' Joe pointed fore and aft. 'Those are the rotary sails. The cables are to hold them rigid. They don't act like normal sails, they spin around their vertical axes. The axles connect to a propeller in the stern. A kind of screw. That's our main source of power. The smart thing about these sails is that it doesn't matter what direction the wind is coming from. You can even sail straight into the wind if you want to, though you won't go very fast.'

'Why do you need two of them? You'll have a hard time seeing where you're going.'

'It's to cancel out the torque.'

'The talk?'

'Torque. The force of rotation. One sail spins clockwise, and the other one spins anti-clockwise. If you only had one, the boat would try to revolve around the mast.'

'Which would not be good.'

'Not if you want to go anywhere. When you want to submerge, they can be telescoped down into the hull and sealed off with a hatch. That's if you have time. If not, you can dive anyway – you'll just have to let the sails dry out when you surface again.'

Christopher looked along the hull and sighed.

'Joe, it's a nice idea, but I'll need to see it work before I believe it.'

'Don't worry, you will.'

Joe opened the hatch and climbed down the ladder into the craft. Christopher followed. Inside, it was not as dark as he had expected; a few small, round windows let in some light.

'What the heck's that contraption? Some kind of bicycle?'

'Kinda. We have two sets of pedals. If we're underwater and need to make a getaway, you sit back in those seats there and pedal like mad. You can do a fair turn of speed with them.'

'They'll just shoot us in the water before we can get any-where.'

'Actually, no. We've done tests. If you're ten feet underwater, not even a cannon ball will get through. Water is better than any stone wall when it comes to stopping ordinance. Now this thing here is called the periscope. It lets you look around without having to surface.'

Joe showed Christopher how the device could be turned and focused.

'That's smart, alright.'

Christopher looked around the cramped space.

'Three bunks?'

'That was in the brief. I don't know why. Did the abbot not tell you any more?'

'Nope,' said Christopher. 'Sealed orders. We'll know when we get there.'

'There's a head down the back – pump action. Pure luxury, compared to the Rock. And there's a washstand behind the curtain.'

'The feminine touch.'

'What do you mean by that?'

'Nothing. It's nice. I'm used to roughing it with the men. Did you know it used to be considered bad luck one time, having a woman on board?'

'Well it's a good job I'm not a fecking woman, then, isn't it?' said Joe heatedly.

'Sorry, sorry…' muttered Christopher. 'I'll try to remember.'

'Just you do that. I'm the engineer on board this vessel, and you'd better treat me that way, unless you want to try running this boat on your own.'

'I will, Joe. Listen, I'm sorry, all right? Engineer it is.'

'Joe will do. Long as you remember. Right – let's take her out.'

Christopher stood at the vessel's bow, taking soundings with a line and studying the empty shoreline with suspicion. The sun was low in the west, and the swell was rhythmic and undramatic, with only a slight breeze. The first day of sea trials of the as-yet unnamed underwater yoke had gone well, but it had been a calm and sunny day. *You don't know a boat until she's been in a storm*, thought Christopher to himself. *Or a sailor.*

'One fathom on a falling tide. Not a lot. You wouldn't want to be caught aground in a bay like this.'

'Why not?' asked Joe, standing in the conning tower at the control position, which Christopher insisted on calling the helm. 'Could you not just wait for the tide?'

'I saw a boat beached once off Kinmallon. Caravelle, three-master. The locals were swarming all over her like ants. Salvage, they called it. But she wasn't wrecked, just careened. They claimed some ancient law or other. Piracy, more like.'

'People always have some law handy when they want to act like animals,' commented Joe. Christopher looked up at him in mild surprise.

'You're right there. Anyway, they stripped it of everything, left it a hulk. The crew were lucky to get away with their lives.'

'Good job we don't have anything worth taking, so.'

'They don't know that. And when we take her out for real we'll probably have something valuable on board. We'll have to be careful.'

He hauled in the sounding-line and looked at his timepiece. The brass angel was pointing at Vespers.

'Low water soon. We can see how it goes. If we have enough draught, we can stop here for the night. We'd better furl the sails. Makes us less visible. We can pedal our way out if we have to.'

'They'd hardly be able to see us from here?'

'They could with a spyglass.'

'They might think we were a whale.'

'That'd be no better. They'd be out here with their knives for the whalemeat.'

Joe disengaged the gear mechanism and braked the rotary sails. Christopher began the task of getting them ready to retract into the hull. He sang as he winched in the lines.

'Oh my cock is as stiff as a herring's backbone
But I need a good woman to find it a home..."

'Do you mind?'

'Sailors sing while they work, Joe. You want to be a sailor, you have to sing.'

'Well sing something a little less vulgar, would ya? You're supposed to be a man of the cloth.'

'How about *The Holy Ground*? You can't get holier than that.'

Christopher launched into the song, which was not in fact very holy at all, and was slightly surprised when Joe joined in.

We will sail the salt seas over,
And then return for shore
To see again the girls we love,
And the Holy Ground once more
Fine girl ye are!

'You can let go the anchors now, Joe.'

Joe released a capstan and the boat juddered as the chains played out fore and aft. The anchors were light and the chains short, designed only to hold the boat in relatively calm conditions and shallow water.

Stowing the rotary sails was a procedure that took a good ten minutes. Christopher was tightening the last bolts on the aft hatch, humming the song under his breath, when Joe reappeared on the deck, barefoot, wearing his cloak and carrying a towel.

'I'm going to take a wash. No looking!'

Christopher held up his hands in acquiescence, and stood up to go below. He was just clambering down into the conning tower when a larger than usual wave hit the boat broadside on, causing it to rock violently. He made a grab for the ladder to steady himself. There was a truncated cry from the stern, followed by a lot of splashing. Christopher stood still in the tower, resisting the urge to look over his shoulder.

'Help me, you bollix!' came the shout from behind.

Turning, Christopher saw Joe attempting and repeatedly failing to crawl up out of the water onto the slippery, rounded hull of the boat. He walked over, picked Joe's towel up off the deck, twisted it into an improvised rope, then held it out for Joe to grasp, before hauling him out.

Christopher had known women in his sailing days, though he had rarely seen one entirely naked. Nonetheless, it was enough to finally confirm Joe's gender in Christopher's mind.

'You shouldn't have designed the hull so round,' he said. 'Makes it hard to climb up.'

Joe stood up on the deck and pulled on his cloak angrily.

'Hope you got a nice eyeful!' he hissed as he walked away.

'No bother, you're welcome,' said Christopher. *And I'll let you flipping drown next time*, he thought to himself.

When Christopher climbed down the conning tower ladder, Joe was lying on his bunk with his back turned.

'You all right?'

'Feck off,' replied Joe.

Christopher sighed and sat down at the tiny mess table.

'You ought to be able to swim at least, if we're going on a voyage. I could teach you.'

No reply. Christopher sat staring off into space for a few minutes. The chronometer ticked and the waves sculped gently around the boat. He took a chart off the shelf and began to study it.

'I nearly drowned, once,' he said eventually, half to himself.

Joe said nothing.

'We were on our way home after a night's fishing,' he continued. 'It was winter and still dark in the mornings. I was aft, packing herring into barrels. The rest of the crew were all forward. Then a big rogue wave came over the side, just like with you, and I had my back turned and didn't see the bugger coming. Next thing I knew I was in the water, still hanging on to a barrel. The boat was gone. I tried to swim to shore, but it was too far and the currents were against me. The seas were high, the water was fierce cold and I was losing my strength fast.'

'What did you do?' asked Joe, still turned to the wall.

'I did what anyone would do. I prayed. I said, please God, just get me out of this and I'll dedicate the rest of my life to you.'

'So what happened?'

'I must have passed out. I don't remember. Sometime after dawn, a crab boat came past looking for their buoys and they spotted me, more dead than alive. They hauled me in. Told me afterwards they had to prise my fingers off the barrel.'

He laughed softly to himself.

'So...when I got my strength back, I went down to Kilkiernan Abbey, knocked on the door and told the abbot I wanted to join the teds. A deal is a deal.'

'And they took you, just like that?' asked Joe.

'Eventually. I had to prove my worth. I kept bringing them things they needed: ropes, nails, bits and pieces. They gave me absolution and didn't ask questions. One time I brought them a whole barge full of butter, don't ask me how...'

A thin, humming sound from outside, almost mosquito-like, but with an oddly rhythmic timbre, interrupted the tale. Christopher picked up the spyglass and climbed the ladder.

'What is it?' called Joe.

'Airships. Albans, I think. But that's a queer noise they're making.'

Joe joined him in the conning tower. Christopher handed him the spyglass.

'Three of them. Might be a raid.'

'The Rock, do you think?' asked Joe.

'Could be. They're heading that way. We'd better get back.

This doesn't look too good.'

By the time they had the sails up, a grubby smudge of smoke could already be seen spreading up the sky.

Christopher surveyed the shore through the periscope. The boatshed looked to be undamaged, although there was no sign of life. The raid did not seem to have extended to the mainland.

'We'd better take her in a bit further. I can't see much from here.'

Joe began peddling, while Christopher manned the rudder.

'Hold it!' he said suddenly. 'Thought I saw something moving.'

He refocused the lens.

'It's the abbot. He's waving to us.'

'So much for invisibility,' said Joe.

'He was probably watching out for the periscope. OK, up we go.'

They grabbed the pump handles and began to pump vigorously. When the needle on the gauge had dropped below the 'safe' level, Christopher opened the hatch and went above. The abbot stood on the shore, beckoning them inwards.

'I am relieved to see you,' said the abbot, once they were safely ashore. 'You saw what happened out at the Rock?'

'Only the smoke,' said Christopher. 'They were gone by the time we rounded the point.'

'I thought the Rock was supposed to be safe from airships?' said Joe.

'It used to be,' replied the abbot. 'The wind was too strong for them. But these airships had some kind of propellers that allowed them to stand still – wherever they learned that trick. And weapons like I've never seen before. Incendiaries. They burned everything above ground. Then they sent men down on rope ladders. We managed to get most of our people into the library vault, where the invaders could not come, but three are dead, many injured. They ransacked everything, then they left. Whatever they were looking for, they did not find it.'

Christopher looked anguished.

'They were looking for our Ignatian weapons. My Lord Abbot...forgive me!'

'Brother Columba, this is not your fault. And you warned me that this day would come. Perhaps I should have paid more attention to you. The Albans would have come sooner or later, the weapons story was just an excuse. They know that they must break our Church if they are to conquer this land. They have accused us of every heresy – Ignatianism was just the latest. And to be frank, right now, our greatest danger comes not from our enemies, but from our friends.'

'The McCarthys?' asked Joe.

'The same. They have pre-emptively occupied the peninsula to protect it, as they say, against the Albans. And quite coincidentally, that also includes the silver mine and the brewery. So now we are left without an income.'

'What will happen now, Father?'

'Negotiations with the McCarthys for tithes or compensation. But from a position of weakness, now. Never mind, it is not your concern. You two must concentrate on your mission, which must begin at once.'

'We had planned to hold a naming ceremony next month,' continued the abbot, 'but under the circumstances we will make do with a blessing.'

He turned to the boat and made the sign of the cross, muttering a benediction:

'Most gracious Lord, who numbered among your apostles the fishermen Peter, Andrew, James and John, we pray you to consecrate this boat to righteous work in your name. St Brendan the navigator, guide her across the waters. Holy St Christopher, watch over her crew and bring them to a safe return. And the blessings of God Almighty, the Father, the Son and the Holy

Ghost, be upon this vessel and all who come aboard her, now and forever. Amen.'

He looked distracted for a moment.

'Name. We need a name.'

'How about *Paloma*?' said Christopher. 'Iberian for dove.'

The abbot looked pained.

'Could it not be something Anglian?'

'*Dove*, then? *Pigeon* doesn't really cut it. And *Columba* is taken.'

'All right, *Paloma* will do,' said the abbot. 'Does anyone have some holy water?'

'I have some here,' said Joe, producing a small bottle from the hood of his habit. Christopher looked at him and raised his eyebrows. Joe shrugged.

The abbot emptied the bottle across the bow of the boat.

'I name this vessel *Paloma* after the Holy Ghost, who appeared to the Saviour in the form of a dove. May God bless all who sail in her. Now you'd better get going.'

'Er...Father Abbot, we have no provisions on board,' objected Christopher. 'And we don't know where we're going,' he added as an afterthought.

'That is taken care of. You will be taking the island route north. You can stop at the monasteries and take on provisions there, it is all arranged. But there are some other things that you must take with you. Come and help me lift them.'

Between the three of them, they managed to install two small but heavy wooden chests on board *Paloma*, through the expedient of removing some of the boat's stone ballast. It quickly became clear why a coracle had not been an option for this mission – it would never have got off the ground. The abbot then handed Christopher a vellum envelope and a map.

'The map marks your route. Destroy it at once if you are captured. The envelope must not be opened until you arrive at your destination. Remember, your mission is vitally important – much depends on it. Good luck to you both, and may the blessings of God be upon you. I can no longer stay.'

And with that, he turned and hurried off.

Christopher studied the map thoughtfully.

'Well, we can give it a try,' he said at last. 'Though to tell you the truth, I don't give a seagull's fart for our chances.'

Extract from *Collected Folk Tales of the Westlands*, ed. K. Madurmann (2375)

[Told by an elder of the Halsanga tribe]

The West Wind was quarrelling with the East Wind over who owned the North Pole. The West Wind had a sword that was more powerful than any on Earth. Its name was Vindicator. The West Wind challenged the East Wind to battle. The East Wind had a bow that could pierce any armour, but Laski the trickster had broken all the arrows. So the East Wind threw three rocks at the West Wind. The first rock landed and made Lake Kaskin, deeper than any lake on the surface of the Earth. The second made Mount Tapitcha, where no tree grows and no bird sings. The third caused the North Pole to melt, and all of the seas flooded across the land.

When the North Pole melted, the West Wind dropped Vindicator, and it disappeared beneath the waters. It is said that he who can retrieve it will rule the world.

No-one remembers who won the battle.

CHAPTER FOURTEEN

'And what will all this cost, Clockmaker? I hear that building the locomotive kept you and more than thirty men comfortably employed for several years.'

She gave me one of her sceptical looks. I had spread my designs out on the library table ready for the King to inspect, but to my surprise the Queen had arrived first and had asked to look at them.

'Majesty, this will be a very low-budget project. Nothing like the clockwork locomotive, I assure you. I estimate the cost will be a few thousand sovereigns at most.'

'Then you had better make sure it stays within budget. The sagas tell of ancient kingdoms going bankrupt trying to explore the cosmos. That fate must not befall Kantarborg. We are stretched enough as it is.'

She tapped the drawings impatiently.

'You believe that this contrivance will help us gain access to iron and blackstone?'

'I cannot guarantee that, Majesty. No-one can.'

'Yes, I thought as much. And if I were to say I am surrounded by dreamers and tricksters, would you contradict me?'

'Majesty, I would not presume…'

'Oh do shut up, Clockmaker, you fatuous fool. It's no wonder this kingdom is in the state it is! Idiots!'

And with that, she made her exit.

The King's reaction was rather more positive. He was particularly pleased with the overall form: the spherical capsule and the small platform supported by four legs.

'I like this, Karl! I like this very much. I can see you have taken inspiration from the ancient mooncraft designs.'

'Yes, sire. My assumption was that the ancients probably knew best about what is required to land on the lunar surface.

It's called a LEM.'

'It's called a *what*?' (The word has several meanings in Kantish, one of which is 'male member'.)

'That's what the ancients called it. I don't know why.'

'Just don't let the Queen hear you calling it that.'

'It is my impression that Her Majesty is a little unenthusiastic about the project?'

'Yes. Well. That would be a bit like saying that a cat is a little unenthusiastic about dogs. But not to worry, I will deal with that. You just concentrate on giving us a moon vehicle. A LEM.'

During the weeks that followed, as the grey and wet autumn slowly turned into a grey and wet winter, I constructed a small wooden model of the LEM in 1/25 scale, and demonstrated in the Rose Castle courtyard that it could indeed be lifted by a half-inflated hydrogen balloon, provided that we made the balloon very large indeed. The balloon flew high up and got entangled with one of the castle's copper spires, from where it had to be retrieved by a servant leaning out of a turret with a broom, which did not amuse the queen. The LEM model delighted the King, however, who kept it on his writing desk. (Partly, I suspect, in order to irritate his wife.)

I then put together a small team. For the balloon, we would clearly need someone experienced in the manufacture of rubber goods; Karsten Mellik, a technician from the Dragonfly bicycle factory, was selected and given the King's seal. Lieutenant Tharup of the royal airship, *Freya*, became our aeronautical expert. Mikkel Tillonsen, a young assistant horologer, was assigned to me to help me build the clockwork devices. These included a small dirigible propeller, powered by a miniature Hansen pod with a compressed spring inside, and an on-board clockwork calculating engine of my own design, which would measure wind speed, atmospheric pressure and compass direction, and use these to gauge the rough position, height and course of the craft.

One thing we lacked was an astronomer – but Brorsen, the

Astrologer Royal, was still enhuffed on his island in the Sound, and curiously, no-one at the University seemed willing to take his place. So I would have to handle that part of the job myself. The first issue to be considered was the actual landing site. To the team, I expressed the opinion that, as on Earth, the centres of civilisation on the moon were likely to be found alongside bodies of water, and as rivers on the moon were too small to be seen from the Earth, it made sense to select the shore of a lunar sea. The others concurred with this reasoning, and after some discussion it was decided that the air mariner should attempt to bring the craft down on the shores of the Sea of Rain – which name, given by the ancients, surely suggested a fertile area.

Now we had to find our pilot. I was a little worried that the King might suggest that I myself might fly the vehicle, and so I quickly proposed Erik Kramer, who had been on my old design team and had been the first man to drive the clockwork locomotive. He also had the advantage of being quite small and light of build.

Kramer was contacted and quickly accepted, on condition that he would not be bound by the King's seal once the project was completed. If he was going to be the first Kantarborgan to set foot on the moon, he wanted to be able to boast about it to his friends afterwards. This seemed a reasonable request, given the danger we were asking him to expose himself to, and the King readily agreed to it. We little suspected what trouble it would lead to later.

Tharup pointed out that Kramer would need to be able to see where he was going in order to navigate the moonship, and so, rather reluctantly, I included more small portholes in the design of the craft, through which Kramer could aim his telescope. With their brass frames, however, all of this was of course adding to the weight, and so I had to keep expanding the size of the balloon section, or the lifting vehicle as we called it, to compensate. At some point the size of the balloon began to exceed that of the Rose Castle, so I realised I would have to come up with something else.

The answer came to me one day when one of the electric bulbs in the Round Tower apartment burned out. I unscrewed it from its socket and found that it was quite strong and light, resembling the glass baubles that people hang from their trees at Yule. I began to think about pressure and weight.

A visit to the Royal Porcelain Factory followed, where the manager assured me that, although such a large mould-blown glass item had not been attempted since the giant punch bowl of Nikolai III, it was by no means impossible. The hatch would not be a problem – it was actually easier to make a sphere with a round hole in it than one with no insertions at all. He gave me a rough calculation of the weight, which left me satisfied that it would be considerably lighter than a metal sphere of the same dimensions. And the cosmos mariner would be able to look out in any direction.

I then got the King to authorise purchases of high-quality horological equipment, and set about installing a small work-shop in the tower. Somewhat to my own surprise, I found I was beginning to take this project seriously. Perhaps Johansson had been right – maybe I had missed being in the thick of things after all.

The final design of the LEM was given to the royal carriage-makers, who were asked *not* to add their usual flourishes, but to keep the vehicle as light and stringent as possible. I had to per-sonally intervene to stop them installing velvet upholstery. Nonetheless, the finished LEM, when delivered to the Rose Castle, was rather more richly decorated than its ancient counterpart had been, with fine marquetry, curlicues and scrolls in the woodwork, graceful curving legs of polished walnut, brass fittings, and the royal coat of arms etched into a small brass plate on the outside. In fact, to my eyes, it looked more like a piece of ornate court furniture than one of the moon landers from the ancient books. Rather like a cocktail table, in fact.

Standing in the courtyard of the Rose Castle, more than twice the height of a man, the LEM looked rather grand. We kept it under canvas to protect it against the weather, and in some feeble attempt at secrecy. Despite this, the rumours of course began to circulate in the city – one of which was that the King was building a giant clockwork spider.

But then, just when things were running along quite smoothly, we encountered a problem. Our airships had up until then used gasbags covered in cowgut. Recently, the navy had also been experimenting with linen coated with gelatine, which had proved a workable and cheaper alternative. But such materials require a rigid structure to support them, and as our balloon was expected to expand quite dramatically in the upper atmosphere, they would not do. The balloon would have to be made of a highly flexible material – which meant, of course, rubber. But neither the navy nor the two bicycle factories in the kingdom had anything like the amount of rubber that would be required. It would have to be imported specially.

The rubber would also have to be in an extraordinarily strong quality, capable of being stretched to a considerable degree. Fully inflated, it would also be very thin, which worried me. A bird could simply peck a hole in it, or land on it and burst it with its claws. Of course it was unlikely that there would be birds in the interplanetary void, but the balloon would have to get up through the sky of our Earth first. We could not make the rubber much thicker, as this would add too much weight. I therefore made two suggestions to the King. First of all, we should have several smaller balloons rather than one big one; in the event of one balloon bursting, the craft would then still be able to retain most of its buoyancy. It would require more rubber material and cables, and thereby sacrifice a little of the craft's lifting capability, but it would be a lot safer. I estimated that four balloons would be sufficient. Secondly, we should enclose all of the balloons in a light cane structure covered by a linen shell, to keep birds away. Inside, each of the balloons would have room to expand outwards.

The King readily agreed to my suggestions, and asked whether temperature, as well as pressure, would be likely to affect the balloons.

'Heat would certainly cause the gas to expand, Majesty.' Entering into the spirit of things, I added: 'So perhaps we should try to ensure that the craft does not get too near the sun.'

'Don't be ridiculous, Nielsen. The sun is millions of leagues away.'

The order for the rubber was divided up and placed with five different suppliers, in an effort to conceal the extraordinary amounts involved. This was for economic rather than security reasons: any merchant who gets wind of a substantial public commission will as a rule automatically triple his prices. But merchants, as I well knew, tended to socialise together, and word was bound to get around. For this reason we also imposed a very short deadline for acceptance: three days in the middle of the working week. The companies were no doubt puzzled, but they complied, and we settled down to await the shipments.

'What is the delay now?' asked the Queen, observing the lack of activity around the moon vehicle in the courtyard.

'We are awaiting an order from overseas,' said the King. 'Our LEM is rather large you see, my dear, so we will need quite a lot of rubber for it.'

I knew better than to smile.

'But we must use this hiatus productively,' said the King to me. 'I have been meaning for some time to show you some of the relics we have uncovered from ancient times. I will come to you tomorrow morning. Meet me at the bottom of the tower at ten.'

I thought it odd that the King did not simply ask me to meet him wherever these relics were, but I was ready at the bottom of the tower the next morning. He arrived with Johansson, who was carrying a large key and a lantern. Lanterns in the middle of the day always make me nervous.

'Did you see this?' asked the King, pointing at the hand-painted notice beside the locked door that had puzzled me when I had first arrived in the tower.

'*As above, so below*. We found it when we were restoring the plaster. We assumed at first that it was of some religious significance, but it has turned out to be a message of quite concrete import. The spiral walkway ended here, but I began to wonder. So I asked some of our archae…knowledge miners to excavate. And this is what we found.'

He took the heavy iron key and unlocked the door. As he drew it back, a dank, musty-smelling draught swept out from the other side. Johansson wound up the lantern and held it up. Beyond the door, the spiral walkway could be seen descending into darkness.

'As above, so below,' said the King delightedly. 'The tower's spiral continues down into the Irrational Layer! So, are you ready for this, Nielsen?'

Like most Kantarborgans, I have a deep, almost uncontrollable terror of the underground, where demons and nightmares are reputed to reside. And yet every time I have had dealings with the King, I have ended up sooner or later having to descend into the depths. Afraid my voice would betray me, I merely nodded mutely.

The three of us walked down the spiral ramp for what seemed like an infinite space of time. Here there were of course no windows, but otherwise the walkway was in every respect identical to that of the tower above, with brick walls and a cobbled floor.

'It was probably built at the same time as the tower itself,' said the King, 'and then lost for centuries. But I believe it was later found again and in use during the Cataclysm.'

'How many storeys are there, Majesty? When will we get to the bottom?' I called out.

'The Irrational Layer is full of stories, Nielsen,' laughed the

King. 'We can never get to the bottom of them all.'

I felt dizzy, caught in the illusion that there was no end to the spiral, and that we would simply keep walking downwards forever. But at last, the King stopped at what looked to be a side tunnel of some kind.

'From here on down, the spiral is flooded,' said the King. 'We have no way of knowing how far it descends into the subconscious of the Earth. But at this level we found something rather interesting.'

I could feel myself trembling, which I hoped the others, if they noticed, would put down to the cold. In the side tunnel was another thick wooden door, clearly ancient this time. It was half open.

'Take a look inside!' said the King.

Johansson held up the lantern, and I poked my head into a large, dusty, concrete-walled cell with a barrel-vaulted ceiling. At first I could see nothing, then my eyes began to make out some box-like shapes.

'We have found tombs like this all over the city.'

'Tombs!'

'Yes; small concrete rooms under the ground, with no windows, what else could they be? Most of them are much closer to the surface than this, and are empty. We must assume that grave robbers got there first, centuries ago. But in some, like this one, we have found both bodies and grave goods.'

Bodies. I looked around, and in the gloom, my appalled eyes began to make out the shapes of four or five skeletons against one wall. They were in an unusual position: crouching, huddled together. As though terrified. Of what?

The King brushed past me into the room.

'The grave goods are very peculiar. Extraordinary, what people chose to take with them into the afterlife. There are fragments of newspapers from the twenty-first century, and a musical instrument, a first aid kit, bottles of alcohol…undrinkable now, unfortunately. And look…look at this!'

He picked up one of the objects and brought it over to the doorway. It was a square box of polished wood, with a hinged lid. Inside was a seemingly random collection of cogs and mechanical parts.

'What do you think this was, before it disintegrated?' asked the King.

'It is clearly a clockwork device of some kind,' I replied, intrigued despite myself.

'Yes indeed! I think we have found something exceedingly valuable here. But let us take it up into the light so that you can take a good look at it.'

To my relief, we once again ascended the walkway. It took us a good five minutes to get back to the entrance to the tower, where Johansson placed the box on the floor, and I opened it again.

'Well, what do you think?' asked the King eagerly. He was looking at me as though he were expecting me to announce that we had found the Holy Grail. But the box of random bits and pieces gave me no clues.

'I don't know,' I said eventually. 'It could be anything.'

'But can you reassemble it?'

'Well…I can try. The parts are very rusty, and some of them may well be missing. I can try to work out its original function.'

'Could it be some kind of ancient calculating machine?'

'I don't know. It's possible. Give me a few days and I'll tell you what I think it is.'

'I look forward to hearing your report, Clockmaker!'

But the following days left me little the wiser. The chassis into which these parts must once have fitted was gone, so there were no clues to be had there. I tried fitting the cogs together in various combinations, but there were not many of them, and some seemed to be missing, which meant that the possibilities were almost unlimited. Eventually I managed to reassemble what could only have been a primitive kind of governor, so I knew the device was meant to operate at a fixed speed. It presumably must have had a spiral mainspring at some stage, now long gone. I made one up in my little workshop, and found the winding shaft to which it must originally have been fitted. So far, so good. But some parts left me baffled – this strange curving metal arm, for instance, what on earth was *that* for?

With several parts missing, it was hard to make much more progress with the mechanism. Indeed, it was difficult even to speculate on what the missing components might be. I began to wonder whether there might be some more pieces hidden away at the bottom of the tower. It was an unpleasant thought, and one that I kept pushing away, but after another day of frustration I screwed up my courage, took the key, a lantern and a wooden crate, and made my way back down to the underground chamber. I did not want to stay there longer than absolutely necessary, so, looking away from the skeletons, I simply scooped up as many of the various objects as I could carry and piled them into the crate, my heart palpitating in my chest. In my panic I accidentally picked up a human femur, and dropped it in horror.

Back in the apartment, however, I found that most of the items I had brought up were useless. There were some old tools, what appeared to be a small medical kit of some kind, a pack of cards, a crank handle, a few odd-shaped glass objects, and some kind of horn from a musical instrument.

But then, at the bottom of the crate, I found something else: a metal frame, which might well be the chassis I was looking for. I tried it in the wooden box for size, and wonders, it fitted! So now I could work out where the spring and the governor were supposed to go. The spring seemed to be mounted vertically, which was odd – in such an enclosure, I would have thought a horizontal mounting would make more sense. Then I noticed a round hole in the side of the box, presumably for the key.

Alas, there was no key in the crate – although I could easily have made one. But I began to wonder about the metal handle that I had found. I tried it in the hole – and it slid in and caught the axle perfectly. So the spring could be wound up with the handle, and a ratchet mechanism stopped the spring from slipping. But as far as the function of this device was concerned, I was still very much in the dark.

In the Rose Castle, the King was keen to hear about my progress.

'I feel sure it must be a *computer* of some kind,' he said.

'A computer, Majesty?'

'That's what the ancients called their calculating machines. They turned their knowledge into numbers and used the calculators like libraries, did you know that? And they stored it all on discs. Most ingenious.'

'But surely they were electric machines, Majesty? This is a clockwork device.'

'But before they developed electricity, they used clockwork devices. Have you ever heard of the Antikythera Mechanism?'

'I'm afraid not, Majesty.'

'An ancient mechanical calculator. Used to calculate the phases of the moon, eclipses and so on. It was made long before they had electric machines, if we can believe the sagas. But what I'm wondering is – what if they also had clockwork computers *after* they had the electric ones?'

'I'm not sure I follow, sire.'

'Well, imagine the situation. All your knowledge is stored on these machines. But now civilisation is falling apart around you, the machines are breaking down and can't be repaired, the electricity stops working. What do you do?'

'Well, I suppose I would try to develop an alternative.'

'Exactly! One that doesn't need electricity, and that you can repair with local parts. And I think that's what you have in your workshop. A clockwork computer.'

'I don't quite see how it would be possible to retrieve any… information from it, sire.' (*Nor make any calculations, for that matter*, I thought to myself. The mechanism was nothing like complex enough for that, and bore no resemblance to the calculating engines that I had myself designed and used.)

'Well, we'll see what you come up with. I put my faith in you, Karl!'

Sometimes I fervently wished the King would put his faith in someone else. Nonetheless, his remarks got me thinking. The mechanism was simple, certainly, but he had said that the ancients stored knowledge on discs in their 'computers'. If he was right about people needing to replace electric computers with mechanical versions during the Cataclysm, it would make sense for them to create a clockwork disc device. So perhaps it was not a computer in itself, then, but part of one? A disc player?

Working on this idea, I found it would be easy in theory to get the mechanism to turn a disc horizontally. But the rotational speed, as I could work out from the governor and the gearing, would be approximately eighty rotations per minute, and that made no sense at all. Nonetheless, having no better theory to work on, I completed the mechanism on the basis that that was what it was meant to do. I manufactured the missing gears and carved a small wooden turntable, put the whole thing together, oiled it, and wound it up. As expected, it turned quite well and steadily. Now what? It could as easily be a potter's wheel as anything more sophisticated.

The metal arm that I had wondered about had an axle which fitted into a hole in the frame. If this was where it was supposed to go, it could move back and forth across the turntable, and could be lifted up and replaced on it. If I dropped the arm down on the turntable while it was rotating, it made a peculiar scratching sound. I realised that if the device really were a disc reader, such an arm would allow access to any part of it. *Random access* – the Anglian phrase rang a bell in my memory somewhere. I looked it up and found that the ancients did indeed use this principle in their computer designs. It was beginning to look as though the King might be right.

Then I began to wonder about the musical instrument that I

had found. It looked to be some kind of horn, with a rounded tube, and was missing its mouthpiece. The diameter of the mouthpiece end, however, matched that of a round hole on the metal arm. For a moment I thought that perhaps the whole thing was just some kind of mechanical trumpet-playing machine, but I could see no means by which air could be blown through it.

I went through the crate once more to see what else it contained. I tried out *everything* I found to see if it would fit somewhere on the device: glass bottles, small metal figures, bits of jewellery. As a result, some very peculiar machines were created that evening, and I was glad there was no-one around to witness my experiments, or they might surely have doubted my sanity.

I had success with one thing only, and that was with a box of steel needles that I had at first assumed must have belonged to a sewing-machine. But these needles had no eyes. To my great surprise, one of them fitted perfectly into the end of the metal arm, though without improving the scratching sound that the turntable gave off – except that now, with the trumpet attachment, it was a good deal louder.

I had now had a functioning machine that, as far as I could see, could do nothing useful at all.

I gave this discouraging news to the King, who did not react at all in the way I expected.

'A disc player! Yes! I do believe you are right. Eighty rotations a minute, you say? Could it be 78?'

'It could, Majesty. The rotational speed is not precise. Why?'

'I believe that the figure 78 held some ritual significance for the ancients. I have seen it before, on certain items we have unearthed from our excavations. Bring the device over to the Rose Castle on Thursday afternoon at three, to the Throne Room. I think we will try a little experiment.'

The machine was a heavy and awkward thing to carry, but luckily the distance from the astronomical tower to the castle is not far. The guards were not curious – they knew their king, and were used to seeing all manner of peculiar things being brought across the moat bridge. Getting it up the spiral staircase was more of a problem, but at last I managed to manhandle the thing into the Throne Room on the second floor.

There, a surprise awaited me. Not only was the King present, but also the Queen, her counsellor Arkdur Andersson, several courtiers, and a churchman in full clerical frock.

'Andersson you know of course, and this is the Most Reverend Harald Arbinger, Archbishop of Ros. I have invited them here to view the demonstration of your marvellous machine.'

'Majesty, I…I very much doubt that the machine will produce anything very remarkable today.'

'Well, we shall see about that. You can set it up on that table.'

I did as the King asked, with memories of the catastrophic public demonstration of the clockwork locomotive flooding my mind.

'Clockmaker Nielsen has reconstructed a most fantastic machine from the ancient past! A disc player, you said?'

'It would appear to be so, Majesty.'

'We know that the ancients used computers with discs to store knowledge,' the King continued, for the benefit of the audience. 'Most of these were electric, but some apparently ran on clockwork. It is in any case my belief that we may learn much of value about the ancient past from this machine.'

'But Majesty,' I objected, 'we do not have the discs!'

'Oh but I think we do, Clockmaker. Try it with *this.*'

With a sly smile, he walked to the table and returned with a large flat disc made of some strange black, wax-like material, with a small hole in the middle. It had a label in the centre with writing in Old Anglian, most of it faded and indecipherable, but the number '78' was written in large numerals and was clearly legible.

'We found several boxes of these recently at one of the excavation sites. Give it a try.'

I placed the disc on the turntable, where the hole fitted perfectly over the small spindle in the middle, and turned the handle of the machine until the spring was fully wound up. Then, as the turntable began to revolve, I lifted the metal arm and with trembling fingers dropped it down onto the edge of the disc.

The result was dramatic. A loud blaring noise erupted from the horn, producing a startled gasp from the observers in the room. After a moment, the sound of some kind of orchestra could be identified. This was interrupted by the voice of what sounded like a child, singing in Anglian:

'Aba, daba, daba, daba, daba, daba, dab
Said the chimpie to the monk
Baba, daba, daba, daba, daba, daba, dab
Said the monkey to the chimp...'

A tremor of shock and alarm spread through the room. Had the clockmaker somehow secreted a child in that small box? It must have looked like witchcraft.

'Then the big baboon one night in June
He married them and very soon
They went upon their aba daba honeymoon!
Aba, daba, daba, daba, daba ...'

'Take it off!' shouted the King. 'For the love of God, take it off!'

I pulled the metal arm off the disc, producing a loud tearing noise that made everyone wince. It seemed that this machine might not turn out to be the fountain of knowledge that we had hoped.

'Try this one,' said the King, handing me another disc. He looked rather more nervous now, and the archbishop had gone a shade of clerical purple.

I placed the disc on the turntable and did as before. This time a quite different piece of music emerged, with a rapid, pulsating rhythm. A man's voice sang:

> *'I know a fat old policeman*
> *He's always on our street*
> *A fat and jolly red-faced man*
> *He really is a treat!*
> *...HA HA HA HA HA HA HA HA HA!!'*

'Devils! Devils from hell!' shouted the archbishop, unable to restrain himself any longer. He marched across the room and gave the table a solid kick, sending the machine flying across the floor into a corner. The maniacal laughter ceased, to everyone's relief. There was a silence.

'Well,' said Arkdur Andersson, 'that was interesting. Perhaps we can use it as a weapon of war one day.'

'Or of torture,' said the Queen, walking towards the door. 'Do take your toy with you when you leave, Clockmaker.'

The rest of the audience followed her out, leaving the King and I alone.

'I had rather hoped the demonstration would go a little better than that, Nielsen.'

That was not fair. I turned to him angrily.

'You sprang that on me, you gave me no warning! You have no-one to blame but yourself!'

I strode out, leaving the machine, and walked back through the wet streets to the Round Tower – wondering whether my indignant words might cost me my liberty. Or, indeed, my life.

CHAPTER FIFTEEN

The good thing about sailing, thought Christopher, is that it can help you to think, or it can help you not to think. It kind of works both ways. *Paloma* was making its usual painfully slow progress across a wide bay, with the object of making landfall at the monastery of Kilfeane on the opposite shore by nightfall.

The wind was choppy today, south to south-west. Maybe a chance of squalls later, keep an eye on it. The glass falling. He liked battling the salt wind and the currents between these mountainy headlands: bring it on. It made him feel alive. *Back where I belong*, he thought.

The thing he couldn't get used to was that it didn't matter what direction the wind was coming from. By pure instinct, he kept wanting to add a touch or two to the rudders when he felt it change direction. She went a bit faster with the wind behind her, but it was extraordinary how well she went even against the weather. But these damn levers he had to steer with – he would have much preferred a proper wheel and a single rudder, not two.

· The other thing was being this low in the water. The cockpit screen kept the worst of the spray out, but every so often a wave would wash right over the boat and leave him drenched and spluttering. A seaman is used to getting wet, but there were limits. You'd catch your death in this thing in cold weather. Still, she bobbed up every time like a cork, just like Joe said she would. Fair play to the man, he knew what he was doing. Wherever the heck he had picked it up, because he was no sailor, that was for sure.

Joe. That fellow was a bit of a conundrum all right. It wasn't so much the fact that he was a woman, but that he was both a woman and a man. Christopher couldn't get his head around it. *They are all men*, the abbot had said. *For administrative purposes, at any rate.* So how many more of the monks he had spent the past few years with had actually been…? Brother Damien, he had slender hands. And an angelic face that turned the heads of some of the old fellas. *Stop this. Concentrate on your sailing.*

It would be eight bells soon, time to wake Joe. But perhaps he would just leave him rest for a while. Joe was no great enthusiast for taking the helm, and Christopher was enjoying the morning and the solitude. They'd hardly make Kilfeane before nightfall, this rate. They'd have to moor offshore in the dark and send in the dinghy. Risky business. They couldn't leave the boat unattended. He could maybe send Joe in and stay on board. *You can't send a woman into danger alone,* said a voice in his head. But that was the thing. How was he supposed to treat this fellow?

Here they were, on a long voyage, forced into greater intimacy than any man and woman ought to be, unless they were lovers. A man with a woman's name, and a woman with a man's name. Sure you couldn't make it up. Joe didn't seem to mind unless he was reminded of his gender. And then he did mind, very much. Christopher still thought of Joe as the young man he had met in Garrystown. Most of the time, anyway. All right, the memory of Joe's naked body sometimes floated unbidden into his mind. The slim, pale limbs, the small breasts, the rounded hips, the shock of red hair at the crotch. It was hard to forget. It wasn't that he had had any lascivious thoughts at the time, he was just trying to get a fellow crewman out of the water. But since then, he had been a lot more careful around Joe, and had avoided getting too physically close to him.

It wasn't even as though men and women were all that physically different, really, he thought. *And yet for this, men will sell their souls.* He'd seen them do it. Baba at the House, that time with the cleric. Never saw a man so obsessed. Used to hang around her day and night. But she'd fixed him good with a word to the bishop. Off to the missions with him.

Terence of Bath, he had once read, held that all women were the creation of the devil, placed on Earth for the sole purpose of corrupting men. Terence of Bath was a moron. You grow up in a brothel, you learn a thing or two about women. Although he was no expert. He could still founder on the rocks. He had once encountered a very enthusiastic raven-haired young lady in Garrystown who had tested his vows sorely. Afterwards, at confession with the abbot, he had broached the subject of the Church's attitude to the female sex.

'They most certainly are not the creation of the devil,' said the abbot. 'The devil creates nothing. All he has to work with, to his great frustration, are what God has made. So he will take whatever mankind delights in and give it a twist. That is his joy. If you love food, he will try to make you a gourmand, so that you no longer know the pleasure of simple eating. If you enjoy sports, he will give you competitions and bitter rivalry. If you love your country, he will make you a patriot and sell you guns.'

(Christopher glanced up guiltily at this point, but the abbot did not seem to have guessed anything.)

'And he takes the natural attraction that exists between human beings and tries to complicate it and turn it against them, so that they become miserable. As monks, we choose to avoid those complications in order to concentrate on the spiritual life, but that does not mean that the urge itself is evil. On the contrary, it is of God. It is evil only when it is selfish and uncaring.'

(Given what he had felt for the raven-haired beauty in Garrystown, it might be that the abbot had indeed guessed something there.)

'But what if I fall in love with a woman, Father?'

'If you cannot live without her, you must leave the order. Our lives here are demanding and require single-minded devotion. But we have had monks in the past who have abandoned the monastic life in order to marry, or for some other reason. The idea that a vocation is necessarily for life is one that belongs in the ancient past.'

Well, at least there was little danger that he would fall in love with Joe. The little bugger was far too irritating for that. The closest Christopher was likely to come to love was the sneaking respect that he couldn't help feeling for Joe's ingenious designs. And for his self-discipline. But then again, it's easy enough for some people to be self-disciplined. You can't be tempted by what you can't even imagine. Perhaps he could introduce Joe to the joys of rum on this trip, it might help him loosen up a bit. But most likely he would just refuse. *Joe's the kind who sees relaxing as letting down his guard*, he thought.

A glint of reflected light a league away caught his eye. Christopher took the spyglass and focused. Damn and blast. Might just be traders, sailing in convoy for protection. Or it might be something much worse. He yanked on the cord that rang the bell below deck.

'What's up?' asked Joe sleepily as he emerged from the hatch. Christopher nodded towards the horizon and handed him the spyglass.

'We'd better take her down,' he said. 'We won't be able to get far enough away in time.'

By the time they had the sails stowed, the approaching ships were looking threateningly large and persuasively Alban in cut and measure. They scrambled down the ladder and began to pump the air out of the buoyancy tanks.

'Save, lest we sink beneath the waves!' sang Christopher lustily as he worked. Joe gave him a look.

'What? It's a hymn!'

At one fathom below, Christopher raised the periscope. The ships were very close now, the bow of the nearest one almost filling the lens. But they were behaving a little oddly. They were spreading out. It looked as though the outermost vessel would pass them to starboard, while the other two would pass on their port side. It reminded him of that time up in the mountains when he had watched a couple of sheep dogs working a flock, responding to the echoing whistle of the shepherd across the valley. The tranquil memory provoked a sudden, chilling realisation.

'Joe, how far down can we go?'

'If we shut off the air pipe we can go down about five fathoms. We did that in tests. Don't know after that.'

'Right. Let's do it. Now.'

'Why, what's up?'

'*They're hunting!*'

Joe reached for the stopcock and closed off the air valve. In the next second they heard the boom of a cannon, then another. Joe watched the depth gauge as they desperately pumped most of the rest of the air out of the buoyancy tanks. Ten minutes later, exhausted by their efforts, they were at four and half fathoms, in complete darkness. They could still hear the cannon reports above, though they had become rather muffled.

'Full fathom five thy father lies,' said Christopher, panting.

'What…in the name of feck…are you talking about?' gasped Joe.

'Sorry, never mind. Are we safe here?'

'Should be. There's no weapon I know…that can penetrate that much water.'

'They'll make one soon, though, I bet,' said Christopher. 'When it comes to killing, men are as inventive as the fiends. How the devil did they know where to find us?'

'You tell me. Someone must have snitched.'

'Joe, is it my eyes, or are walls bulging in?'

'It's the pressure. Don't worry about it. They'll hold.'

'I hope so. So, are we going cycling?'

'I think we should keep still. Lie down boss, we need to conserve air. They can't see us, they'll think we're gone.'

After three hours underwater, Christopher and Joe were

gasping for breath. Pumping out the tanks to raise the boat proved to be unexpectedly hard work, almost more than they could manage. By the time they reached periscope depth, they were nearly spent.

Joe opened the air valve and gulped in the fresh air, while Christopher scanned the scene. The ships were gone. But so were the landmarks. Rotating the periscope, Christopher searched for the mountain peaks against the horizon. The boat was rocking wildly about in turbulent seas.

'Ah blast, we're miles out. We must have been carried out by the tide. We're out in open water. We'll have to head due east and try and get back on course.'

They climbed onto the deck, into what had become much rougher weather. It was a struggle to get the sails up in the strong winds – the waves were growing and *Paloma* rolled threateningly from side to side. Rain began to fall.

'Here, watch yourself back there!' called Christopher, throwing Joe a line from the cockpit.

Joe tied the rope around his middle and struggled with the bolts around the aft sail hatch.

'Remind me to put more handrails on her next time, willya?' he called back.

Finally the sails fore and aft began to revolve, although it was impossible to see whether *Paloma* was actually moving. The rain was coming down now in thick, heavy sheets.

'Get down below and keep an eye on the compass,' shouted Christopher. 'I can't see a thing up here.'

Joe went below and sat at the instruments.

'Over to starboard ten degrees. That's it. You're heading due east now, boss. Better close the hatch or we'll be swamped.'

Christopher kicked the hatch closed. It was all he could do to hold on as the wind and water battered the craft and swung her first one way, then another. Wave after wave washed over the boat, soaking him. He tried to read the compass, but the rain stung his eyes and raindrops covered the dial. After half an hour of fruitless efforts, he opened the hatch and shouted down to Joe.

'It's hopeless. I'm going to have to come below.'

Below decks, the water sopping from his clothing, Christopher could only steer the boat more or less east and hope for the best. Joe manned the periscope, but there was little to see. *Paloma* bucked as though she were trying to vomit her crew out. Both of the mariners were bruised from being thrown around inside the vessel. Perhaps because of the buffeting, the compass was also acting strangely, the needle swinging around in the dial.

'I've no idea what way we're going. You see any sign of land, we'll head for it,' shouted Christopher. 'There might be a bay where we can shelter.'

'Right you are. I can see something up ahead. Twenty degrees to port.'

'We'll head for that, then. She'll surely not take much more of this.'

'She will,' said Joe confidently. 'It's more whether we will.'

Ten minutes later, Joe called out again: 'It's land right enough. I can see a hill. Could it be a headland?'

'Too far out for a headland. Might be an island.'

'I think I can see a harbour wall. Keep going, I'll look for the entrance.'

'Thanks be to God. You guide me in.'

'Ninety to port now. That's it. Straight on. It's a harbour all right.'

'OK, let's go above.'

They opened the hatch and climbed up into the cockpit. The rain, though still heavy, seemed to be easing off as they directed the craft through the harbour mouth, which towered above them on both sides. The harbour wall was constructed from large granite stones and concrete, and looked ancient, with iron mooring rings that had almost rusted away. The inner harbour space was vast, but deserted of other vessels. There was no sign of life. In the shelter from the wind, a near-silence descended.

'It looks like an island.' Joe's voice was subdued. 'But why'd they build such a big harbour, so? Who would have big ships out here?'

'Look at all the ruins. There must have been lots of people here once.'

Joe looked around. The harbour was surrounded by the roofless remains of three and four-storey brick buildings. This had been an important place. Probably centuries ago. But one group of buildings looked like it had received a new roof in the not too distant past.

They found a suitable mooring spot beside a set of concrete steps, tied off the boat, and, breaking their own watch rules, fell asleep. It had been a very trying day.

When Christopher awoke, the rain had stopped. He found Joe up in the cockpit, studying the chart.

'What I don't understand is why this place doesn't seem to be marked anywhere on the map.'

'How's that?'

'We were about two hours in the storm, right? So even if we were driven due west, we can't be further out than about here...' he pointed out the area. 'But there's nothing there. Just open sea.'

'It must be there somewhere.'

'Nearest island I can see is Cairnglee, about thirty miles north of our last position. We can't have sailed that far in the time.'

'Give me a look.'

Christopher studied the chart thoughtfully. Joe was right. There were a few skerries and isolated rocks marked here and there, but nothing this size. It was odd all right.

'I've just been up to look for the mainland,' said Joe. 'I think I could just about make out some of the peaks to the east, but we're a good bit out. If we can take our bearings off them we could work out where we are.'

'Can we get a meal on first?' asked Christopher. 'I'm famished.'

'I'll go see if I can find some firewood.'

'You'll be lucky to find anything dry. Maybe over beyond in the ruins...'

He stopped. They both heard it: a groaning, echoing clamour, the sound of metal against metal. It ceased as suddenly as it had started. They looked across the harbour, but there was nothing to be seen.

'Be not afeard; the isle is full of noises,' said Christopher.

'Ya wha´?'

'Never mind. Take the axe with you. I'm going to go see what made that racket.'

In the late afternoon light, the birds had begun singing their evensong in the bushes. Christopher made his way carefully around the harbour's edge, clambering through undergrowth that in places almost concealed the quay itself. Beneath the nettles and brambles he could make out the remains of old, rusting machines everywhere – some them recognisable as cranes or winches, others of indecipherable purpose.

The creaking, groaning sound returned, louder now. It seemed to be coming from the other side of the harbour. It took a lot of scrambling and climbing to get any closer, and he was sweating by the time he could get near enough to see more. There was an inlet from the harbour here into some kind of short canal, which led into what looked like a tunnel going into the hillside. The remains of a wire fence crumbled beneath his fingers, and he edged his way through onto a ledge above the water. From here, he could look into the tunnel mouth.

Back at *Paloma*, Joe had returned and was loading firewood and twigs into the iron stove at the back of the cockpit. Satisfied that they had enough for a small cooking fire, he went below to fetch the matchsticks. Then, as he climbed the ladder again, he heard a click. As of a gun being cocked. He looked up and found himself staring straight into the barrel of a musket. A small, grey-bearded man in a broad-brimmed hat was standing on the harbour wall, pointing the weapon at him.

'Who are you?' asked Joe.

'Never mind who I am,' said the man. 'You're on my land.'

'We…I just wanted to ride out the bad weather. I'll be on my way directly.'

'You're going nowhere,' said the man. 'Put your hands up and get up here.'

Joe, his hands raised, stepped carefully along the hull of *Paloma* towards the harbour steps. The man tracked sideways, keeping the gun pointed at him. But then, for no apparent reason, he suddenly took a flying leap off the harbour wall and landed in the water with a loud splash, where he flailed about, coughing and cursing. He looked about desperately, but the musket was nowhere to be seen.

'You'll pay for that firearm! You'll pay for it, damn you!'

Christopher appeared at the top of the wall.

'We will of course, Grandad.'

Joe threw the man a line and drew him in, and then, with Christopher's help, bound him firmly with it. Christopher retrieved the man's hat from the water and patted him down to check for other weapons. Then they manoeuvred him down the ladder and into *Paloma*'s hold.

'Right, why don't we introduce ourselves?' said Christopher. 'We sort of got off on the wrong foot there, so to speak. Sorry about the kick. We are brothers of the order of St Michael, on a mission of the Lord. Who are you?'

'I'm the King of Holy Island. King Barney. This is my island.'

'Do you know what? I think I've read this saga. You have a daughter here somewhere, don't you? And a monster.'

The man looked at Joe.

'What's he blethering on about?'

Joe shrugged. 'I dunno. He says things.'

'There's no-one here only myself.'

'But there were lots of people here until recently, weren't

there?' asked Christopher. 'And pardon my effrontery your Majesty, but you're no king. I know a security guard when I see one.'

The man stared defiantly back.

'Why isn't this place marked on the map?' asked Joe.

'Course it is. It's on all of them,' said the man.

Christopher held up their chart.

'Sure that's an old chart,' said the man. 'Probably from back before the Cataclysm.'

'So what?' asked Christopher. 'Islands don't just come and go.'

'The ancients didn't want it showing anywhere. They had secrets out here.'

'What kind of secrets?'

'Wouldn't you like to know, now?'

'Would these be secrets involving something called Vindicator?' asked Christopher.

Joe gave him a puzzled look. The man glowered and said nothing.

'So, where did they all go? All the workers?' Christopher continued.

'They died. The whole lot of them. This island is cursed. You're going to die, too.'

'You look to be all right.'

'I stay out of the cave, is why. I don't go meddling with the underground. There's a monster down there all right, he'll get you. Yeah, you can laugh, mister. Just wait.'

'All right, it's none of our business,' said Christopher. 'Just point us in the right direction and we'll be on our way.'

The man gave a bitter laugh.

'Ye won't get far.'

'Why's that?'

'I know who ye are. The Jarl's men are out looking for ye. There's a price on yeer heads.'

'We have no business with the Jarl.'

131

'Well now, he says ye do. He says ye're Ignatians, and that ye have a secret weapon on board this boat, and ye're trying to smuggle it into Alba to blow up King Malcolm.'

Christopher laughed.

'Look around you, old fella. You see any secret weapons here?'

'I don't know what ye have or ye don't have. It might be the size of a matchbox. But I know ye won't get further north of here. The Jarl's men will have ye.'

Christopher nodded at Joe, and they went up on deck to confer. The evening air was cool now, a gentle breeze blowing. The air on the island was fragrant, seductive – quite different to the stiff winds of the Rock.

'What do you think?' asked Joe.

'They found us out in the open sea. They must have known where we were heading. I'd say they know the whole route, all the stops we've planned. They'll have men waiting at all of them.'

'What is it they're after? They don't really think we have secret weapons, do they?'

'Maybe we do. We don't know what's in the chests. Either way, they're throwing everything at us. They must really want to find us.'

Joe sighed.

'How about if we made a straight run through Alban territory?' he asked. 'No stops for supplies along the way, just the odd anchorage for the night. Could we do that?'

'We could try. It would take us a good few days' sailing, and we'd have nearly nothing to eat. We'd need to stock up here. There's a pump over by the ruins, we can get water before we go. Do you reckon King Barney has a stash of spuds somewhere? Maybe even a side of bacon?'

'I'm sure he does. But isn't stealing supposed to be a sin?'

'I'll give you absolution when you get back.'

'Me?'

'I'd better stay here and watch the old fella. You check out the island. We have a couple of hours yet before it gets dark. He must have a house here somewhere, it shouldn't be that hard to spot. Take the rucksack.'

When Joe was gone, Christopher went below and sat down opposite the bound man.

'Now, your kingship, let's you and me relax a while. Was that a hip flask I felt in your waistcoat, or were you just glad to make my acquaintance?'

'Thieves, that's all ye are,' said the man, as Christopher deftly removed the flask from his pocket. 'Nothing but common thieves.'

'Hey boss! CC! Wake up!'

'Hi Joe...'

'Thank God, I thought you were dead...what are you doing lying out here?'

'Ah well Joe, we are all in the gugger, but somfus...'

'Jesus Christ, are you *drunk*?'

'Ah, I wouldn't say that. I wouldn't say that, now.'

'Where's the prisoner?'

'I think he went home.'

'You think...you fecking imbecile! You let him escape!'

'Sure he won't do any harm.'

'No harm! He's probably halfway to the mainland by now. God almighty, we have to get out of here *now*. The Jarl's airships will be on their way soon. Give me your arm.'

'Heh...are you taking me up to the 'ministration again, Joe?'

'Just shut the feck up. Don't talk to me! Fecking eejit.'

'Joe, listen. Listen to me now. I've figured it out. How he did it.'

'How who did what?'

'How our Lord fed the multi...all the people. With the loaves and fishes. He just used a bloody big fish! Like the one in the cave.'

133

CHAPTER SIXTEEN

By tacit agreement – and somewhat to my own surprise – the unfortunate disc player incident was never mentioned again. The King, however, was becoming something of a fan of the ancient '78' discs – although, as he confessed to me, there was little real knowledge to be gleaned from them. Most of the ones they had found in the city turned out to contain songs in old Anglian or Kantish, some presumably humorous but quite obscure in meaning, many more romantic, together with a great deal of fast-paced, rather frenetic music that the King told me was called *jazz*.

'It seems to have been the preferred music of the aristocracy,' he said. 'It was composed by counts, dukes and earls, even a few kings. But the language is mostly indecipherable, it must have been some kind of code.'

Nonetheless, the King made determined efforts to learn the Anglian dialect of his forefathers, and often walked around in the Rose Castle humming the ditties to himself.

'My baby want a hep cat, hep cat, hep cat, zap a doody mama, that's what I say.'

'Would you please STOP mouthing that inane gibberish!' the Queen almost screamed.

The King grinned at me.

'Put my crazy mama on a tin can cot, way down yonder in New Orleans.'

With a gasp of exasperation, the Queen strode out of the room. The King shrugged.

'Bird gotta fly, boat gotta float, bye bye baby that's the way that it goes.'

The King also tried to interest me in the ancient music, but, to be honest, most of it sounded like a dreadful cacophony to my un-aristocratic ears. There was however one instrumental piece by the Duke of Ellington that I quite liked, called 'Take A Train' – apparently inspired by some ancient railway or other. The King fantasised about getting it scored for a military brass band, though thankfully nothing came of that idea. The reaction of the generals would have been something to see.

Four of the five ships arrived in March. The fifth was never heard of again. So we would have to be even more sparing and precise in our use of the precious rubber. At high altitude, when the balloons were fully inflated, their skins would be very thin indeed. Mellik assured me it would hold, but I was far from convinced.

The large mould for the balloons was carved from wood by the royal carriage-makers. This was cylindrical, with a rounded top. (The King laughed heartily when he saw the shape.) The balloons would be cast one half at a time, and then the halves welded together with molten rubber in the middle, which Mellik said was the right way to go about it. It did strike me, though, that the weld line would inevitably be weaker than the rest of the material. If one balloon burst Kramer would still have three more, which would permit him to land safely but would not be enough to lift the LEM again, with its heavy wooden landing legs. In such a situation, unless he could obtain help from the moon-dwellers, Kramer might be left stranded on the moon. I therefore made a design decision: the spherical capsule would be detachable from the landing gear. Once on the moon, Kramer would be able to unscrew a number of bolts and fly back to Earth with the capsule alone. That could be lifted by just two balloons, which greatly enhanced his chances of survival.

Kramer had never flown before, so he was temporarily assigned to the crew of *Freya* as a rating, in order that he might become acclimatised to air travel. It would not do, after all, if he went into a panic the moment the LEM cleared the ground. But he was reported to be a natural air mariner, with a good head for heights, remaining calm even when the airship had to make an emergency landing with a punctured gasbag on the

Northlander side of the Sound. It looked like we had the right man.

The clockwork calculating engine to be installed on board the LEM was taking shape in my workshop at the tower. I tried to base it on the old calculating machine I had used on board *Freya* on our trip to the north – a truly beautiful contrivance of polished wood and brass. But the new machine would also have to be highly accurate, able to collect information on air pressure, airspeed and compass direction from a variety of sensors, and combine this intelligence to provide a rough estimate of the craft's position – at least relative to its point of origin. As a further refinement, it would also plot this course on a map by means of a mechanical pencil-holder. My assistant Tillonsen and I installed a prototype on *Freya* that proved reasonably successful, although after a couple of days it began to be wildly inaccurate. The calculator would clearly be no substitute for traditional chart-reading and bearings, but as the voyage was likely to last for several days, it could provide a kind of substitute navigator while Kramer was asleep. I had also hoped that it would be able to automatically steer the craft itself, but this proved a touch ambitious, and would involve mechanical devices that would greatly increase the weight of the moonship. In the end I simply equipped the machine with dials and the paper spool, which would provide Kramer with the necessary information to be able to adjust the course himself. (Nonetheless, this was research that I could see might one day have considerable potential for the automatic steering of airships and marine vessels, so I kept careful records and notebooks.)

The plan was that Kramer would navigate in the first instance by means of ordinary landmarks on Earth, and then switch to lunar landmarks at the approximately halfway mark. Since we had no idea of how long it would take to reach that point, Kramer would have to measure the apparent size of the moon and judge when it had doubled in size. To assist in this, a scale was painted on the inner glass of the capsule, to be visible from the mariner's chair.

It looked like we would be ready within a few months, so we set a tentative launch date for the last week of May, weather permitting. At that time the moon would rise at around eight in the evening, which would give Kramer plenty of time to orient the craft in the right direction. It would also be full moon on 1 June, so the landing site would be fully illuminated.

I had been sorely missing Marieke, especially when Yule came and went. She was barely a day's journey away, but the passage was expensive and I would need every penny I could earn if I was to pay off my debts. She had sent me a Yule card, with a letter in her idiosyncratic Lowlander Northlandish:

I hope all is good with you. I am at the house of my father. Yesterday a man came, he said he was a friend from you. He wanted money. My father hunted him away. But you must not concern, I can look after myself.

It was disturbing that they had found out where she was living. I had some money, but it would most likely be robbed if I sent it through the post. Eventually I went down to the market, listened for Lowlander accents among the stallholders, and found a cheese merchant from Sandviken who knew Marieke's family. For a small fee, he agreed to take a bag of coins back with him which would at least pay off some of the interest. I did not doubt his honesty, as I knew the Sandviken Lowlanders to be very close-knit.

Since the project now looked as though it were going to succeed (at least as far as getting the thing off the ground was concerned), the King decided that the time had come to make it public. It would be good for his standing in the city, he reasoned, and perhaps improve the general opinion of him. His counsellors warned him of the risks involved, but as usual the King was contemptuous of danger. To assuage them, however, he agreed that he would unveil the project in the park of the Rose Castle, the King's Garden, where he would be far from buildings where assassins might lurk, and where a goodly supply of the King's Men from the adjacent barracks could provide adequate protection against any rowdiness. A temporary wooden podium would be erected, with the LEM being displayed alongside. The public would be admitted through the park gates, after being checked for weapons. The King showed me the speech he was planning to make, so that I might correct any scientific inaccuracies. As usual, his rhetoric was faultless.

'It is a most excellent speech, Majesty, I congratulate you.'

'Not too populist, I hope? Did I get the details right?'

'You might want to change "Travel to heaven" to "Travel to space".'

'Ah. Good point. No need to get the archbishop riled up again.'

The Saturday morning on which the King was due to present the project was sunny, if rather cold. I was getting ready, standing shaving at the glass, when I thought I heard knocking. I ignored it at first, putting it down to the many peculiar noises emanated by the old tower, but it persisted. Eventually, patting my chin with the towel, I went to open the apartment door. Outside stood Erika Thorne.

'What are you doing here? How did you get into the tower?'

'Never mind. I had to see you, Karl.'

'Well, I'd like to see you, too, but…now? I have to attend the King's presentation in an hour.'

'The King will not miss you.'

'I am to stand beside him on the podium. I am quite sure he will notice if I am not there.'

'He has plenty of counsellors and courtiers to keep him company.'

'Erika, I must go.'

She put her hand on my chest.

'No. You must stay.'

And with that, she kissed me.

We Kantarborgans have never been afraid to take on difficult tasks. Now, we are attempting a feat that many other, more timid nations would regard as impossible. But it is precisely because they would deem this task impossible that we are taking it on. Because we are Kantarborgans! Today, we stand on the threshold of a new age, the age of travel through the cosmos. The risks are many, but the potential gains for this nation will be incalculable. We are a trading nation, a nation of boat-builders and merchants. We know that in order to beat the competition, we must be daring. Like St Christopher Columbus, we must seek out new lands and new opportunities...

'What is she like, your wife?' asked Erika, stretching her naked body back languidly against the pillows. Our lovemaking had been every bit as intense as I remembered it from our student days.

'No, let me guess: she's a plump little Northlander peasant girl with a round face and plaits in her hair. Am I right?'

'Not at all. You're thinking of the Queen.'

That made her laugh.

'Karl, you must be careful what you say!'

'I am lying in bed with a member of the League for Democracy. I think what I *say* may be of rather minor significance at this stage.'

'Do you love her?'

'Yes. Yes, I think so. She is a good woman. But...it's different with you.'

'And with you,' said Erika, putting her hand to my cheek and looking into my eyes. She drew me down upon the bed again.

And that is why I believe we should commit ourselves, before this summer is out, to sending a man to the moon and returning him safely to the Earth. The nation that is first to embrace this magnificent adventure will be first to reap the rewards. And I believe that those rewards will directly benefit every one of you standing here today. I am therefore calling for your support in this great venture: Kantarborg is going to the moon! We are going to travel to heaven!

There was a loud, echoing report from outside, like an explosion. Erika started.

'It's just a cannon over at the castle,' I said. 'The show must be ending.'

She gave a strained smile.

'It's time I was getting out of here, Karl. Before I am discovered.'

She slipped out of the bed and began to struggle hurriedly into her clothes.

'By your lover?'

'Not by him. By the King's Men.'

'What would he do if he knew you were here? Would he challenge me to a duel?'

'Oh, he knows I am here.'

'He knows?'

She looked back at me, her hand on the door handle.

'Of course. He let me in.'

NOTICE

All civilian traffic is forbidden with immediate effect in all streets bordering the King's Garden. Costermongers and other persons with business at the Rose Castle must apply for a pass. Any persons contravening this order will be subject to arrest and confinement without trial at the pleasure of His Majesty the King.

By order, R. Rachlinsen, Watch Commander

It was a week before I was allowed to visit the King. I was a little nervous about what mood I might find him in, but I need not have worried.

'Karl, good to see you,' he said weakly, lying propped up on pillows in his four-poster bed.

I had not seen the King's bedchamber before. There were many drapes and velvet coverings, a few paintings – it was softer, less robust, somehow, than I would have expected of him. We were not, of course, alone – his equerry kept a sharp eye on me from the end of the bed. Everyone, now, was being treated as a potential assassin. The King looked rather less vigorous than usual, but that was only to be expected. His head and midriff were heavily bandaged.

'And you, Majesty. I have brought you some flowers.'

'Thank you. Not poisoned, are they? I'm becoming a little paranoid, you understand.'

'No, sire.'

He looked at me for a long moment.

'I have to tell you, Karl. Certain accusations have been levelled against you. Your absence from the event was noted.'

'I was suddenly taken ill, sire. Some stomach bug that I must have caught from the street vendors. Most unpleasant.'

'You should stay away from that stuff. I will send you a cook. But it was rather a lucky stroke for you, wasn't it? You would have been caught up in the explosion otherwise. There were even those who said you must have been behind it. But do you know what I told them ..?'

He paused, wincing in pain as a coughing fit took him.

'I said…if Karl Nielsen were behind this, the damn thing would have worked! It was underneath the podium, you know. An inside job, probably. Personally, I suspect the Queen. Oh God, I must not laugh, it hurts like the devil.'

I could only smile. His demeanour was remarkable, given

what he had experienced. Perhaps it was the knowledge that he had once again cheated death and his enemies that made him so cheerful.

'So, how are things with the moonship?' he asked.

'The balloons were fitted last Thursday, and the canopy. Now we just need to install the calculating engine and the clockwork motor. I think we will be ready on time. But should we not delay the launch until your Majesty is fully recovered?'

'Not at all! I intend to be out of this bed by the end of the week. We must proceed with all possible speed, and launch her to heaven! Oh and by the way, you were quite right.'

'About what, sire?'

'I should have changed that phrase. I said, "We are going to travel to heaven!" and disappeared in a cloud of smoke. It was most unfortunate timing.'

The launch of the craft could not now be the public event that the King would no doubt have preferred. Due to the tense security situation, the LEM was to be sent up from the parade ground of the barracks next to the Rose Castle, and attendance would be very restricted. Only the project team, a few courtiers, the King's Men and the King himself would be there. Archbishop Arbinger had also agreed to attend the launch, and to christen the vessel – somewhat reluctantly, as he regarded the whole business of sending men up into the heavens as theologically dubious. And he was not all happy with the name that the King wished to bestow upon the craft.

'That, my liege, is the name of a breed of dog.'

'It is also the name of a famous vessel of the ancients, your grace.'

'The vessel of a man whom the Church has always regarded as a heretic.'

'Archbishop, perhaps I did not make myself entirely clear. As defender of the faith, I decide what is heretical or not. Just as I decide upon the ecclesiastical appointments in the Church. Your own among them. I regard it as politically important to have the Church on board, and you will kindly do as I request.'

The Archbishop looked alarmed.

'Not literally on board, man. It's an expression. Not that I wouldn't consider it under the right circumstances, mind you. Don't tempt me.'

'I see. Very well, your Majesty. As you wish.'

In the last week of May it rained for the first few days, but the Thursday dawned sunny and warm, with just a few clouds in the sky. We gathered on the parade ground beside the moonship – the King, much to his annoyance, confined to a wheelchair at the insistence of his physician. The LEM had been polished up for the big day and looked magnificent, its wood and brass gleaming; above it, the vast balloon canopy, painted in the royal colours, flapped in the breeze, straining skywards like a hunting dog on a leash.

No-one said anything. It should have been a festive occasion, but the atmosphere, with the group of us standing around in the open like that, was to my mind distressingly reminiscent of a funeral. I fervently hoped I was not sending a man to his death. I liked Erik Kramer and would not wish to see any harm befall him. But when the little man marched up, dressed in his green flying suit and 'CCCP' helmet, he looked cheerful and confident. There was some desultory applause. Kramer smiled confidently and waved to us all, then ascended the small ladder to the platform surface of the LEM, where Tillonsen was waiting to help him get through the hatch.

'Now, Archbishop,' said the King from his wheelchair, once Tillonsen had climbed down.

The Archbishop stepped forward and pronounced: 'May the blessings of God be upon this vessel in all its journeys.'

'And the name, please, Archbishop.'

'Er…and I hereby name this craft the *Beagle*, after the ship of Charles Darwin, a man of science who also set out to discover new worlds and new life.'

'Thank you, your grace.'

'Are you going to do the countdown, Majesty?' I asked.

'The what?'

'It's an old tradition of the ancients. You're supposed to count backwards aloud from ten and then launch it. It will bring luck to the voyage.'

'Superstitious nonsense, if you ask me. Oh very well, then: Ten, nine, eight, seven, six, five, four, three, two, one – go! Cast off!'

The King's Men let go of the restraining ropes. At first nothing happened, then, very slowly, the craft began to rise above the parade ground. I exhaled a sigh of relief; I had calculated correctly. The watching soldiers cheered.

At this point, to my surprise, the hatch of the craft opened, and Kramer poked his head and shoulders out and waved cheerily to us all.

'He'll overbalance it!' muttered Tharup, beside me. 'Get back inside, you fool!'

Indeed, the LEM was beginning to rotate slightly, one of its legs almost hitting a tree in the King's Garden before it stabilised and began to rise straight up into the air. Kramer, determined to make the most of his moment of fame, continued to wave, and I fancied I could hear a cheer go up from somewhere in the city. He had no doubt told all his friends to watch.

We remained standing on the parade ground until the craft had disappeared into the blue.

'Well, that's that,' said the King. 'Now all we can do is wait.'

He turned to me.

'Now for the next job, Nielsen!'

'The next job, Majesty?'

'Indeed. We are far from finished with your services yet. I have yet to tell you of my Grand Plan.'

'I rather suspected as much, Majesty.' I smiled as though forbearingly, but his words were a relief. I still needed to earn a great deal more money before I could pay off my debts.

That evening, the King held a small reception at the Rose

Castle to celebrate the successful launch. I was in expansive mood and partook rather freely of the wine. On the whole, I felt, things had gone rather well. My design had worked, and I was feeling quite pleased with myself. Standing by himself in a corner, I noticed Professor Artison of the University's astronomy department, and I went over to buttonhole him about the lack of co-operation we had received from the University.

'We could have used someone on the team with knowledge of the cosmos,' I said to him. 'But it seems no-one from your department was interested in the job.'

He regarded me with a grim expression.

'It is difficult to refuse a king, as I'm sure you are aware,' he replied. 'But we were having some success in dissuading him from this absurd course of action. Until you came along.'

It was not the reaction I had been expecting.

'But surely Professor, this was a project worth pursuing? To gain knowledge of other worlds?'

'A *balloon* to the *moon*? He came to us with that ridiculous idea two years ago. We told him it was impossible. That's why he wanted to build a giant spring-loaded human cannonball device instead, and sent for you. He gets the most insane notions. He should not be encouraged.'

'But why should it be impossible? We know the ancients went to the moon. And a balloon seems as reasonable a transportation device as anything else.'

'You are working outside your field, Clockmaker, and the results are what one would expect of an amateur. First of all, it is highly unlikely that the ancients ever really travelled to the moon. The distance is vast – far greater than you have ever imagined. And secondly, have you for one moment considered what happens to a balloon in a vacuum?'

'A vacuum?'

'Yes, Nielsen, a vacuum! In the outer void there is not a single molecule of oxygen or any other gas. If your air mariner does not die of asphyxiation, he will die when the balloons burst and he falls to Earth. You have killed him, Nielsen. As surely as if you had held a gun to his head and pulled the trigger.'

And with that, he turned away.

On board the *Beagle*, Erik Kramer was enjoying being ruler of his tiny spherical kingdom, further away from other human beings than he had ever been in his life before. He had been in the air for some hours now, travelling on a more or less vertical path, drifting just a little to the east. He ate a sandwich, wound up the calculating engine and studied its readout. There was no need to make any course adjustments yet, so there was little to do. He amused himself by looking down at the Earth through the viewing port in the centre of the floor. He could already see all of Kantarborg, all the way to the Old Capital in the west, and right across the Northland peninsula to the east. It was almost silent in the mooncraft, except for the creaking sound that told him the balloons were beginning to reach their maximum capacity. The air inside the capsule was also growing thin, and he found himself frequently taking puffs from the compressed air flask. Although the sun was shining intensely, the sky above was growing dark. That was a wonder. The Earth below was tinged in blue, and he fancied he could make out its roundness at the horizon. What a marvellous thing to behold. He kept a watch out for angels – this, after all, was reputed to be their domain. Who knows what he might see.

For a sunny evening, it was surprisingly cold in the capsule. He wondered how cold it was going to get in the void. Clock-maker Nielsen had assured him that in space the sun shone all the time, even when it was night on Earth, but that sounded hard to believe. And at any rate, he would have to get to space first.

The moon had risen and could be seen through one of the

portholes. Using the scale painted on the glass, he noted its apparent size in his notebook, together with the time. Did it already look a little larger than it did on Earth? He thought that perhaps it did, but it was hard to say. Soon it would be time to point his craft in the right direction and start the clockwork motor. He felt proud and excited. He was on his way to the moon.

CHAPTER SEVENTEEN

'What's so funny?' asked Joe. He was standing in the conning tower, smoke swirling around him as he tried to boil some potatoes and cabbage on the tiny iron stove at the rear. *Paloma* had found a secluded anchorage for the night in a rocky inlet. They had not succeeded in catching any fish today, so it would be vegetables only.

Christopher was below, studying the charts.

'I've worked out that if we could walk on water like the Good Lord, we would have covered nearly the same distance by now.'

'You'll be glad of those sails yet. If we'd had normal sails the Albans would have caught us long ago. We got through their territory without a hitch.'

'The sails are grand, they just need to be bigger. And if we could get them inside the hull faster. A few seconds, say. Push a lever and schooock!'

'The bigger they are, they harder they will be to stow. And they'd be much more visible.'

'I suppose. I just wish there was some other way to do this. This rate of progress is driving me spare altogether.'

'Sure aren't you travelling in style, Brother Chris? Sit back, take in the view.'

'Very funny.'

Joe brought down a couple of wooden bowls from the conning tower with the simple repast.

'Bit of bacon would be nice with this,' Christopher remarked.

'It would all right. And some butter.'

'We can dream. But fair play to King Barney, his spuds got us this far. You put out the fire?'

'I did. With water. The smoke is gone. Speaking of King Barney, what was all that about a monster in a cave?'

Christopher looked at Joe. How to put this.

'It's just something I saw in the harbour. In a tunnel.'

'What sort of a thing?'

'I think it was the remains of an ancient boat. Pretty big.'

The thing had been massive. Black. Terrifying. Unimaginably huge. Nightmarish. And shaped like a shark. Something you would need an army of slaves to build. Or to dismantle.

'Jaze, why didn't you tell me? I would have loved to have seen that.'

'Let's say, events overtook us.'

'Yeah. You got rat-arsed and we had to run for it. Maybe we could see it on our way back.'

'I'm sure we could.' *If we come back*, thought Christopher.

Joe looked at the chart as he chewed.

'So where are we now?'

'Right there...last bit of Alban territory before we make the crossing to the Westlands. This is where things get rough. It'll take us a few days to get across, and we won't get much sleep.'

'And what then?'

'Then we head north, up along the coast. It's a heck of a long way, I have to tell you.'

'How long do you think it will take us to get where we're going?'

'A month or so, at this rate. That's the bit that worries me. It's a long time to be at sea, and there's nothing over there: no towns, not even a farm. We haven't even any weapons to hunt with. I don't know what we're going to eat over there. Man cannot live by fish alone.'

'No-one living there?'

'A few tribals. You wouldn't want to wind up in their hands. They eat Christians.'

'You're having me on!'

'It's what I hear. And there are some strange sea beasts up there, too. Swallow a man with one gulp, a boat with two.'

Joe sighed.

'Any idea why we're doing this?'

'Not the slightest. But I'll tell you one thing...' Christopher nudged one of the wooden chests with his foot. 'I reckon that's money. Silver coins. Probably the last of the treasure from the mine.'

'You know what, I'd never have guessed. Of course it's money.'

'How about it, Joe? You and me split the booty and we sail off into the sunset?'

'Get thee behind me, Satan. So what's it for? Are we buying something, do you think? Some precious item?'

'Might be paying off a debt.'

'Why don't you just open the letter and find out? What difference does it make whether we know now or later?'

'It'd make a difference if we were captured.'

'But then wouldn't they just read the letter?'

'We'll destroy it if we can. If they get that, the game's up.'

Joe stretched.

'I'm going to get some kip. You take the first watch?'

Christopher nodded. They had been dividing the nights between them in this manner, worried about the possibility of being seen from the shore. In these long evenings, whatever advantages *Paloma* offered in terms of stealth were somewhat counterbalanced by the oddness of her appearance. They could have submerged below the surface, with just the air pipe poking above, but the thought of sleeping underwater, especially on a fixed anchor and a rising tide, made Christopher more than a little nervous.

He climbed the ladder to the conning tower, taking the log with him to record the day's progress. The evening air was quiet and tranquil. Tomorrow, those mountains behind them would be the last bit of solid ground they would see for a good while, when they took on the Westland Sea. He well remembered what those waters could be like. Joe had no idea. They might not make it at all. Fifty-fifty, he'd give it. But no sense in worrying the lad. He watched as a flock of birds, high up, made their way silently across the darkening sky. He gave a sigh of contentment. Right now, just enjoy the peace, he told himself. Nothing will disturb you here.

And it was at that moment that a giant cocktail table fell out of the sky.

It began as a whistling sound, then Christopher gaped as an enormous piece of furniture scythed through the air and smashed into the sea not twenty yards away, throwing up a huge plume of spray. Some rags on strings floated down above it. The wash from the impact spread out and rocked *Paloma* violently back and forth. The Beagle had landed.

CHAPTER EIGHTEEN

The professor's words had put quite a damper on my mood as I walked back through the King's Garden to the tower. I was furious – with him, with myself, with everyone. Kramer knew the risks, of course, before he took on the job. And we had deliberately chosen a man who did not have a wife and children. But even so; he had seemed so brave, so innocent, somehow. *He trusted me*, I thought. And I had led him to his death. Artison was right, I was a complete amateur. I had allowed myself to be seduced by my own cleverness, by the joy of solving an engineering problem, and had utterly failed to see the bigger picture. God, what a fool I was!

I had but one hope, which was that when the balloons burst, they might do so one at a time and not all at once. That way the craft might descend more slowly, and Kramer might survive. It was the best I could hope for.

The guards checked my pass, with the King's signature – they did that even for departing guests now – and unlocked the gates. The streets around the park were deserted – it was not yet curfew, but the order of the Watch was being obeyed. After the warmth of the day, the wind was starting to feel cool and biting. I hurried in the direction of Woolmerchant Street, anxious to be back in the tower and well away from all human machinations.

So the King had gone to the University with this idea two years ago. And they had told him the simple truth: that it was impossible. Then why the devil had no-one said anything to me? They had just stood back and let me make a fool of myself – and put a man's life in danger. Because they wanted me to fail, of course. Court life was all about jockeying for status, for position, for money – had I not learned that by now? The King for his part had chosen to ignore the advice of the experts, and had put me in charge of the project, simply because I did not know any better and had agreed to do it. And now he had a grand plan, and he wanted me to be part of it. Well, whatever it was, I was resolved not be manipulated again. By anyone.

She was waiting in the shadows by the tower. She smiled as she stepped forward, but her eyes were serious.

'Karl, we need to talk.'

'It seems I owe you my life,' I said as I unlocked the door.

'I know what you think. It's not true.'

I looked at her.

'It wasn't…just for that reason,' she said.

'I do not approve of political murder,' I said, rather stiffly.

That made the fire flash in her eyes.

'Oh, so you do not *approve*? And the slaughter of civilians, what would you call that? Is that not political murder? Your own brother, Karl!'

Her words echoed in the tower as I closed the door behind me.

I would not betray her, she knew that. And anyway, what, exactly, could she be accused of? It could all have been the merest coincidence. If I avoided the maelstrom that was forming around me, I might yet have a chance of preserving my life. But the spiral walkway suddenly felt as though it had become much steeper, and my body heavier than lead. Every force on Earth seemed to be drawing me back down; back to her, and death. I turned back.

'Magnificent, isn't it?' The King's words echoed in the cavernous space. The roof of the hall arched high above us, almost like an inverted boat hull, covered in wooden tiles. Four such halls had been newly built, arranged in a square pattern. Twelve more were under construction nearby.

'It is indeed marvellous, Majesty – but why out here in the

wildwoods?'

'Well, that's the plan, you see, Nielsen. One day there will be no more wildwoods.'

'I don't quite follow, sire.'

'Right now, our kingdom consists just of a few islands of civilisation in a sea of anarchy. The capital itself, plus Ros and Alsina. That's it, more or less. But in ancient times, believe it or not, the Kingdom of Kantarborg stretched all the way from here to the Anglian Sea. And all of that land was covered with farms, not forest. It supported a huge population – millions, not thousands. You look sceptical.'

'It is a little hard to imagine, sire. Can we always trust the sagas?'

'I believe on this point, we can. And the archaeological evidence certainly supports it. There is scarcely a tree in this forest whose roots are not tangled around some ancient object. Bricks, tools, even vehicles.'

'I was taught in school that all such things proceed from the Irrational Layer. That the Earth dreams as we do, and brings forth these strange artefacts.'

'Well, that was when the Church had control over the places of learning. I hope we are a little wiser now. The Irrational Layer is certainly real enough – you and I have seen what it can produce – but I do not believe the Earth dreams of such trivial things as construction materials. Besides, the old maps show hundreds of towns all over this territory. We know that the ancients were prone to exaggeration, but I don't think *all* of those places can have been mythical. They are just lost now, beneath the undergrowth.'

'So what is your plan, sire? Cut down all the trees?' *As well try to paint the sky*, I thought.

'Small steps, Nielsen, small steps. First of all, we connect our towns by railways, so that we do not always have to sail from one to the other. Then, all along the line, we place small settlements, each with its own garrison to protect it against wild men and outlaws. We invite people to come and clear the forests, and start farms and businesses. Forges. Dairies. Bakeries. Breweries. Why not? The railways will take their produce to the cities. The network will gradually spread until we take it all back. This land belongs to us, it is our birthright, and we must reclaim it. It will take a very long time, perhaps centuries, but this country will be great again. Where now there are bandit-infested forests, there will one day be pastures and fields of corn. And the population of Kantarborg will be among the largest of any nation in the world, perhaps half a million or more. That is my vision.'

'It is a very noble vision, Majesty.'

'But?'

'But...ambitious. Building such railway lines will require vast amounts of labour. And many tons of iron. Where is that to come from? And how would we pay for it? The kingdom is somewhat strapped for cash, I am led to understand.'

'For the iron, if we cannot access the mines of the Northlands, then we must look elsewhere. I have an idea for how we might be able to do that without it costing the kingdom anything at all. As for the workforce to build the railways, my plan is to import foreign labour. They are cheaper than Kantarborgans and will be glad of the work. That is what these halls are for. Solid, clean, waterproof housing. Nothing but the best for our guests. They will have good food and lodgings for as long as they stay with us. Though naturally, we will have to keep them outside the towns, for their own protection. Kantarborgans are not keen on strangers, as you know.'

'And you believe that they will come here, sire? Far away from their own countries and families?'

'I know they will. People who are hungry will travel far to look for work. You saw that in the iron mines – and that was a much more remote place than here.'

It sounded a bold and imaginative scheme. But as I left the complex, I noticed that the men were erecting a palisade of sharpened stakes around the circular ramparts. The foreign workers clearly needed protection.

CHAPTER NINETEEN

Cracked. Touched. Round the bend. Off his rocker. Christopher was running out of ways to describe the ambassador.

'He just got a bad bang on the head,' said Joe. 'He'll be all right.'

'Joe, he thought I was the King of the Moon!'

'Says the man who saw an elephant playing a trumpet.'

'It was a mouse, actually. The elephant blew fire. You think he's been beatified, then?'

'I don't know. He could be. He talks like one of the blessed, all right.'

'You don't really believe he came from another world?'

'That's what he says.'

'*On a flying table?*'

Joe shrugged.

'I don't know. Do you have a better explanation?'

Christopher did not. He liked to think of himself as a rational man, but he'd never seen anything like this before. Giant furniture falling out of the sky. It defeated his logic entirely. It annoyed him even to think about it.

The stranger was lying on the spare bunk. His clothing was bizarre: just the one grey-green garment covering him from head to foot. And that strange helmet he had on when they found him! He did look like someone from another world, there was no denying it. Above the man's heart, a label was sewn on with some lettering on it.

'Ekramer? Do you think that's his name?'

'Must be, I suppose. Unless it's his job.'

'Maybe it means 'ambassador' in his language.'

The ambassador stirred and began to mumble something.

'What's that, your excellency?' asked Christopher.

'My craft…it is damaged?' He had an odd accent. Anglian

clearly wasn't his first language.

'Ah, you could say that right enough. Pretty much a write-off, to be honest with you.'

The shattered remains of the *Beagle* had sunk shortly after they had rescued its occupant. The ambassador looked distressed.

'Can you…can you get me to Earth?'

'Oh, I'd say we could all right. We started out from Earth, at any rate.'

Ekramer relapsed into unconsciousness.

'Has he said anything that made any sense at all?' asked Joe. 'What did he say when you opened the hatch?'

'He said, "We come in peace",' said Christopher. 'Which is nice to know, I suppose. Then he said he was an ambassador, and he asked me if I was the King of the Moon. But he was already rambling at that stage, I think he was concussed.'

'I don't like the look of that cut on his head,' said Joe. 'I've washed it, but it looks like it might be getting infected. He's very hot, I think he has a fever. We don't have the medicines to treat him.'

Christopher considered.

'What we used to do with sick sailors is put them ashore somewhere. But the question is where. We can't leave him here, and we can hardly just drop in on the Albans. King Malcolm thinks we're a couple of assassins, on our way to bump him off with a secret weapon.'

'Nowhere on the Westland coast that would do?'

'There's nothing there. He'd just die. Or be eaten.'

'Maybe we might spot a ship that could take him?'

'Not too many ships in these waters. And we'd have to be careful. We don't want anyone getting too curious about us. If there *is* money in those chests, we'd be ripe for plunder.'

'Set him adrift in the dinghy near a ship, then? We could watch through the periscope to make sure he gets picked up.'

'We'll need that dinghy in the Westlands, when we go

foraging for food. We can't take this boat close enough in to the shore.'

'A raft, so? There must be wood in the Westlands, surely?'

'There is, and plenty. I suppose that might be our best bet all right.'

It was far from a perfect plan, but Christopher could not think of a better one. They began to make *Paloma* ready for the crossing.

Twenty-four hours later, Christopher was wondering if he was about to die. No matter how many times you've done it, nothing prepares you for it: the swells that tower above the vessel, the screaming, stinging wind that seems to have taken a personal dislike to you, the endless series of vast waves that slap down upon the boat like the hand of some giant gambler glee-fully claiming his winnings. The spindrift on the crests told him it was a regular gale. It had sprung up on them on the morning of the second day, just when Christopher was beginning to think they might be lucky this time. The wind was so strong that it was hard to turn your head to windward – even, at times, to breathe. The weight of the water crashing onto the deck felt like it might break your neck. They had to tie themselves to the hatch to avoid being washed overboard. Taking turns in the cockpit, Joe and Christopher found they could each endure no more than half an hour before the cold water numbed their limbs so much that it became impossible to steer. They switched watch regularly; but below decks was almost worse, with the craft pitching and rolling as though the crew were dice being shaken in a cup. Everyone had been sick again and again – it was impossible to clean it up, so the hold stank. Their clothes never had time to dry out, and the constant cold was wearing them down. Christopher found he was shivering continuously. Climbing the ladder, Joe had been thrown aside and had suffered a heavy blow on his left arm that had almost dislocated it. The ambassador, bound to his bunk for his own safety, was groaning and wild-eyed with fever. God knows where he thought he was.

Paloma, however, had one great advantage over more conventional vessels, which was that she could submerge occasionally to give the crew a break. At five fathoms, the pounding was much less intense, and Joe and Christopher could catch a couple of hours' sleep before lack of air drove them to the surface again. Each time they had to stow the sails and rig them again, with the wind and waves constantly threatening to pluck them off the hull bodily and devour them whole. By the compass they were keeping to a roughly easterly course, but they had no real idea of where they were, or how much longer they would have to endure this.

Joe was worried about the pressure on the rotary sails.

'If we lose one, we're finished,' he shouted. 'We'll just go round in circles.'

By partially retracting the sails, they managed to reduce the amount of sailcloth exposed to the gale, and thereby the strain on the axles. But the sail masts were still bending worryingly, and spinning so fast that there was a real danger the sails might be ripped to pieces.

Early on the morning of the fourth day the bow sail mechanism jammed, so Joe had to shut down the aft sail, too. From now on they would have to rely on pedal power, and otherwise just go where the wind and currents took them. They stowed the sails, with great difficulty, then tied themselves into their seats below deck and pedalled as best they could, while the boat leaped and dived from giant peak to gaping trough. The noise was unbelievable, mind-numbing, merciless, unceasing. Joe was chanting prayers, over and over. In the darkness of the hold, Christopher found he was beginning to hallucinate: as he pedalled; he felt as though the craft were flying through the air, soaring and diving like a seabird.

Then, as the fifth day dawned, the incredible happened. The clouds parted and the sun came out. The wind eased to a stiff breeze. The wounded *Paloma* lay rotating gently on the foaming, undulating surface. Christopher and Joe dozed where they sat, lost in exhausted dreams, with the ambassador occasionally shouting out something in his alien language.

Christopher woke to find he was achingly thirsty. He found the water flask, drank his fill, and gave some to the ambassador. The man was still hot to the touch, and after gulping down the water he collapsed back onto his bunk with his eyes closed. At least he was alive, thank God. It would be a poor end to a visit from another world if they had had to throw his corpse overboard. And that was a thought – was he baptised at all? For safety's sake Christopher poured a few drops of the precious water onto the man's forehead and made the sign of the cross, baptising him Ekramer in the name of the Father, Son and Holy Ghost.

He found he did not have the strength to mount the ladder, and so he looked out through the periscope. But what he saw there greatly revived his spirits.

'Joe! Joe, wake up!'

'Boss…what is it? Are we alive?'

'We are indeed, Joe, and more than that – I can see land!'

Joe joined him at the periscope.

'Thanks be to God and all the saints for deliverance. Watch out there or you'll have us on the rocks. We'd better look for an estuary or something. What day is it?'

'The feast of St Boniface.'

'Who was he?'

'A monk in ancient times. He sailed from Anglia to convert the heathen tribes of the north.'

'Brother Columba, it is a miracle!'

'It would seem so, Joe, it would seem so. Do you think you can get the sails working?'

'I don't know. They took a bad beating. I can try.'

Joe, despite his injured arm, sprang up the ladder with a vigour that made Christopher feel suddenly old. He followed slowly. One step at a time.

CHAPTER TWENTY

Extract from the diary of Johannes Brorsen, Astronomer Royal

This morning I was surprised by a visit from two young people, a man and a woman. I had retired late the previous night, having spent the small hours observing the moons of Jupiter, and so was rather tired. Nonetheless, this isle being somewhat wanting in sources of entertainment, I was not entirely displeased to receive guests. How they managed to gain entrance was something of a mystery to me at first, none of my staff having announced them – the explanation for which I was to discover later.

They were both personable and respectful; she bare-headed and quite handsome; he wearing the hat and cape of a peasant, but with the gait and bearing of a soldier. She spoke Anglian very well; he, Kantish, though with an accent. They stood before my library armchair as though it were a royal throne, until I invited them to sit.

They would not say their names, but introduced themselves as officers of what they called the republican council, though how a woman can be an officer, I do not know. Perhaps she commands a regiment of women.

I asked them how things were in Kantarborg, and the young man informed me that the King has installed that idiot Clock-maker Nielsen in my apartment in the Round Tower, and grants him great favour, plying him with foreign sweetmeats and spar-kling wines – the like of which he never once did offer me! – and in general treats him like a pet monkey, to the great chagrin of the generals and scientists.

I hope I am not a jealous man, but this did put the fire in my blood. To think that that *shopkeeper*, a man of no noble family, a mere engineer who probably needs a clock to discover the phases of the moon, was occupying my home like a lord, drinking my wine, reading my books, sleeping in my bed! I need not tell you I was much aroused.

But worse was to come; for now, the young man said, the King had taken it into his head to declare Nielsen a scientific genius, and had of late chosen to ignore the scientific advice of the University itself, and had commissioned him to build a balloon to visit the *moon*, no less! And that, further, they had actually built such a device, and had sent a young air mariner aloft in it, who had not been seen since.

I was, of course, flabbergasted. The whole thing would be farcical if it were not tragic.

'And meanwhile,' said the young man, 'the people are suffering greatly, from cold and hunger, and from the effects of the late predations of the Northlanders.'

'That is most disturbing to hear,' I said. 'But I am hardly surprised at the doings of that family. There is madness in it, you know. His father was much the same.'

'We are convinced that the only remedy for this canker is to uproot the bush upon which it grows,' said the young woman. 'The King must no longer rule in Kantarborg.'

'Indeed, if things are in such a parlous state as you describe, then that might appear to be the only solution, radical as it may be,' I replied, making a small joke that I am sure none but I appreciated. 'But I cannot see how such a man as I could be of any help to you in that endeavour.'

'Are you not related to the King yourself?' asked the young woman.

'Distantly,' I replied. 'A cousin of a cousin. Why?'

They looked at me in silence, and I at them.

'Oh no,' I said. 'Oh no, no, no, no! Put that thought out of your minds straight away. I assure you, I would rather sit on one of the thorn bushes in my own garden than upon the throne of Kantarborg.'

'What we had in mind,' said the young man, 'was more of a ceremonial position. A kind of head of state.'

'While the real power would be...?'

'In the hands of an elected assembly.'

'Mob rule? It's been tried, you know. Never lasts. Ignorance always wins out in the end. People don't want to decide things for themselves, they want rulers who will tell them what to do. They want to worship someone. They want magic, and pageantry, and flags, and guns, and war. The fools.'

'But you are a man of noble blood and reputation, who commands great respect in Kantarborg.'

'You flatter me, young man. I suspect I am quite forgotten in the city.'

'That is not true, my lord. You are known as a scientist of great learning. Your almanacs have a wide circulation, and your predictions are heeded.'

'Popular nonsense, those almanacs,' I said. 'But they have their uses, I grant you.'

'Would you be willing to publish a new one? With certain predictions?'

Their attempts to manipulate me were hardly subtle. But I saw possibilities in this.

'Well, that is worth considering, certainly. None has been printed this year, as you know, and I am told the farmers of Agaholm and the southern Northlands are most concerned, not knowing when they may best plant and reap. I have already done the calculations, so it would be a simple enough matter. And there is one particular astronomical event due this year that I think might be most useful, if handled with skill.'

'Then I think we should proceed with that plan,' said the young man. 'We will require the necessary documents from you.'

I looked at him.

'You did not come here alone, did you?'

'No, my lord.'

'I thought as much. Then you leave me no choice, it seems.'

'No, my lord.'

'Very well then, I will give them to you. But I must ask you to publish them anonymously. I have no desire to find myself confined to a prison cell at my age. If you attempt to link my name to them, I will say they were stolen from me by a band of ruffians. Which would appear to be little short of the truth, under the circumstances.'

'Indeed, my lord.'

The young woman was looking out of the window, at the distant coastline of Kantarborg.

'Why does the King not arrest you now?' she asked. 'This island offers little defence, and your opinions are well known. Is it because you are a relative?'

'Good grief, no. The King would happily strangle his own mother if she got between him and the throne. I suspect it is simply because I am not very important to him. And perhaps also because I am under a certain degree of protection.'

'From the Northlanders?'

'No, ever since those two monstrous families united their bloodlines, I am, as the Kantish saying has it, like a louse between two fingernails. What little protection I have left stems from one of my former employers: Pope Nicholas of Birmingham.'

They looked blank. The name of the Anglian pope had not, it seems, penetrated the gloom of the schoolrooms of Kantarborg.

'It is, I grant you, more the protection offered by custom and tradition than by military might. The King has broken with the true Anglian Church, and the Church itself is suffering grave persecution from many sides, so I can hardly expect the Papal Guard to come to my rescue. I have my own guard here, and they are loyal and true, but they would hardly be of much use against the King's Men.'

I fancied I saw the young man smile a little at that. It was only after I had given them the papers they wanted and they had gone that I found out why. All of my staff had been efficiently bound and gagged by, they claimed, a party of at least thirty rebels, men and women. They had not moored in the harbour, but at a small jetty we use for rowing-boats, and had moved swiftly and silently. Most of my people had been left in peace, but the captain of the guard, who happened to be wearing the colours of the King, they treated most uncouthly. They will make a Royalist of him yet, I fear. 'Pirates', he calls them, and spits. His anger is understandable; yet he does them an injustice. Had they been pirates, they would have slit my throat, taken whatever gold they could find. But precisely what they were, I have yet to fully discover. Time, no doubt, will tell.

CHAPTER TWENTY-ONE

'God forgive me, but I am heartily tired of fish. My kingdom for a potato,' said Joe.

'Eat it and be glad of it, you ingrate. Further north there might not be any food at all.'

Paloma had sought the shelter of the first available fjord to give Joe a chance to attack the foremast with his toolbox. An afternoon's work had got the cogs turning again. Christopher had meanwhile taken the dinghy out, and had caught a fair-sized cod.

'What's this, some kind of cabbage?'

'Sorrel. It's good for you.'

'Come back, King Barney, all is forgiven. What about himself? Is he eating at all?'

'I gave him some of the broth, he got a bit of it down. He's still away with the fairies, though.'

'Did he say anything?'

'He said thank you. More gratitude than I get from some.'

Joe smiled ruefully. 'I gave him a poultice on that sore. Dandelion and comfrey. But he's still very hot. He was talking about some very important letter he was supposed to give someone. But he doesn't have it on him, I checked. If there was one, it went down with his craft. Then he just starts rambling again in his own language.'

'Doesn't sound too good. Maybe his own people might send someone to take him back?'

'Yeah, watch out: they might drop a chest of drawers on us next time.'

'Or a giant piano. Can you imagine?'

Joe looked around at the fjord, at the silent water and steep slopes covered in pines.

'I think I'll go take a wash,' he said.

'OK, I'll go below.'

'No…don't go below. Stick around in case I need help. Just… don't stare at me, all right?'

'All right.'

Joe brought a towel up from below and went to the stern of the boat, where he pulled off his monkish habit and stuck a foot in the water.

'Jaze, the cold!'

'Straight down off the mountains, Joe. That's cold water all right.'

Christopher busied himself with the spyglass.

'Thought I saw some goats up there. Might make a change from fish.'

'I think I'm getting the hang of this swimming lark. You just kick your legs and wave your arms around, right?'

'Pretty much.'

'What if you're drowning?'

'Same procedure.'

Christopher focused the spyglass on the mouth of the fjord. There was a motion there, just at the waterline…

'Holy…Joe, you'd better get out of there! Come up here, quick!'

Joe scrambled up the side of the boat, drew the towel around him, and climbed into the cockpit.

'Every flipping time. What is it now?'

Christopher passed him the spyglass.

'I think it might be showtime.'

The biggest ship either of them had ever seen was slowly and silently entering the fjord. A four-masted warship.

'What class of a flag is that?'

'Kantish military.'

'And who are they, when they're at home?'

'Kantarborg. Small kingdom. Mostly pirates.'

'Can they see us?'

'I don't think so, we'll just look like rocks to them over here.'

'What are they up to, do you think? There's feck all in this fjord.'

'I don't know. But if they go in, they'll have to come out again sooner or later. There's no other way out of the fjord. So maybe it's time to try your plan.'

'Do you think that's a good idea, though? Handing the ambassador over to pirates?'

'We've no choice, Joe. There's not many ships in these waters – this might be the only chance we'll get. And it's a military vessel, they'll have a doctor on board.'

After rowing ashore in the dinghy, it took Joe and Christopher a couple of hours to construct a reasonably serviceable raft, made of pine logs lashed together. For visibility, they gave it a mast and a 'flag' made from a red rag.

'Looks a bit rickety.'

'It'll only have to hold together a short while. And the waters are calm enough in here. Right, let's get him up on deck.'

But lifting a semi-comatose man up the ladder and through the narrow hatchway turned out to be no easy task. The ambassador moaned and protested.

'It's all right, your excellency. You're going to be safe now.'

They laid the man on a small bed of willow branches that they had placed on the raft. Joe reached around the back of his neck, undid the clasp of a chain, and slipped it around Ekramer's neck.

'What's that?'

'St Christopher medal. Safe journey, ambassador!'

Proceeding slowly and carefully, with the raft in tow, they sailed *Paloma* further into the fjord. Eventually they could see the Kantish vessel moored at the far end, close to what looked like a small beach, where a crowd appeared to have gathered.

'Who are all those people?' asked Joe.

'Must be natives. Let's get the sails down,' said Christopher. 'We don't want them catching sight of us. We'll pedal her in as close as we can.'

'What way is the tide?'

'It's coming in. And the wind is behind us. That's what we want. OK, that's close enough. Cast him off.'

Joe undid the line that held the raft while Christopher turned *Paloma* to port. The raft drifted slowly away, turning gently.

'Right, let's take her down.'

By the time they had pumped enough air out of the tanks to submerge their craft, they could only just make out the raft through the periscope. But it seemed to be heading in the right direction.

'Come on, somebody see him,' muttered Christopher.

The red rag was still visible, fluttering in the breeze.

'They've spotted him! They're putting out a boat.'

Joe took a turn at the periscope.

'They have him. They're taking him in.'

'Thanks be to God.'

'There's an awful lot of people on that ship, chief.'

'Give me a look.'

Christopher put the spyglass to the periscope for better magnification.

'Civilians. Tribespeople. I don't like the look of this.'

'Slave ship, do you think?'

'Could be. They're not in chains, though, far as I can see. But if the Kantarborgans are mixed up in it, it's probably something murky.'

'Let's hope they look after the ambassador properly, at least.'

'Let's hope so, Joe. But we've done all we can. Now we'd better get out of here before they start wondering where the heck he came from.'

CHAPTER TWENTY-TWO

I answered the hammering on the door in the early morning to find Johansson standing outside.

'I'm to bring you to the Rose Castle at once,' he said, gasping for breath. 'Something's happened.'

'What?'

'Erik Kramer is back.'

'What? No! Really? He's alive?' I grabbed my jacket from the hall stand.

'He's fine. Come on, I'll fill you in on the way.'

We hurried through the empty streets and through the iron gates into the King's Garden, which was still shrouded in mist at this hour.

'What happened? How is he? Is he in good health?' I asked as I ran to keep up. I could scarcely believe it.

'He has been unwell, but is quite recovered,' said Johansson. 'It's the strangest thing. He was found floating on a raft in the Westlands. But he claims to have visited the moon, and that the moon-dwellers brought him back to Earth.'

'Couldn't the LEM just have fallen from the upper atmosphere?'

'That's what I thought, but there are several eye witnesses – trusted officers of rank – who report that they saw a strange craft in the fjord just before they picked him up. But when they looked again, it had vanished without trace.'

'Men see strange things at sea sometimes.'

'They do. But he must have had assistance of some kind. Kramer was in a bad way, half dead from what I hear. It's all a bit of a mystery.'

'Where did they find him?'

'In Irdai territory. One of our naval vessels was there, *Ariadne...*' Johansson seemed about to say more, but stopped.

'Quite a stroke of luck for him.'

In the Rose Castle, the King and Queen were already seated on their thrones. This was to be an official audience. Archbishop Arbinger was also present. But Kramer was not in the least intimidated; when summoned, he strode into the hall like a man of privilege, and addressed us almost as underlings.

'Greetings to the King of Kantarborg from the denizens of the moon!' were his first bombastic words. 'I bring tidings of great joy. Word of a new age, of a new dominion. There shall soon be a great dawn upon the Earth, and mankind shall no longer know war and want.'

The King looked somewhat nonplussed at this announcement.

'That is as may be, Mr Kramer, but I sent you on a very specific mission. We are anxious to hear the response of the King of the Moon to our request. In particular, in relation to the urgent need of the Kingdom of Kantarborg for iron and blackstone. What news do you have on that front?'

'The citizens of the moon, sire, do not deign to dig beneath the surface of their world. For they are like as to the angels, and have no need of earthy things. Their concern is with the spiritual welfare of mankind. For we have fallen into grave sin, into the very cesspit of the underground, and have abandoned the virtues of our forefathers. Therefore their message to us all is: Repent, and leave the Irrational Layer behind!'

There was silence for a few moments.

'All right, let's go back to the beginning,' said the King. 'You landed on the moon, in the Sea of Rain. What then?'

'The hatch was opened. And I heard a man's voice calling me.'

'Did he speak Anglian? What exactly did he say?'

'He spoke Anglian, sire, of a kind. He said, "Who are you?"'

'Exactly that?'

'Well, "Who the feck are you?".'

The King and the Archbishop exchanged glances.

'And then he told me he was Christopher Columbus. And he was accompanied by an angel.'

'How did you know it was an angel?' interrupted the Archbishop sharply.

'It was neither man nor woman, your grace. As the good evangelist tells us angels are.'

'And did this angel have a name?'

'Yes, your grace. It was Joe.'

'The angel Joe? Doesn't quite have the ring of Raphael or Gabriel, does it?'

'I don't know, your grace.'

'And the man told you he was St Christopher Columbus?'

'He did, your grace.'

'Not St Christopher, patron saint of travellers?'

'No, your grace. St Christopher the Navigator, the saint who flew the *Hindenburg* to the Americas.'

'I see. Mr Kramer, how well do you know your Bible?'

'I warrant I know it as well as any plain man, your grace.'

'Was the angel clad in raiment white as snow, as in the Gospel of Matthew? Or was it clothed in linen with a belt of fine gold, perchance, as the prophet Daniel describes?'

'Neither, your grace. Both the angel and the saint wore but the humble garb of monks.'

'They were dressed like monks? Did they have haloes? Rings of light around their heads?'

'Not that I noticed.'

'Well, I think you would probably have noticed if they had. And these two…beings, they brought you back to Earth in their craft?'

'Eventually, your grace. But first we travelled through a wild and windy country, with many mountains. And they took me up to great heights, and showed me all the cities of the moon, and they were wonderful to behold, and they showed me the Garden of Eden…'

'Just a moment,' said the King. 'The Garden of Eden, you

said. It's on the moon?'

'Yes, Majesty. That's why mankind has not been able to find it again.'

The Queen let out a guffaw and tried unsuccessfully to disguise it as a cough. Kramer continued unperturbed.

'It was for our original sin of digging beneath the ground in search of the golden apples that mankind was banished to the Earth. So if we wish to return to the moon, our true home, we must repent. We must cease to burrow into the underground after earthly riches, and instead seek our riches in heaven and in the things of the spirit.'

'They told you all this?'

'Yes, sire. Though without speaking, and all in signs and visions.'

'I see. And what happened then?'

'The saint gave me food to eat, and it was good, and unlike any food I have ever eaten before. And the angel placed its hands on my brow, and behold, my wound was healed.'

Kramer pointed to the scar on his forehead.

'And then they brought you back to Earth and set you adrift on the sea?'

'Yes, sire. They brought me to Earth on a strange craft like no other I have seen before. Then they placed me on the raft near our ship, and the angel gave me this, and wished me a safe journey.'

Kramer took the medallion from around his neck and handed it to the King.

'A St Christopher medal,' said the King.

'This was to be a sign to you that my story is true.'

The King examined it expressionlessly.

'Is it not good, sire?'

'Well, I rather wish the angel could have chosen something a bit more singular. A signed letter from the King of the Moon would have been nice.'

'There is no King of the Moon, sire. Except the Lord our

God.'

With that, Kramer joined his hands and looked reverently down at the floor.

'Yes, all right. Thank you, Mr Kramer, I think we've heard enough for now. We will talk to you again soon.'

When Kramer was gone, the King turned to the rest of us.

'Well, what do we think of that?'

The Queen gave a scornful laugh.

'I think you've wasted your money,' she said.

'Kramer is no liar,' I said to Johansson, as he opened another bottle of the astronomer's wine. (The tower's wine store was by now much depleted, though there were still a few bottles left.) 'He was one of my finest team members when we worked on the locomotive. I know him for an honourable and truthful man. I don't know what happened, but he must truly believe what he says.'

'From what I hear in the city, he has become something of a popular hero, fêted wherever he goes,' said Johansson, placing the bottle on the chessboard. 'The first Kantarborgan to visit the moon. And thanks to our bungling, he is not bound by the King's Seal. He can say what he wants.'

'So do you believe he visited the moon?'

'I don't know whether he did or not, but whatever the truth, it puts the King in a very embarrassing position. He sends a man to the moon to investigate its mineral resources, and the man comes back and says that all mining is immoral! Just when we need iron above all, he tells us that going underground is a sin in the sight of God, exactly as the Church always claimed. The Queen would have him strung up, if she had her way. Only the King stays her hand. And I think he is right to do so. It will not do, as a general rule, for a ruler to declare someone a hero one day and have him executed the next. The King knows that.

Kramer is well-liked in the city, and you can be sure that if we make a martyr of him, then it will not be long before some old woman claims that she was cured of her arthritis by praying to him, and then they will collect his relics and venerate them, and make a saint of Kramer, and a villain of the King. Such things have happened before.'

'What was *Ariadne* doing in the Westlands, anyway? Do we have business with the Irdai?'

'She was picking up volunteers for the King's railway-building programme.'

'Volunteers?'

Johansson smiled grimly.

'Well, in a manner of speaking. If you offer someone – What is the Kantish phrase? Gold and green forests? – they will follow you anywhere. For the Irdai, the King of Kantarborg is their messiah, and he is leading them to the promised land. Except that they will find the promised land involves quite a lot of physical labour. He's more a kind of messiah in reverse, really. Taking them out of the promised land to build the pyramids.'

'They're slaves, in other words.'

Johansson said nothing.

'He told me they would be well cared for,' I said.

'Of *course* they will be well cared for, Karl! A slave is a valuable commodity. If he dies, you lose your investment. So they are well housed and fed. The King is looking after them in the hope that this injection of cheap labour will save the economy of the kingdom.'

'But you cannot build an economy on slave labour!'

'What on earth makes you think that? Of course you can. It's been done many times in the past. You just have to make sure they can't escape and go home. And the Irdai are perfect for that – they have no possibility of getting back to their own country. Unless they hijack *Ariadne*, I suppose.'

'Aren't you supposed to be captain of *Ariadne*, anyway? Why weren't you there in the Westlands?'

Johansson took a sip from his glass before replying.

'I did not join the King's Men to be a slaver, Karl.'

I stared at him.

'Surely you have not resigned your commission?'

'No, I pleaded special responsibilities here at court, helping out with the excavations at North Gate. The King granted my request.'

'But you have always been…flexible in the past. You haven't become an idealist, have you?'

'Not really. I'm more of a practical man, Karl. A sailor usually knows which way the wind is blowing.'

Extract from *My Journeye to the Moone* by E. Kramer

[…] Now, it was at this great height, whence I could see, as the poet says, the round Earth's imagined corners, that a great joy began to come over mee, which did not desert mee in all the time I spent in the heavenly realms. For I could sense presences all about my little craft, that did help mee upon my journey, and that did guide my mooneship entirely without my intervention. And they were of great comfort to mee. 'Fear not,' they said, 'for we have come to take you to the Holy Ground, there to receive a message of great import for all humanity.' And I knew not of what they spoke.

As I neared the Moone I fell as though into a reverie, and I could feel my craft gradually attaining a great and unnatural speed, and then I felt it falling down into the depths, and I landed in the sea upon the surface of the Moone, the force of which did utterly destroy my craft, but mee it did not harm, except that I received a great blow upon my forehead. And I was greeted and welcomed to the Moone by St Christopher Columbus and an angel.

Now of these two, the saint was small and strong, and had tattooed upon his arms signs and images most wondrous and strange, while the angel had the appearance of a young man, but was as comely as any maid, with hair as red as blood and skin as white as snow. They were dressed in humble garb, like that of monks. And they brought mee into their craft, which was like no other I ever have seen, being shaped like a fish, and dark inside.. Like Jonah I spent three days and three nights in the belly of this great fish, until like Jonah I was spewed out upon the Earth to preach repentance to the citye and the King.

I was at first greatly afeared that I should not be able to return to my own world, my craft being gone, but the angel said to mee, 'Fear not, childe of man, for from Earth have you come, and unto Earth you shall return'. And the saint sang to mee a song, to comfort mee in my affliction, and that song was such sweet music that it brought tears to mine eyes, though I could not discern the words, except that it was a song of the Holy Ground and of longing to see it again. And then they showed to mee great signs and wonders; for they did take mee on their craft across the Moone, up to great mountain peaks and down into terrible depths, and there I did see wondrous cityes and marvellous temples, seas full of fish, and fields of golden corn, and the great Garden of Eden itself, whence our ancient father and mother were banished for seeking the Golden Apples beneath the soil.

And it was in this manner, all without words, that they did reveal to mee the nature of our sinne, and the means whereby we might once again attain the path of heaven. For Man, seed of Adam and Eve, has ever burrowed into the Earth and stolen of its riches, that hee might be spared a life of labour, and not have to eat bread in the sweat of his brow, as is decreed by the Good Book. And it was for this sinne that the Great Cataclysm engulfed the whole world, and for this that the great punishment of God lay upon the Earth for a century or more, which we call the Dark Ages.

And I heard a voice say, 'Beware, childe of Adam! For your race has sunk into iniquity, and has begun once again to steal the treasures of the underground and to burn the blood of the Earth. But there shall soone appear a great portent in the heavens, and all that shall see it shall wonder, and this shall be the sign that a great kingdom shall fall, unless that it turns away from sinne ...'

CHAPTER TWENTY-THREE

The King had summoned Johansson and I to a meeting. He was not in a good mood.

'What the devil is this?' he demanded, throwing down a small pamphlet on the table.

'Kramer's book?' asked Johansson. 'I hear he is attracting quite a following with his tall tales.'

'Not that lunatic, this is something else entirely. It's Brorsen, I'm sure of it.'

I picked up the little publication. On its cover was printed the familiar design of the Round Tower.

'An almanac? I thought none had been printed this year.'

'Well it turns out that one was. And of course it's full of seditious nonsense.'

The King snatched the book out of my hand and opened it at a marked page.

'Listen to this: "*October: A great sign in the heavens portends the fall of a kingdom. A ruler who sins and does not repent cannot be saved.*" Well, you know who that's about, don't you? Me! I am a sinner, it seems, because I am trying to bring much-needed resources to this kingdom. Which, of course, chimes in very conveniently with Kramer's ravings. This is the rebels' work, and Brorsen is in league with them.'

'Brorsen says his papers were stolen by bandits a month ago,' said Johansson.

'He does, does he? The traitor! I will see him in Sythorn for this.'

'Majesty, might I counsel a slightly different approach? Brorsen's almanac has been published for many years and enjoys wide respect in the kingdom. To imprison him now, however greatly he may have offended, might make it look as though we were trying to silence him. And that would only tend to lend credence to his absurd prophecies.'

'So what do you suggest, Johansson? We can hardly allow vituperous nonsense like this to circulate freely.'

'Well, two can play at that game, can they not? We could produce our own almanac with entirely different prophecies. And at the same time declare that, from now on, only the official almanac, with the stamp of the Round Tower, will be permitted. That would also make all other almanacs forgeries. And for forgers, if I might remind your Majesty, entirely different and rather more punitive decrees apply. We have some old statutes that prescribe the removal of certain parts of the body, for example. That would surely deter even the greediest printer.'

The King's mood changed instantly.

'Johansson, have I told you before that you are a damned clever fellow?'

'Frequently, sire.'

'Well, you are. Nielsen, what's all this nonsense about a sign in the sky? Is something special going to happen in the heavens in October?'

'I don't know, Majesty. I can try to find out.'

'Do that, and we will print that almanac. In fact, no – we'll go further. Build me a clock, Nielsen! A planetarium clock, like the one in the Round Tower. But this one must be on public display, so that all can see the configuration of the planets and their benevolent portents for the King. And let it give praise every hour to God and to his appointed ruler here in Kantarborg! By the devil, if they want a war of the stars, we will give them one!'

Back in the tower, I reflected that the King could conceive of an idea in half a second that could take me half a year or more to realise. Still, the work was very welcome. I had asked for my salary to be paid to me monthly in gold coins, and I now had a permanent arrangement with the Lowlander cheese merchant in the market. The regular consignments to Sandviken would hopefully help to keep my Marieke safe from harm. Lowlanders are not enthusiastic correspondents and although I wrote to her regularly, I had heard no more from her since her last letter, with the exception of a greeting on my name day, in which she reassured me once again that she was safe, which I was very glad to hear. I calculated that if I remained in the King's service, then within another half-year I should have paid off my remaining debts, which would be a very great weight off my shoulders. And then, if all went well, I could go home.

At least this new project lay more or less within my area of expertise. However, cogs and gears are one thing – astrological calculations are quite another. In Brorsen's library I found a number of handbooks on the casting of horoscopes, and with some difficulty I began to work my way through them.

I could of course have sought help from the University, but after my brush with Professor Artison, it seemed unlikely that they would be willing to co-operate. Not one of their staff had so much as requested to use the tower's telescopes in all the time I had been staying there, despite the fact that they were probably the best astronomical instruments in the kingdom.

There was in any case no time for me to become a skilled astrologer before the almanac was published. It was already late in the year, and so it would have to be printed as soon as possible, with retroactive effect. That at least made some of the 'predictions' rather easy: there had for example been an unexpectedly heavy fall of snow on two days in April.

'It will make our almanac seem all the more trustworthy,' laughed Johansson.

'But people will see right through it!' I protested.

'No they won't. People love to be fooled by this kind of thing. You'll see. Just don't be *too* accurate. A little bit of vagueness and no-one will be suspicious.'

A quick examination of what we had begun to call the pirate almanac made it fairly clear what the 'great sign' in October was supposed to be: a lunar eclipse was due on the 24th.

'Is that so unusual?' I asked Johansson. 'I seem to recall

seeing one or two.'

'Yes, so have I. But they can look quite dramatic on occasion, with a red hue, as though the moon were covered in blood.'

'Let's hope that it is a cloudy night, then.'

The need to check Brorsen's calculations in the pirate almanac – and to make sure they had not been manipulated – gave me an excuse to spend some nights in the observatory, learning how to use its instruments. This was a great delight to me, as the telescopes were very finely made, as well as being very beautiful – the very best the kingdom could afford. The moons of Jupiter were clearly visible through the largest of them, and for the first time, I also saw the rings of Saturn – a wondrous sight.

I also discovered what the large concave mirror in the middle of the floor was for. It was aligned with one of the telescopes, in such a way that it reflected a magnified version of the night sky. When the roof was open and all other light in the dome was extinguished, I could thus sit and observe the heavens in the observatory floor as though they lay both above and below me – creating the illusion that I, like Kramer, were flying through the firmament. It would be a marvellous thing, to be so isolated from humanity and all its travails. Surely one day we would build a balloon that could manage it.

As far as I could tell from my observations – and after double-checking them against other published tables and the navigational ephemerides – the positions of the planets recorded in the pirate almanac seemed to be accurate, although the rebels had of course interpreted them in entirely their own fashion, with much doom-laden prophecy about the fall of kingdoms and rulers, etc. The date of the assassination attempt on the King was for example rendered as "*A bright new morning is marred by a dark cloud. But dawn must come, even after the darkest night*". This was of course published after the event, and so involved no great prophetic powers, but might well serve to convince the credulous. As Johansson had remarked, vagueness, not accuracy, was the key. ("A bomb will fail to kill the

King" might doubtless have aroused a little more suspicion.)

Inspired by this, I began to pen my own poetic aphorisms and insert them as appropriate among the recommendations of the best days to sow potatoes or harvest beets. *"A villain behaves with cowardice; a great ruler acts with courage"* was for example my own 'prediction' for that fateful day in the King's Garden. (After all, whatever else one might say about the King, his courage has never been in question.)

Sooner or later, though, I had to start making predictions about the actual future, and this was, as you might imagine, a rather more demanding task. I had learned from the astrological works in the tower that oppositions between planets were generally viewed as being rather negative, or at least a source of tension – depending on the actual planets involved – whereas conjunctions tended to be rather more favourable and mutually supportive. Then there were other relations; squares, trines, sextiles, etc. I have always enjoyed mathematics, and this part of the business fascinated me – drawing the horoscopes and calculating the angles. From these calculations, with the aid of what were called 'houses', it was relatively easy to discern which days would supposedly be good or bad for planting crops, or for trade, human relations, etc. So – leaning a little on the pirate version – I was soon able to concoct a series of plausible-sounding prophecies that could mean almost anything: *"Danger from the east. Do not travel"*; *"Something that was lost will be recovered"*; *"Luck for the seller – ill fortune for the buyer"*, and so on. I devoted special attention to those ominous days in October when the rebels had foretold dire portents; in my version, the lunar eclipse promised, on the contrary, nothing less than doom for the King's adversaries: *"A red moon – calamity for the enemies of a great man. Anarchy is averted by wise action"*.

I would be lying if I claimed it did not bother my conscience. *You have become a mere propagandist*, said the now-familiar voice in my head. But I did at least make an honest attempt to get most of my predictions to accord with the astrological conditions for the day – reflecting that, if the clock-making trade should fail, I could always make my living as a market day astrologer.

The official almanac for the year was finally published in July, with the stamp of the Round Tower and its imprint on the front cover. I was named as its compiler. Sales were limited – the pirate version had by this time been out for more than a month, and if I knew anything about farmers and merchants, they were hardly likely to fork out for an almanac twice in the same year. But the clamp-down on street sales of 'seditious' publications at least meant that our version was free from open competition.

That task completed, I could turn to the rather more dignified project of designing a planetarium clock. If this were to have the desired effect on the public mind, it would have to be something very special. My first idea was to render the heavens astrologically, which is to say, as they would appear from Earth. This would meet the King's demand of showing at a glance the astrological situation, but it rapidly became clear to me that God seemed to be having something of a joke at the expense of the astrologer – or the horologer. Yes, the planets move in relatively simple orbits about the sun. But the problem is that we do not live on the sun, we live on the Earth, and relative to the Earth, the apparent movements of the planets in our sky, which is what determines the horoscope, are complex in the extreme. Reluctantly, I abandoned the idea of an Earth-centred planetarium in favour of a more traditional depiction of the planets 'from above', with the sun in the centre. It would still be a complex mechanism, but not impossibly so. The only disadvantage of this arrangement was that it would make the astrological context much more difficult to read – in fact, I was not at all sure that it could be directly read at all. How, then, to convey the benevolent influence of the King?

I began by drawing some half-dozen different designs, but grew quickly frustrated and dissatisfied with them all. After a few fruitless hours of pacing about the apartment in something of a huff, I remembered the marvellous astronomical clock that was reputed to have existed in the kingdom of Bohemia in ancient times, and which I had heard about in my student days. I went looking for illustrations of this legendary contrivance in the astronomer's library, and was lucky enough to find, not just pictures, but also a detailed account of the mechanism. This most ingenious device displayed not only the time of day and the positions of the sun, moon and stars in an elegant and attractive manner; it also struck the hour with musical chimes and a procession of carved and animated figures, which is more or less exactly what the King had asked for.

But it was also, of course, horrendously complicated, telling the time in reference to five different systems, and with an eccentrically placed zodiacal ring in the middle, which rotated about its own axis once a year, and about the clock's centre once a day. The time of rising of the sun and the phases of the moon were also indicated with small models of these bodies, but it did not show any other planets. If I was going to produce a working mechanism within a reasonable period of time, I would clearly have to adapt and simplify the design, and reduce it somewhat in size.

Then there was the question of location. I would have liked to place the clock in a city square, like the clock in Sandviken, but this was out of the question – the plan was that an effigy of the King would emerge on the hour to wave to the people and signal that all was well in the kingdom, and in any such public place in these times, the figure of the monarch might lose its head quite quickly. There was only one spot where the clock could be safe from vandalism and still be on public display, and that was at a good height on the side of the Round Tower itself. This also meant that there would be quite a long drop for the weights inside, giving more power to the mechanism – and of course more work for the winder, unless we installed a windmill on the tower to do the job.

In the centre of the arrangement would be the clock itself, with several superimposed dials, as in the Bohemian timepiece, to represent both the hour and the astrological situation. Below this would be a second circular dial, indicating the positions of the planets relative to the Earth. Then, above both of these dials, would be a pair of doors that would open on the hour for a procession. Traditionally, the figures used with such clocks are either saints and characters from the Bible, or else personifications of the virtues and vices, etc. Apart from the figure of the King, though, something told me that this particular clock needed something a little bit special and specific to Kantarborg. But what should it be?

In the old days, when I needed to think, I used to pay a visit to the public bathhouse – a rather grand, temple-like building near the University. I had resumed this habit lately – the plumbing facilities in the tower being somewhat primitive – and had been pleased to find that the place had escaped the worst effects of the bombardment, and had barely changed. And sure enough, lying there in the warm water, surrounded by green plants and marble columns, an idea occurred to me that I felt was quite inspired, and which would surely confer upon the King great political advantage. The only problem would be convincing him to do it.

'You want to put HIM on the clock! I don't understand.'

'I hope that all will become clear, Majesty, when I have explained myself.'

'Yes, I hope so too!'

'You can see the basic idea in this drawing, sire. Above the planetary dial, on either side, will be two globes, representing the Earth and the moon. The model of the moon rotates to show its various phases. Every hour, as the clock strikes, a model of the moonship takes the figure of Kramer from the

Earth, *here*, to the moon, *here*. There, he is welcomed by the figures of St Christopher Columbus and the angel. Their arms will move in greeting. And the angel's wings.'

'Why does the angel have wings? And those robes?' interrupted the King. 'He said it was dressed like a monk.'

'Because that's what people expect angels to look like, sire. Then the moonship, by cunning contrivance, turns into the alien craft – actually it just rotates and shows its other side – and Kramer is brought back to Earth. All of this is presided over by your benevolently waving figure here at the top, and by the approving images of God and the apostles around the sides. And a lot more angels.'

'So you are proposing that we celebrate a man who is calling me a heretic and a sinner?'

'What we cannot change, sire, we must turn to our advantage. This clock will stand long after both we and Kramer are gone, and in the future, sending a man to the moon will be remembered as one of the greatest achievements of your reign. Along with the clockwork railway, which we will show *here*, traversing the mountains of the north, and *here*, passing through the wildwoods to realise your Majesty's Grand Plan.'

'But what about Kramer's message? That we may not use the fruits of the underground? If we honour the fellow like this we shall have to accept his doctrine, and then the Grand Plan is doomed.'

'I suggest we simply ignore it, Majesty.'

'Ignore it? But how?'

'We concentrate on the fact that you sent him to the moon and that he returned. What he actually says is of lesser importance. It cannot, in any case, be shown on a clock.'

'I still don't see it. It sounds like gross recklessness to me.'

'If I may point out, Majesty,' interjected Johansson, 'this is exactly what the Church has always done with awkward zealots like this. Venerate their memory, and ignore what they actually said. It has proven to work quite well in the past.'

The King looked thoughtful.

'You may have a point there. I suppose it might be one way to deal with the fellow, short of bumping him off. But what if Kramer objects? Says he is being misrepresented or something?'

'Majesty, he will be delighted,' I said. 'What have we done but immortalise him and his story? And there is nothing here to suggest that you and he were ever in disagreement.'

'I must admit, you have grown quite cunning, Nielsen. I can see I shall have to keep an eye on you in future. Very well, we shall do as you suggest. I just hope that you are right about the consequences.'

CHAPTER TWENTY-FOUR

'No way. Forget it. I am not going in there.' Joe stood with his arms folded outside the tunnel in the hillside.

'Well, you were the one complaining about the food,' Christopher replied. 'I'm telling you, I've seen tunnels like this in the Westlands before. The ancients used them as stores. I bet you we could find a great load of tin cans in there.'

'And why can't you do it yourself?'

'I told you, *because I'm not allowed.* Monks can't go underground beyond sight of daylight, that was laid down by the founder of our order. You're a lay brother, it's all right for you.'

'Oh right, go all pious on me now! When did you last say your office, will you tell me that?'

'Look it, when I'm on operations, I'm on operations. Everything I do then is a prayer to the Lord. I'm sure he understands.'

'I hope the Lord approves of thieving, so.'

'To know all is to forgive all,' replied Christopher. 'And you're a know-all, so it should be easy for you.'

'Very funny. This is probably a sacred site for one of the local tribes. I'll end up being roasted on a spit.'

Christopher handed him a wind-up torch and a basket.

'Take the lamp. And if you see any bottles in there...'

'Yeah, right. So you can get hammered again. Some man of the cloth you are.'

'To quote the Good Book, Joe: I came to you eating and drinking, and they say, "Here is a glutton and a drunkard".'

'Well I'm not carrying you back to the boat again, just so you know. You can lie here and get eaten by the natives.'

Still grumbling, Joe disappeared into the darkness. Christopher busied himself gathering firewood for what he hoped might be a halfway decent meal. Further south the stores had all been plundered, but boats rarely ventured up here, so there was a good chance. He had found a can of baked beans once, back when he was a sailor. Told no-one. Most delicious thing he'd ever eaten. His mouth still watered at the memory. And then there was the tomato soup that time in Mercia. The crew were fighting over it, they got about a mouthful each. Don't know why, it's not like they couldn't have made tomato soup themselves. But the ancients had some trick to it, it was a strange thing. Tasted fantastic. You had to be careful, though – if the can is dented or too rusty, throw it away. A bad can could make you very ill. Whole crews had died that way, sometimes.

The bracken-covered hillside beneath his sandals dropped away sharply, down to where *Paloma* was anchored below in the tranquil fjord. All around, mountains and silent pine forest stretched to the distant horizon. Most beautiful country in the world, thought Christopher. Damn the place. Snow and darkness half the year, and the rest of the time you'd nearly be eaten alive with the insects. Most of the crews he had known hadn't even bothered coming ashore in the Westlands; there was no salvage worth the taking, and no human life either, except for a few tribals. Still, a fair few people must have lived here once. Down by the shore, among the trees, they had been stumbling over ancient remains all over the place: walls, roads, buildings, all burned down now and overgrown. Must have been a good life while it lasted. Vanity, all is vanity, says the prophet.

'You're a right bollix, is what you are!'

Joe threw the full basket on the ground.

'What?'

'There were *dead bodies* in there, you fecker! You knew that, didn't you?'

'Bodies?'

'Skeletons.'

'Oh, right. Sorry, should have warned you. You get them too, sometimes.'

'It was *horrible*, man. Twenty or thirty of them, children and all. All bunched together, like they were trying to hide. Poor bastards. Wonder what got them?'

'Don't know, Joe. Terrible things happened in the Dark Ages. The Church says they let loose monsters from the depths. That's another reason why we're not allowed to go underground.'

'Yeah, let the poor sodding lay brothers do it,' said Joe. 'Anyway, you were right, they had cans down there. Don't know what's in them, the labels are gone. Robbing corpses, Jesus, what's become of us…'

'Sure they can't use them, we might as well. I'll get the fire lit.'

Once the cooking fire was going, Christopher produced a small hook-like metal device from the purse at his belt and showed Joe how the cans could be opened.

'This is the way the ancients used to do it. I bought one of these on the docks in Garrystown. Handiest thing ever. Saved my life a few times.'

'Should I get some pots from the boat?'

'No need. You just put the cans in the fire.'

'That's smart all right.'

'The ancients were smart people, Joe. We don't know the half of what they had back then.'

Later, after a somewhat perplexing meal of spaghetti hoops and stewed prunes, Christopher and Joe sat by the fire, mulling over the gastronomic tastes of the ancients.

'I swear, that was the most peculiar food I ever tasted in my entire life,' said Joe.

'It's the cuisine of the ancient aristocracy, Joe. The kings and the nobles. Not everyone would be able to afford food in metal cans like that. Did you see the workmanship?'

'I suppose t'would be an acquired taste.'

'Well that's just it. You'd nearly have to be brought up eating it. Like, you know, swans and stuff that only kings and queens eat. Then you probably couldn't get enough of it.'

'I think I've had enough of it already,' said Joe, getting up. 'I need to go visit the bushes.'

When Joe returned, he found Christopher standing at the

fire with his back turned. He had one hand behind his back and was gesticulating to Joe to stay back. Joe looked past Christopher and saw a large animal standing at the other side of the fire, staring straight at him.

'Sure it's only a dog,' called Joe. 'Throw it a stick or something.'

'Stay where you are, Joe. Don't move.'

The animal stared at Christopher for a few seconds more, then turned and trotted off into the undergrowth.

'I suppose where there's dogs, there must be people,' said Joe. 'Maybe we'd better get a move on.'

Christopher began kicking out the remains of the fire in an agitated manner.

'What's up?' asked Joe. 'Are you worried the tribespeople might be coming after him?'

'That was no flipping dog. That was *canis lupus lupus*.'

'Ya wha?'

'A wolf, Joe. It was a wolf. And wolves live in packs.'

'Wolves? I thought they were only myths. They don't really exist, do they?'

'A lot of strange things live up here in the north, Joe. Including some things that don't really exist. We need to get back to the boat, quickly.'

They gathered up their things and bundled them into the dinghy. Joe sat in and Christopher pushed off from the shore.

'That was one peculiar wolf, though,' he said, picking up the oars. 'I've seen them before, but only at a distance. Never saw one come up close to human beings like that. Almost like it was interested in us in some way. Sizing us up for dinner, maybe. Gave me the creeps. We'd best get under way.'

'Sun's going down,' said Joe. 'We'll put her on the rocks if we try to take her out in the dark. First light tomorrow, that'd be the best thing.'

'All right,' said Christopher. 'But we'd better keep a watch tonight. Those buggers can swim.'

They climbed up onto the hull of *Paloma* and pulled the dinghy up after them.

'How far north are we now?' asked Joe.

'Another few days and we should be there. If the weather holds.'

'And then what?'

'Then we open the letter.'

'Bet it says, "Ha ha, fooled you!"'

'The abbot of St Michael's Rock is not known for his sense of humour, Joe, fortunately for us. The monks threw all the resources they had left into this. So it must be something important.'

'I suppose. I'll take the first watch if you like.'

'Grand, I'll turn in then. And tomorrow to fresh woods, and pastures new.'

'Ya wha?'

CHAPTER TWENTY-FIVE

My design for the planetarium clock was almost finished, and if I say so myself, it looked rather splendid. I was particularly proud of the mechanism that transported the figure of Kramer to the moon and back. In the model, I had rendered the LEM without the balloon, so that it could more easily transform into Christopher Columbus's craft for the return journey. I had no idea what the alien craft looked like, of course, but the men on board *Ariadne* had said it resembled a whalefish, so I designed it in a fish-like form, with a long tail for visibility. The clock would also have a slightly simplified inner face within the walls of the Round Tower, showing the precise planetary positions for the benefit of scientists and academics. If the whole contrivance worked as I hoped, it would be most impressive.

I had built a small wooden mock-up which seemed to work satisfactorily, but there was no way of knowing whether the whole machine would function correctly until all the pieces were assembled in full size. So, mindful of the need to test the device before installing it, we erected a huge temporary wooden scaffold at the foundry, and began mounting the pieces on this almost as soon as they came out of the moulds. The whole structure looked vast standing there in the foundry yard, and gathered quite some attention from passers-by along the canal, but it would hopefully seem less dominating once we had it mounted on the tower. The wooden figures had been carved for me by sculptors who normally worked with church carvings. As the figure of the King would be furthest away from the observer, I had drawn it particularly large – which also facilitated the installation of the hand-waving mechanism inside it.

It was while I was up on the scaffolding, supervising the fitting of this figure to the mechanism, that I noticed something odd down below in the yard. A large stack of iron rails had appeared in one corner. They appeared to be quite new – not the rusty ancient type that was sometimes melted down here – and were clearly intended for the new railway lines. But I had not seen any new rails being made at the foundry.

I climbed down and asked the foreman about them, who told me that the rails had arrived in a shipment from abroad, and that there would shortly be more on the way.

'Alban vessel, Mr Nielsen. First time I've seen one. Small enough to come up the canal, so they moored right outside the gates.'

This news surprised me greatly. If true, it would radically alter the situation.

'Albans? Did you know where they got the iron? Is it mined?'

'One of my men asked the ship's master, but he spoke no Anglian – they don't, you know, as a rule. He said only one word that my man could understand: Vindicator.'

'Vindicator? What does that mean?'

'No idea, sir. Your guess is as good as mine.'

If the King had suddenly found a new source of iron, it was strange that he had said nothing to me about it. It was puzzling.

It had become the custom of people who wished to see me for one reason or another to post a message on the door to the Round Tower. On this day, when I returned home (as I now called it), I found a note which said simply: *Need to see you urgently. J.* It could hardly be Johansson, since I saw him almost every day. And the visitor had not posted any details of how I could get in touch with him. It was rather odd.

It was only when I had almost reached the top of the tower that I realised who it must be. And where I could find him.

My brother Jonas was waiting for me in The Thimble. He had grown thinner, and was bearded, wearing a wide-brimmed hat pulled down low over his head. Our greeting was cordial, but under the circumstances, could hardly be warm.

'I hope that perhaps after this latest escapade you have seen the true nature of the King,' he began.

'The moonship? Well, who knows? The King may yet turn it to his advantage.'

'Karl, the man is a crackpot. He is bankrupting the kingdom and starving its people.'

'He is doing his best for the kingdom. And he has never betrayed me.'

'I did not betray you. Whoever put you in Sythorn, it was not me.'

'No. I know. It was the King. Though inadvertently.'

'And yet still you serve him? I don't understand.'

'It's complicated. It's a matter of personal loyalty.'

'And of money, no doubt.'

'That, too.'

'Well, that is a matter for your own conscience. I did not come here to discuss that with you. I bear a message for the King from Ulrika Häkonsdotter.'

That took me very much aback. My brother was, after all, a minister of the Anglian Church.

'You are with her faction? Reindeer herders and witches? I am amazed, Jonas.'

'Not as amazed as I am to see you with the King. But do you want to hear the message or just regale me with your cultural prejudices?'

'Yes, of course I want to hear it. Go on.'

'The King knows the military situation in the north. As you do not, perhaps. The war is over. The Häkonite forces have control of the northern provinces from coast to coast, including the iron mines. The King wants iron. Ulrika Häkonsdotter has iron. What she wants now is recognition. As Queen of the North, and as the first and only true spouse of the King.'

'Spouse? What are you talking about? He was with her for one night, in a tent! How could that possibly make some tribal witch the wife of the King of Kantarborg? For all I know, he may have lain with fifty women in the past, or a hundred.'

'Karl, there is much more to all this than you know or

understand. Just give him the message. Here it is in writing, if anyone should doubt you. You can say a stranger gave it to you.'

From his knapsack, he produced a scroll with what looked like a royal seal, and handed it to me. Then he got up to leave. For a moment, in the light from the window, he almost looked like my brother again.

'Are you keeping well, Jonas?'

'Thank you for inquiring. As well as can be expected. It has not been easy, this past time. But I think we may finally be on the right road again.'

'You heard about William?'

'Yes. Another of your king's crimes. Your niece is being cared for.'

'Jessica is with you?!'

He nodded, and left without another word.

It was almost curfew when I left The Thimble, which meant I had to wait until next morning before delivering the scroll to the Rose Castle. This happened to be a Sunday, and the King was at service in St Marilyn's church, so I left it with a servant and went back to the Round Tower. That afternoon, Johansson called on me – no doubt at the urgent instigation of the King. I told him the whole story, except the identity of the courier. (I could hardly throw my own brother to the wolves, even if he was probably well gone from the kingdom again by now.)

'He claimed the war was over,' I said, as I fetched the wine-glasses from the scullery, 'but I don't understand. How could a bunch of tribal warriors defeat regular soldiers in battle?'

The sun was shining through the stained glass windows, but even in high summer, it always seemed rather dank and chilly in the tower. Dust motes in the sunbeams fled from our breath as we spoke. Johansson placed the wine bottle beside the chess-board and sat down in his usual armchair.

'Well, first of all, you have to remember that the tribes know every inch of the terrain. They know the valleys that you can or can't cross when it snows or rains. The ravines where you can ambush your enemy, how to get away without being pursued. All of that. And they are skilled hunters, which means they shoot straight. It's not that hard to imagine how such a force could defeat soldiers who are cold and far from home. Especially if they have a charismatic leader. And Ulrika is certainly that.'

He moved a white pawn to Q4. I mirrored the move.

'And then of course, they are not just tribal. King Häkon was by all accounts a popular monarch, so his daughter has the backing of a great many ordinary Northlanders, too. And more to the point, several major noble families are waiting to see which way the cards will fall. So she is a contender, no doubt about it.'

He moved a knight to QB3.

'But why is she making this absurd claim to be the wife of the King?'

'It may not be all that absurd. Don't look so surprised. I'll tell you what I think; I think there may have been more people around that day in the mountains than just the ones we saw. There could have been other witnesses.'

'What difference would that make?'

'Are you familiar with the requirements towards a valid wedding in the eyes of the Church?'

I laughed.

'Well, surely there has to be a church ceremony, for a start?'

'Not at all.'

Johansson counted off on his fingers.

'First, the intent to wed; second, the consent of both parties; third, the presence of a church minister and at least two witnesses to hear the promise spoken; and fourth, the consummation of the marriage. In a normal wedding that last bit occurs off stage, so to speak, but the marriage can be annulled if it doesn't happen.'

'So?'

'So let's imagine that they had a clergyman and some witnesses spying on them while they were in the tent. Peering through a hole in the canvas, something like that. Now Ulrika, I think we can safely assume, is a woman skilled in the arts of love. So she taunts the King and teases him until he's almost mad with passion. At the same time, she's probably saying things like, "Will you do this to me? Will you do that to me?" You know what such women are like.'

I nodded, though I had no idea what he meant.

'All in Anglian, no doubt, for the benefit of the witnesses. And all the while he's saying, "Yes, yes, yes I will, yes." And then, at the crucial moment, she says in a loud and clear voice, "*Will you make me your queen?*" And of course the poor man says "Yes, yes, yes!" So there you have the promise and the consent, and the consummation is obvious. A wedding. Somewhat un-orthodox, perhaps, but arguably valid. Performed in front of witnesses, and in the presence of the clergy.'

He lifted his glass from beside the chessboard and took a sip. Our wine was red today – we were down to the last two bottles in the astronomer's store. Soon we might actually have to buy some. I moved a knight to KB3.

'It's just my theory, mind you,' he went on. 'But it would explain a lot. And they drugged you and me to make sure we would sleep through it all.'

White pawn to K3.

'They drugged us?'

'Of course,' he smiled. 'Never drink anything in the house of a witch, Karl! Or perhaps you thought it was just tribal hooch that made us pass out like that in a hut full of yelping dogs?'

I thought about that. It made sense, certainly.

'But why go to all that trouble? Ulrika is a princess. She has power of her own. And now she has won a war.'

I moved a pawn to KN3.

'That's what I've been wondering. Well, for one thing, her people are few in number, so they cannot occupy large areas. They would be spread too thinly. That's why the war has ground to a halt now, when she has control of the northern provinces and the iron mines. But she's not finished yet. She has her sights fixed higher, Karl. How high, I don't yet know.'

'I still don't understand. Her quarrel is with the Northlands. Why is it important to her to be the wife of the King of Kantarborg?'

'If you ask me, I don't think she gives a damn about being the wife of the King of Kantarborg. Her target is Ingeborg.'

'The Queen!'

'Yes; Ulrika's cousin – the daughter of the man who ousted her father. Think about it. If Ulrika's marriage to the King is recognised by the Church, that would make the King a bigamist and annul his marriage to Ingeborg. And if Ulrika has in the meantime borne a child by the King, that child would then in principle be the sole legitimate heir to the throne of Kantarborg. Even if the claim is never realised, its mere existence would be the sweetest revenge. With one move, Ulrika turns the Queen into a whore and her coming progeny into bastards. And all this with the blessing of the clergy, mark you, because now that the King has thrown out the Anglian hierarchy, the Church has every reason to look favourably upon Ulrika. They will no doubt be prepared to overlook her heathen tendencies if she will promise to restore their privileges.'

'So you think she has borne a child?' I asked.

'I'm sure of it. That's why she's making her move now. Karl, the plain fact is that she has outfoxed us all, right from the very beginning. We're only seeing the start of her plans.'

Johansson moved a bishop to QN5.

'Check,' he said.

CHAPTER TWENTY-SIX

'*Dreamed Me A Dream Last Night*? A bit mournful, don't you think?' said the King.

We were discussing what melody the chimes should play as the figure of the King emerged from the clock. He had made no mention of the message I had delivered, which I took to mean that it was not a matter he wished to discuss with his clockmaker. And that, I must admit, suited me very well.

'How about the opening bars of *In The Mood*? Tar-de-dah-dah-dah-dah-dah!'

'With the greatest respect, Majesty, I suspect that that tune might not be sufficiently dignified for the purpose. The clock does after all have a religious theme, as well as an astrological one.'

'Seems such a waste. If one is going to be standing there in effigy for centuries, one might be in need of a little entertainment. What about *It's Only A Paper Moon*? Dah-dee-dee-dah, dee-dah-dee-dah…Pretty little tune. No?'

'Sire, your figure will be waving and turning from side to side. We would not want to give the impression that it is…'

'Dancing. No, I suppose not. Damned shame, though. Oh very well, *Dreamed Me A Dream Last Night*. Dismal melody, if you ask me.'

'But Kantish, sire, and traditional.'

The King sighed.

'Mm. Like flour dumplings. And just as boring.'

As I rolled up my drawings, I took the opportunity to ask the King about the rails I had seen in the foundry yard.

'Well, Nielsen, until we re-take the iron mines and get supplies of our own iron again, we will just have to trade for it, won't we?' he said.

'I heard they were from Alba. Do the Albans have iron

mines?'

'No, but they have recycled iron at a good price. And foundries that can produce rails of the type we need.'

'But how are we paying for it, Majesty?'

'No need to concern yourself with that, Nielsen. Just get the clock finished. That's your first priority right now.'

I put the drawings into my shoulder bag.

'And how is your Majesty's Grand Plan progressing out in the wildwoods?' I asked, as casually as I could.

'Very well, Karl, very well indeed!'

'You have managed to attract some foreign workers?'

'Yes, we have already filled up the first camp. They have been busy clearing the forest, and now that we have some good rails, they can begin laying tracks.'

'Johansson mentioned that they were Irdai?'

'Many of them are, yes. Excellent workers. The sad truth is that Kantarborgans have grown lazy, Nielsen. We have grown fat on the Sound Dues for far too long, and people no longer want to do an honest day's labour. Those foreigners, on the other hand, they'll work from dawn to dusk without complaint. Quite remarkable.'

'And it is actually *paid* work?'

'Of course it is. Don't look at me like that, Clockmaker, I know what you are thinking. I am no slave trader, I'll have you know!'

'So they are free to go if they wish?'

'They can go wherever they like once they have paid off their passage.'

'Their passage?'

'Well, as you know it costs a lot of money to ship them down from the Westlands, so obviously they have to work to pay that off. And then there is the cost of accommodation – building those fine halls wasn't cheap, you know – and their food and so on.'

'It does *sound* rather like indentured labour, sire.'

I had learned the term from Erika, never having heard it before. The King, on the other hand, seemed to be quite familiar with it.

'Nonsense! They get the best of everything. Why, they probably eat better than I do! They get to travel and see a foreign country, and they sleep in warm huts at night. And they love it, you know – I heard that there were more volunteers lining up in the Westlands than we had room for on *Ariadne*. And no wonder – if I were from the Irdai, I can tell you I would much rather be well taken care of like that than trying to scratch out a living in the forest!'

And with that, the King turned and swept out. It was clearly not a subject he wished to discuss further.

I was on my way out of the castle library when I was ambushed by the Queen, who grasped my elbow and steered me back inside again. Arkdur Andersson followed us, in his black tunic, his expression unreadable.

'You delivered a message to the King yesterday,' she said in a voice that was low but urgent. 'You were seen receiving it from a man in a tavern. Who was he?'

'A stranger, Majesty. As I have said.'

'Don't play the innocent with me, Clockmaker, or I will have you spiked this very afternoon. You have previously been seen in that same tavern in the company of that League for Democracy woman. You are thick with the rebels, aren't you?'

'No, your Majesty. I am a loyal servant of the King. I knew Erika Thorne from my student days. It was a chance encounter.'

'Followed, it seems, by another chance encounter. With some strange person who gives you a scroll with a Häkonite seal.'

'I do not know who he was, Majesty. He told me to give the scroll to the King.'

'You must think we are fools, Nielsen.'

'No, your Majesty.'

'So what did your mysterious friend tell you was in that

message?'

'I do not know the details, Majesty. He said it was from Ulrika Häkonsdotter.'

'I know who it was from. *What was the whore's message?*'

I hesitated. I did not want to be the one to bring the Queen this news. But neither, apparently, did the King. The Queen stared at me intently and spoke in a quiet, undramatic voice.

'Clockmaker, if you do not tell me I promise you most sincerely that you will not see another dawn.'

'I believe…she is claiming to be His Majesty's first wife.'

The Queen eyes widened, then she laughed in incredulity.

'Really? And did some kind of heathen wedding ceremony take place in the mountains of which I am unaware?'

'No, your Majesty. I do not know what foundation she has for that claim.'

'Then she has lost her reason. Lies and sorcery. Well, I will see that witch burn!'

She strode out, leaving me trembling. The noose, it seemed, was closing about my neck. On the other hand, she and Andersson could not have any real evidence against me; if they had, I would surely be in a dungeon already. *Now might be the time when a wise man might flee the kingdom*, I told myself as I walked on slightly unsteady legs down the long corridor to the exit. But then again, a wise man would not be here in the first place.

CHAPTER TWENTY-SEVEN

The skies were growing lower and lower. To Christopher, standing in the cockpit in the early morning, it felt almost as though the clouds were closing in above *Paloma*, shutting around the boat like a trap. The wooded fjords and islands of the Westlands, which had appeared almost bucolic in sunlight, looked rather more ominous now under grey skies. The tall pines of the south were giving way to scrubby, stunted birch. Many of the mountains were snow-peaked, even now, in what was supposed to be late summer, and there was almost no darkness at night, but only a kind of drawn-out blue twilight. Seals lay everywhere among the rocks, watching them in mild curiosity as they passed. Once, in the far distance, Christopher thought he saw the tail of a mermaid slap the water, but it was gone before he could call Joe. Their supply of tin cans was running low, but they had fish in abundance – *they'd nearly leap out of the water at you* – and they had the best part of a sack of oats still, for porridge. Christopher, fearing sailor's scurvy, insisted that they made frequent stops at the islands to supplement their diet with herbs and berries. There was lots of angelica here – a good and healing plant – and the lingonberries were plentiful and ripe.

The further north they sailed, the less reliable their charts were becoming – even though they were supposed to be based on ancient originals.

"It's the copyists at Kilkiernan," he complained to Joe. "I keep telling them: You can't augment ancient admiralty charts with hagiography. Just because Brother Benjamin says he landed on an island inhabited by two-headed dragons doesn't mean you should draw it in where you think it's supposed to go. It's bad enough putting Birmingham at the centre of the world."

He waved the chart in frustration, where some monkish

scribe had also embellished the northern seas here and there with sea monsters and the odd volcano. But while monsters had clearly grown scarcer since the time the map was drawn, unmarked islands and headlands seemed to appear out of nowhere, while others that should have been there had apparently vanished. At one point they had wasted a whole day, following a long fjord that had ended blind instead of providing a channel between the islands. Every now and then sullen black rocks reared up ahead of them in the mist, forcing *Paloma* to alter course sharply, or to retreat and find an alternative route. In ancient times, Christopher mused to himself, these landscape features might have been domesticated and borne cheerful, man-made names, like the Devil's Armchair back home. But now they had reverted to their primordial anonymity: aloof, disdainful, keeping their own counsel and their own secrets. *Names are how we tame the world*, he thought. Because without names, the world is a threatening and alien place.

Between the islands, the winds were capricious and unpredictable, and not for the first time Christopher was glad of Joe's rotary sails, which made the actual wind direction less important. *This must be what it's like to sail a steamboat. Though I bet they go a bit faster.* According to the chart – if they could trust it – they ought to be very close to their destination by now. *And then the real trouble starts.* For what on earth were they really heading into? Missions were one thing, but this was something else again. What could possibly be so important that the Church would devote much of its precious resources to sending them all the way up here? And without so much as a shotgun to defend themselves if things went wrong. It had been an evil chance that had destroyed his munitions store at the old monastery, there had been plenty of handy weapons there. All that work, gone for nothing. Even King Barney's old musket would have been better than nothing, a pity they lost it. If nothing else you could bag a few rabbits with it.

The wind was freshening from the west, causing the sails to

hum gently as they spun. A few drops of rain fell upon his face. Good sailing weather, if they could just get a clear run at it.

'Morning,' said Joe, climbing up from below. 'Bad watch?' he asked after a minute.

'Not the best. Too many shallows, rocks just below the surface. Maybe we should take her out to the open sea. It's getting to my nerves, this.'

'Don't worry, she'll bounce if she runs into something.'

'Ah, the confidence of a man who's never been shipwrecked!'

'We can take her out further west if you want. There won't be much shelter, though, if we run into another gale.'

'The chart is all over the place. It's too risky to stay in these shallow waters.'

'Right you are. I'll steer west, then. Windward of the islands.'

'Then north-east when you get out into the open sea. Watch out for a line of mountains to port. When you see them, give me a shout.'

'I will.'

He hadn't slept more than a couple of hours when Joe called him back up on deck again.

'Is that them?' He asked, pointing north, where a row of ridges marched to the horizon.

Christopher took the spyglass and studied the prominences. 'Looks like it.'

'So what do we do now?'

'We find an anchorage. And then, I think, we can open the letter.'

That evening they found a suitable bay, and anchored *Paloma* in the shallows by a small beach.

For the better light, they rowed over to the beach in the dinghy, where Christopher took out the scroll, and, without further ceremony, cut through the seal with his knife and unrolled it. But what it revealed was a shock.

'What the hell is that?'

The message seemed to be written in some kind of code:

46 49 4e 44 20 54 48 45 20 51 55 45 45 4e 2e 20 45 58 43
48 41 4e 47 45 20 59 4f 55 52 20 47 49 46 54 53 2e

'That's it? No key? How are we supposed to work it out?'

Christopher gave a gasp of exasperation. It was not a pleasant thought – that they might have come all this way, only to be unable to proceed any further. What had the abbot been thinking?

Joe took the scroll from his hand and studied it for a moment. Then he smiled.

'Well chief, now you'll be very glad that I came along on this trip. Because I know what this is, and the abbot knew I would know. But if we were captured, no-one would be able to figure it out. Smart enough. It's hexcraft.'

'Hexcraft? Some kind of sorcery?'

'Kinda. It's a sacred code of the ancients. They used it to cast spells and stuff. In Kilkiernan we used to copy them out and try to decipher them. Most of them were just nonsense, though. "Begin...do...end".'

'So what does this one say?'

'I can't tell you that from memory. I can see it's six words, but it's a bit complicated. I need to write out the code tables.'

The tide was receding and had left an expanse of wet sand. Joe picked up a sharp stone and began writing in it. After ten minutes, he had produced two large tables.

'That one over there, that's called asky. The other one is the hexcraft. You have to convert the one into the other, and then into the alphabet.'

'How do you do that?'

'Hex codes are written in pairs. You multiply the first number in the pair by 16, then add the second number.'

'But some of them aren't even numbers.'

'They are, though. A is ten, B is eleven, and so on up to sixteen.'

'Why sixteen?'

'The sixteen holy teachers. The twelve apostles plus the four evangelists.'

'Oh, right. What then?'

'That gives you the number of the letter to look up in the asky code.' He pointed to the second table in the sand.

'So 1 is A, and so on?'

'Not quite. The alphabet starts at 41 in hexcraft.'

'Why on earth would the alphabet start at 41?'

'Magic number. Seven plus nine plus twelve plus thirteen. Though of course it's not really 41, it's actually 65.'

'Okay, now I have not the remotest idea what you are talking about.'

'Don't worry about it. Now, if we take our message and convert it into asky code first, we get this...' – Joe wrote out another row of codes – '...and then we convert that into ordinary letters. Like this.'

In the sand, Joe scratched out the letters one by one. The two crewmates stood and stared at the decoded message. There was a pause.

'And just what do you think *that's* supposed to mean?'

'Search me, chief. I haven't a clue.'

FIND THE QUEEN. EXCHANGE YOUR GIFTS.

CHAPTER TWENTY-EIGHT

By mid-August, the planetarium clock was ready. It had taken a great deal of work to install it in the tower, during which time I had barely slept, supervising the work of the builders at all hours of the day. Each piece was brought in a planned sequence by oxcart from the Royal Foundry and placed in position by means of a winch on the tower roof. A large hole had to be made in the front of the tower to facilitate the work, which caused some muttering among the structural engineers, but the tower's ancient brickwork held up well. A canvas curtain had been hung on a scaffolding around the tower to obscure the clock from public view until the appointed time.

The linkage between the upper dial, which showed the hour, and the lower one, which showed the planetary alignments, was complex and required some further adjustment on site when Mars was found to be going backwards, putting the time out of joint. A set of two cogs that had been installed in the wrong order was found to be the culprit.

Interpreting the planetary positions from an astrological point of view would probably require some considerable training in the arcane art, but at least we could say that everything was openly on display. As an exercise in public transparency, it was surely laudable.

I had considered installing one of our more advanced clockwork mechanisms, a variation of the one that powered the locomotive engines, but as this would involve daily pod changes, I had plumped in the end for the more traditional weights and chains, which would not involve anything having to be brought in. Some poor soul would have to winch up the weights once a week, though, and I was glad that it would not be me. My assistant, Tillonsen, would be performing the job for now.

When the opening day arrived a considerable throng packed

into the narrow streets around the tower, despite the rain and the fact that the King himself would not be present. He was making fewer and fewer public appearances lately, and on the advice of his household guard, his movements were kept irregular and unannounced. It was quite a change from the showmanship of the old days, when he had taken such a delight in public speechmaking.

I stood anonymously among the crowd to watch the spectacle and hear the comments. In truth, I was as excited as any child. In my own mind I was convinced that the clock was a thing of considerable beauty, as well as being useful – but then, I am a clockmaker. I had no idea how the people of the city would react.

As noon approached, the canvas curtain was drawn back to gasps of delight, and Tillonsen set the mechanism going. Then, a minute before the hour, the wooden doors at the top opened and the carved figure of the King emerged, to the accompaniment of both cheers and jeers, and made its way to centre stage as *Dreamed Me A Dream Last Night* played on the chimes. (I had eventually acceded to the wish of the King to allow at least the possibility of the mechanism playing a different melody in future, for example on special occasions.) As the King's effigy waved to the crowd, there were gasps as, just below him, a model of the clockwork locomotive emerged from a tunnel and journeyed across and through the carved mountains of the north. Then the LEM appeared below that, and carried the small figure of Kramer between the model of the Earth and the moon, switching around when it arrived there and travelling the return journey in the form of the fish-shaped alien craft. There was cheering and some laughter among the crowd. It seemed that, at any rate as public entertainment, my device was a success. I need not tell you that I was greatly relieved. It made for a good reason to open the last bottle of the astronomer's wine.

'Showmanship,' I said to Johansson. 'That's the trick. Amaze the crowds. The power of power. I don't know why the King doesn't open up the excavations at North Gate, show them what the ancient kings could do.'

'You wouldn't get Kantarborgans down into that tunnel, they're still terrified of the dark. Anyway, what the ancients did down there is something we could never equal. The architecture is incredible. We haven't explored half the tunnels yet, they seem to go on forever.'

'Yes, they're amazing to see all right.'

Johansson looked puzzled.

'When did you see them? We only began the excavations last autumn.'

'The King took me there from the Rose Castle. By the secret passageway.'

'There's a secret passageway from the Rose Castle?'

'Yes, didn't he tell you? It leads to one of the old station platforms. The kings of old probably needed an escape route.'

'We'd better keep it open, then. The kings of our own day might need it yet.'

That evening, in a slightly intoxicated state, I climbed the ladder up to the observatory and cranked open the roof in readiness for some moon observations. The weather had cleared up and the sky was almost cloudless, which gave me an opportunity to try out something that I had not yet had time to do, namely to take a close look at the moon and see if I could spot anything that might confirm Kramer's story. It was unlikely that I would able to see the Garden of Eden at this remove, but you never know.

While I was preparing the large telescope for this, I happened to glance down at the floor and the concave mirror, which was aligned with one of the telescopes, showing a broad swathe of the stars of the night sky. However, what caught my eye at that moment was clearly not a star. It actually looked more like a hole in the sky that was letting in light from outside the firmament. I stopped what I was doing to take a closer look at the smudged, slightly oval blur. My first thought, of course, was that it was some defect in the mirror. But if that were the case, it would not be visible in the large telescope – so I trained the latter on the same quadrant of the sky, and looked through the eyepiece. And then my heart stopped. There was something new in the heavens.

'With a shape like that, it's either a comet, or else it's a mooncraft on its way to us,' I said to Johansson next day, showing him the drawing I had made. 'Either prospect is rather worrying, I would think.'

'But don't comets return at regular intervals?' asked Johansson. 'If this is one, it should have been predictable. The astronomers would have known.'

'I think they did know. But they chose not to say anything. It's even mentioned in the pirate almanac.'

'*A great sign in the heavens.* So that's what they meant, not the lunar eclipse!'

'It would appear so. And as we wrote nothing about it in the official almanac, that will inevitably tend to lend credence to the rebels' version.'

'Well, there's nothing we can do about it now. We'll just have to hope that people ignore it.'

But people did not ignore it. As the weeks passed, the object in the sky gradually grew larger until it was visible to the naked eye at night. Always a city that loved its gossip, Kantarborg practically lit up with rumours. One was that the King of the Moon was coming on a visit, and that I was secretly building a clockwork elephant in the Rose Castle to give to him as a gift. (Some servant must have overheard our discussions.) More seriously, and particularly galling for me, was the whisper that the planetarium clock I had so painstakingly constructed did not depict the King at all, but rather Satan, who was pictured presiding in delight over the end of the world, no less. According to this story, the fish-shaped alien spacecraft depicted in the clock was actually the comet, the arrival of which signalled the advent of the end time when the Antichrist would be enthroned. A variation on this tale was that the King was himself a Satan-worshipper, who transformed into a dog at night and listened to the orders of the Evil One in code through a mechanical music-box. The proof of this was apparently a label that a chambermaid at the Rose Castle had seen on a music disc, which clearly showed a dog sitting and listening to the device, alongside the Anglian words 'His Master's Voice'. And on top of this came Erik Kramer's prophecy – reinforced as it was by the claim in the pirate almanac – that the strange sign in the sky portended the fall of the Kingdom of Kantarborg.

All of this was of course the most sublime nonsense, but it seems to be a strange quirk of the human psyche that the more outlandish the story, the more people are inclined to believe it – especially if it is officially denied. And in any case, it would have been rather hard for anyone at the palace to come out and *deny* that the King turned into a Satan-worshipping dog every night with a penchant for listening to old jazz recordings. And so the rumours continued to flourish.

There was little sympathy to be had from the University. Yes, of course the astronomy department had known about the imminent arrival of a comet that had last visited almost a century ago, during the reign of the King's grandfather. The failure of official sources to give warning to the public of this celestial event was naturally unfortunate, but if the King insist-ed on appointing a *clockmaker* to compile the almanac, what could be expected? Why had they said nothing about it? Well, no-one had asked them.

'They are trying to blame me for a job they themselves refused to do,' I complained furiously to Johansson as we walked through the castle park. 'None of them was willing to step into Brorsen's shoes and publish the almanac. It is their fault that this has happened.'

'Well, I suppose they could hardly step into his shoes with-out stepping on his toes,' he remarked with a smile. 'One thing you can say for the astronomers – they are certainly loyal. But to their own rather than to the King, it would appear.'

'Then why not fire them? No, I'm serious. Fire them all. They are crown employees, and this is subversive activity that could threaten the stability of the realm. All these ridiculous rumours.'

'Well, it's rather difficult to accuse someone of subversion for what they *didn't* do – more for what they *did* do. That's the way laws tend to be framed. And it would be next to impossible to prove malicious intent here. As they well know.'

'Then cut their budget. Terribly sorry, hard times and all that. Half of you will have to go. You decide who.'

'Which, of course, will set them at each other's throats. Divide and rule. Excellent. Now, my dear Karl, you are finally beginning to think like a courtier.'

That silenced me. Because he was right.

Lying awake in my bed that night, troubled by these thoughts, I eventually realised I had made one very serious error in the design of the clock; the confounded thing chimed all night long without cease, the bells echoing up the vaulted passageways of the tower. I had been able to put up with it until now, but in my sleepless state it seemed unbearable. When it was about to strike midnight I decided could stand it no longer and went down to stop the mechanism, just as the chimes started up again. I could always claim that it had developed a fault, I reasoned to myself. In my befuddlement, however, I failed to notice that I had halted the figure of the King mid-way in his journey across the clock face, giving the impression next day that the clock had mysteriously stopped exactly at the witching hour, with the image of Satan – as it was claimed – standing and leering out across the city. I was beginning to hate that mannequin.

In the following days, I hurriedly made the necessary adaptations – from now on the clock would strike only in the daytime, and the procession would occur only at noon. I also called in the sculptors to try to make the royal figure look a little less devilish – but this, they explained, would be difficult to do without removing the beard, which would mean that it would no longer resemble the King. And I was not about to suggest to the King that he should shave.

Such problems, however, were mere trivialities compared to the misfortunes that then befell us. For, just as though the comet were indeed exerting a baleful influence upon the Kingdom, we began to hear disturbing reports from the labour camps of the King's new railway lines. The Irdai workers were falling ill in large numbers, some seriously. All work had been halted while the King's physicians attempted to identify the cause.

'It does not appear to be infectious disease,' said the King, 'because it affects only those who have been working on the lines. Those engaged in other work are healthy, and no children have fallen ill. And I have personally interviewed the cooks, who assure me that the quality of their food is as good as anything we might eat in Kantarborg. They eat the same food themselves. So it is a mystery. The current theory is that some species of mosquito might be spreading disease out in the Wildwoods – perhaps one to which we Kantarborgans have grown immune.'

'What about the Irdai themselves? What do they think it is?' I asked.

'The tribespeople? Ah well, you have to remember that are uneducated and rather superstitious,' smiled the King. 'They think that there is something wrong with the rails themselves. They are calling it poison iron, and are refusing to touch it. But of course, iron cannot be poisoned. The explanation must be elsewhere.'

But then the foundry workers who had been handling the shipments of iron rails in the city, far from the Wildwoods, also began to fall ill. One man died. Something was clearly very wrong. There were mutterings about witchcraft, and the workers at the foundry warned that they would refuse to accept any more deliveries from Alba. Before they could implement this threat, however, the shipments themselves simply dried up.

The King was beside himself with frustration, striding up and down the throne room.

'I have been cheated, Karl! The Albans assured me this would be iron of the very highest quality, but it is clearly rotten with some foulness. What bacillus can this be, that can infect even base metal?'

'I have no idea, Majesty. I have never heard of such a thing. Could it be something drawn up from the bowels of the Earth?'

'From the Irrational Layer? It is possible, I suppose. Some underground pestilence. Though the Albans told me this was recycled ancient iron, not newly mined, so it would have been some very considerable time since it was underground. But they are clearly untrustworthy. I have kept my side of the bargain to the letter, but they did not keep theirs.'

'If I may inquire, sire – what *was* our side of the bargain?'

'They wanted certain things from us. Our clockwork technology, especially. The airship motors.'

'My designs?'

'Well, yes. They were produced under the auspices of the state, so the copyright rests with the Crown, as you know.'

I did not know. The King caught my look.

'That's the way it works, Karl. We provide the funding, but then we take the profits, if there are any. But in this case we seem to have got ourselves a very poor bargain. It may even be that all the new lines we have laid will have to be taken up again. Oh, this is a disaster for Kantarborg!'

It was certainly a disaster for the King.

Even worse was to come. When the track laying ceased, those Irdai workers who were still in a healthy condition were switched to forest clearing duties. Then a foreman who – as we later discovered – was known to have a particularly brutal reputation was found in the woods with his throat cut. None of the tribespeople could be persuaded to reveal who did it.

Collective punishment was imposed, with rations reduced to gruel only. And so, early one morning, the Irdai workers took their tools, murdered their guards, and disappeared into the Wildwoods. We had forgotten they were a forest people.

CHAPTER TWENTY-NINE

'Right, which of you ladies is the Queen?'

There was no reply. Christopher and Joe kept their hands in the air.

Their destination, as marked on the chart, had turned out to be the remains of a sizeable ancient port, surrounded by dark, glowering, snow-capped mountains. It had seemed a quiet enough place the evening before, when *Paloma* had sailed into it – dull, even. Ruined buildings everywhere, but no sign of life. Joe and Christopher had tied off their craft at an ancient concrete jetty and had celebrated their arrival with a prayer of thanksgiving and a can of soup. But when they came up on deck in the morning, they found themselves surrounded by ferocious-looking females armed with an odd assortment of muskets, flintlock pistols and bows and arrows. Their clothes were equally disparate, being composed of animal skins, feathers, leather caps, motley tunics in startling colours, and fur boots. Their faces were painted, especially around the eyes, which gave them a terrifying appearance.

'Er...we come in peace?' tried Christopher. 'Anyone here speak Anglian? We need to find the Queen. Queen! Oh God, what's Northlandish for queen...*Drottning!*'

One of the women stepped forward. She held a crossbow on her arm, and around her neck, over a red and blue tunic, she was wearing what looked like a host of amulets and charms on chains.

'Are you the Queen?' asked Christopher.

'Shut up!' she replied, in Anglian.

'Right, right, fair enough,' he muttered as she turned him around and tied his hands behind his back. She did the same to Joe, then poked her fingers curiously at Joe's chest, and said something to the others in an alien tongue.

'*What about the cargo?*' hissed Joe urgently.

'I imagine our luggage will be taken care of.'

The two crewmates were marched along the quay and through the ruins of the town. None of their captors said a word. When Joe and Christopher attempted to talk to each other they separated them, placing Christopher at the head of the procession and Joe five yards behind.

The town presented a desolate aspect in the grey morning, with its blackened ruins and indecipherable graffiti. After about twenty minutes they arrived at what might once been a hostelry of some kind, though little of it now remained except the bare walls of the ground floor. Joe and Christopher were taken around the back and down some steps into a cellar with a straw-covered floor. The bolt was slid shut in the door behind them. Their hands still bound, they crouched down against the walls.

'So what now?' asked Joe.

'Now they light the bonfire and get out the cookbooks. Ah, I'm only codding ya. They'll take us to the Queen, I bet you. Or bring her here.'

Joe looked aggrieved.

'You might have shaved, so.'

'I...what?'

'I'm only saying. The message said find the Queen. If you're going to meet a queen, you might have shaved. Or had a wash. When did you last have a bath, could you tell me that?'

'Joe, we're on operations!'

'It's only common consideration. I'm the one who has to share that boat with you.'

'For feck's sake, we are sitting in a dungeon with our hands tied. We might be about to be barbecued! Could we please take this discussion some other time?'

'And now you're going to meet a queen. What kind of an impression do you think you'll make on her?'

'Joe, this is a mission for the Church, not a flipping ladies' tea party!'

The words had flown out of him before he could stop them. Joe gave him a hurt look.

'Joe, I'm sorry, I didn't mean…why the hell am I apologising? You're off your head!'

A guard banged on the door.

'Shut up!' she shouted.

'Ah shut up yourself,' Joe shouted back.

Some hours later, Christopher and Joe had fallen into a doze when they were startled awake by a cacophonous clattering, followed by loud metallic squeals. There was a narrow aperture set high in one wall, which let in a little light. Christopher could just about look through it if he stood on tip-toe.

'God almighty, what class of a yoke is that?'

'What is it?'

'A whacking great machine. I think it's some kind of, what's it called, rail train. Like they had in ancient times.'

Joe jumped up.

'What? Really? Give me a look.'

'You'll need to get up higher. Hang on, I'll give you a lift up.'

Christopher bowed down so that Joe could sit on his shoulder, then stood up.

'Don't fall off there now with your hands bound.'

'I can see it. It looks like a railway train all right. That's amazing. I've seen pictures of them, but I never thought I'd see one in real life.'

Christopher lowered Joe down again.

'So why would they build something like that all the way up here?'

'Search me. There can't be many people living in this neighbourhood.'

Joe sat back against the wall and closed his eyes.

'You're dreaming of building one, aren't you?'

'I am. All the way from the silver mines to Rock Harbour. What's the motive power, do you think?'

'Don't know. If it's steam, we can't build it. It's forbidden to our order to use the fruits of the underground. That's what got Adam and Eve into trouble.'

'What if it's electric?'

'Depends on how they make the power.'

'I'd love to get a closer look at it.'

'I have a feeling we will, Joe.'

Christopher's prophecy came to pass shortly afterwards, when the bolt was slammed open and they were led outside. The locomotive, looking alien and splendid with its incomprehensible pipes and rods and gears, stood waiting on the nearby track at the head of a short train of open trucks.

'Any chance of taking these ropes off us? We're envoys of the Church, you know.'

'Shut up.'

'Right, right.'

They were directed up a plank and into a truck. Their guards motioned to them to sit down; but thankfully, they did at least untie their ropes first.

'What's the betting it's going to be cold where we're going?' said Christopher, rubbing his wrists and looking up at the snowy peaks.

'It's flipping cold enough here,' muttered Joe, lifting his hood and wrapping his habit more tightly around him.

Two of the guards joined them in the truck, holding their weapons at the ready and keeping a tense watch on their surroundings. *Looks like we're in a war zone*, thought Christopher. On the platform, they saw more warriors carrying the heavy chests from *Paloma* onto another of the trucks. The locomotive was being run around on a parallel track. Joe tried to stand up to take a better look, but one of the guards gestured at him to stay sitting down. The machine clattered past the wagon, trailing a cloud of noise. A few minutes later there was a jerk as the wagons were connected, and then, with an alarming thumping, the train squeaked gradually into motion.

'No smoke,' said Christopher. 'It might be of God after all. It could hardly be clockwork – could it?'

'Not unless they've invented some special kind of spring. And how would they wind it up?'

'I've heard stories that these northern tribes know how to catch the wind, bend it to their purpose. Maybe that's how they do it.'

'Could be. But I don't know about going all the way up there in this,' said Joe, looking doubtfully at the mountains ahead.

'Sure aren't we travelling in style?' retorted Christopher. 'Sit back Joe, take in the view.'

'Jaze you're hilarious, you know that?'

CHAPTER THIRTY

Even now, she haunts me. A day rarely passes when I do not think of her. Her hands, the light of her eyes, the way she brushed back a stray lock of hair, the way she fumbled for her reading glasses when she wanted to read something to me from some tract or other. Of course, people would say I hardly knew her, and that is true. And yet I did know her, and she me; thoroughly and intimately, from the very first moment we met. How that can be, I cannot say. But it is so, nonetheless.

But I grant you, I will never understand what she saw in me. Cogs and gears and machinery were very far removed from everything that was dear to her, and I for my part had only a passing interest in words and ideas. But perhaps it was that very fact – the fact that I was not of her world. Nor indeed of the world of the court, either – despite what people mutter. Perhaps that was part of it.

Some say that she used people. I never felt that. Not once. I was an insider at court, I could have been a valuable source of information. Yet she never asked me about my life there, nor about the private apartments at the Rose Castle, the guard routines, nothing. And that was what I repeated again and again, later, to my disbelieving interrogators.

I have no idea how she gained access to the excavation site at Northgate – though now, of course, looking back, it is obvious how she learned about it. Once inside, she would have had to descend a long series of ladders, each some twenty feet in length. She did that, wearing that simple dress and cloak, and carrying that device. Down into the darkness, deep into the Irrational Layer. Then she had to find the long tunnel that led from the old underground railway station of the ancients to the Rose Castle. And finally, she would have had to push aside the heavy cabinet that concealed its entrance in the castle cellar.

The older I get, the harder it becomes for me to distinguish between courage and madness. But whatever you call it, it was a remarkable deed.

But of what lay ahead, I had as yet no inkling. In the autumn of that year, my work, it seemed, was at an end. I had built the LEM and installed the planetarium clock, and the King's Grand Plan was shelved, so I could be of little assistance there. In any case, the troubles of the kingdom, I told myself, were not my concern. I had earned my money, the period of my contract was up, and now I wanted to go home.

The King was writing when I entered his office. Maps of the northern regions were spread out on his desk, beside the wooden model of the LEM. He had reading glasses perched on the end of his nose. When he saw me in the doorway, he quickly removed them.

'Karl! Come in, come in. I was just making some plans for the trip. Lists of supplies. You've heard that I'm going north?'

'I heard some rumours, Majesty.'

'I must try to strike some deal with the witch. It seems we have no choice. We must have iron, if the kingdom is to survive. Will you come with me? I could extend your contract. Johansson is coming.'

'I would prefer not to this time, sire. Your Majesty has several experienced navigators and a clockwork engineer on board *Freya*. I would merely be a passenger.'

The King, of course, guessed my true motivations straight away. He looked at me for a moment.

'There is no civilisation without war, Karl. This kingdom, every kingdom, is founded upon it. The rule of law rests upon the threat of violence. It is just a fact of life.'

'That may be so, Majesty, but I have no stomach for it. I am no soldier. As you know.'

Let him think me a coward if he wished. That, at least, was something he could understand.

He looked down at his desk.

'I hear that your brother died when we re-took the city. I'm sorry.'

'Such things happen in war, Majesty.'

'Indeed. But I would wish that things had been handled differently. Mistakes were made. But rulers have to take chances, you know. Things don't always turn out…as we would hope.'

I nodded. I knew he wanted me to say something, give him some conciliatory word. Rain spattered against the window, and the sound of the midday chimes in the Round Tower floated distantly across the gardens.

'Very well,' he said at last. 'I will sign for your final salary payment. You will receive it tomorrow.'

'Thank you. I wish Your Majesty the very best of luck. I hope things work out.'

'Thank you, Karl. And you.'

He returned to his papers. He did not get up to shake my hand. I bowed and left.

She was waiting for me by the tower, wearing a black cloak and hood. How long had she been standing there in the rain?

'I hear that you are leaving us, Karl.'

'Tomorrow. My work is done. But you'd better come inside, you're soaked.'

She smiled and took my hand. With her left hand. The awkward gesture made me glance down. In her other hand, beneath her cloak, she held a flintlock pistol.

'Don't worry. It's not for you.'

She stopped on the way up the tower to admire the inner face of the clock.

'You did fine work here, Karl. It is a remarkable device. Beautiful. A shame this is such a mistrustful time. In another age, you would be better appreciated.'

I was about to say something, but she gestured to me to be

silent, and pointed up the spiral walkway.

I took her cloak as we entered the apartment. She placed the pistol on the hall table.

'So, what's going on? Why are you armed?'

'Karl, this is all I will say: Tomorrow is a good day to leave the kingdom. Get the earliest boat you can. And now please don't ask me anything else, or I may be forced to reply.'

She smiled and began to unbutton her dress.

'Why tomorrow? Tell me!' I whispered to her in the dark. I felt sure she was awake.

'Well, Karl, as you know the city is unsafe when our beloved monarch is not here to protect us.'

'He said he was going north to negotiate with the witch.'

'And you believed him?'

'Why should I not? He needs iron.'

'Indeed,' she scoffed. 'And where is the King's navy? Have you asked yourself that?'

'I don't know. Do you?'

'Almost the entire fleet sailed a week ago for an unknown destination.'

I was silent a while.

'The north?'

'The word among the men is that they will strike from the east while the King is faking these negotiations. He means to seize the iron mines now, before winter comes.'

'And how do you know what the men are whispering?'

'Never mind. Promise me you will look after yourself.'

Was that a sheen from the moonlight I saw in her eyes?

'Of course I will. And so must you. We will meet again, I'm sure of it.'

She made no reply.

I was woken in the early morning by the familiar rattle of *Freya*'s clockwork engines as the royal airship passed overhead. He had flown directly from the Rose Castle, rather than the Tower – taking no chances in the city, presumably. I looked around for Erika, but she was gone.

I must have drifted off, because when I opened my eyes again, it was daylight and the brass clock in the room showed just after eight. I had slept later than I had planned to do. She had said that I should take the first boat, but that had already sailed. Besides, I needed to collect the final instalment of my salary from the purser at the castle.

I gathered my few belongings together ready for my journey, then left the tower and walked through the King's Garden. The moon hung low in the clear morning sky, and not far from it, above the towers and spires of Kantarborg, I could make out the faint outline of the comet, the harbinger of all our woes – now visible in daylight, too. I was going to miss this city. Despite everything, all the changes, conflicts and devastation, it was still the place where I was born, where my language was spoken. It was home.

When I reached the bridge across the Rose Castle moat, I was surprised to see many more of the King's Men around than usual. The guards examined my papers carefully, but they let me pass. They looked at me a little strangely. Perhaps they had thought I had gone with the King. I entered the castle, went to the purser's office, signed the book and was given my small bag of gold coins.

Then, as I was walking back down the corridor towards the castle entrance, two guards suddenly appeared and seized my arms. My bag of coins fell to the floor.

'What are you doing? Release me!'

'Good morning, Clockmaker. Perhaps now you finally know what hour has struck,' said the Queen.

The guards dragged me up to the throne room, where Ark-dur Andersson was waiting. I tried to concentrate on trivial details, as I had done before in interrogations. It helps a little, sometimes. His hair was thinning. He had a tanned, lined face and a fencing scar beneath his left ear. His beard was going grey. His lapel bore an emblem I had seen only once before: in the far north, in the court of the Northland Queen. It was the order of the Mountain Fox, an ancient Northlandish insignia. He had not worn it while the King was here. His tunic was black, as usual. Did the man never wear any other colour? He showed no triumph, only a kind of sadness at having been proven right yet again about human nature. He spoke quietly and calmly.

'Early this morning, the Queen was assaulted in her bed-chamber by a female person armed with a pistol. It seems the woman gained access to the castle by means of a secret passage, the location of which was known only to you and the King. Fortunately, the Queen's wolfhounds were also present in her chamber, and they defended her. The assailant shot one of the dogs, and was subsequently seized and killed by members of the household guard. It turned out to be a familiar face. The same woman in whose company you have been seen multiple times in the city. I wish I could say I was surprised.'

'I know nothing of any of this.'

He studied my face quizzically for a long moment, as though disappointed in me and searching for a rational explanation.

'Clockmaker, I cannot quite tell whether you are very clever or very stupid. But we will find out soon enough. Everything you know, we will also know, and then you will die. Why make your passing so hard? I could promise you a quick death if you tell me everything now.'

'I will answer any question you put to me, Andersson, but I promise you, you will grow no wiser.'

With an impatient gesture, he motioned to the guards to take me down.

In the castle dungeon, the jailer, a stocky, middle-aged man called Hartwig, whom I had seen before in the castle, told the guards to hold me firmly.

'And now, Mr Nielsen, I'm afraid I'm going to have to hit you.'

The blow slammed into the side of my face, filling my head with white light. My legs buckled.

'Hold him up,' said the jailer.

The next blow landed on the other side of my head. They released me, and I fell to the floor.

'Wait for me outside,' said the jailer. The guards walked out of the cell, and he crouched down beside me and began to speak softly and urgently.

'Sorry about that, Mr Nielsen. Now, let me give you a little bit of advice. Are you listening? *Stay alive.* Tell them the truth, or make stuff up, anything you like, it doesn't matter now. But don't tell them everything at once. Spin it out. If you give them everything straight away you're a dead man. You need to hold out for a few days more. Do you understand? Now rest, because tomorrow you will be giving a concert.'

He walked out and locked the door – leaving me lying on the cell floor, wondering if I had really heard what I thought I had heard.

CHAPTER THIRTY-ONE

Christopher and Joe huddled together in the wagon for warmth as the train rattled up through the mountains. Several times it hurtled through long echoing tunnels, causing Joe to cringe in fear and Christopher to cross himself in expiation for entering the subterranean regions. But each time they emerged again after a few seconds, the way leading stubbornly upwards to new heights. Christopher, despite himself, was lost in admiration for the marvel and mystery of the thing. The monks of St Michael had prided themselves on their technical knowledge, but these people were clearly far ahead of them.

'And we thought they were savages,' he shouted to Joe. 'We'd never have dreamed they had anything like this, would we?'

But Joe's fascination with the technology had worn off, and now he just wanted it all to end. He looked sick and was shivering with cold.

'How much further can this thing go? We must be halfway across the world by now.'

'My guess, it can't be further than a day's journey,' said Christopher. 'I can't see them driving this through the mountains at night.'

Joe groaned and buried his head into Christopher's shoulder as the train plunged into darkness again. Gingerly, Christopher laid an arm around him. Joe did not pull away.

It was late afternoon when the train began to slow. They stopped at a clearing in the forest, and some of the guards on board the train immediately leapt out and began unloading barrels and crates. Others pulled over a motley collection of handcarts and sledges, to which the cargo was made fast. They worked very rapidly, as though they had little time. Then, one by one, they began to drag the loads away, up a forest track. All in silence.

'Now I know what they remind me of,' said Christopher. 'Ants.'

'They'll surely have a queen, so,' said Joe.

Finally, Christopher and Joe were ordered out of the truck and marched up the ascending track between the trees. The path was wet and stony, and the mud clung to their sandals as they trudged upwards. They passed strange carved stones along the way, some with occult-looking inscriptions. Here and there they crossed watercourses in full and noisy spate, balancing on felled logs. The guards were watchful, looking to all sides, including the sky.

'Do they not have menfolk at all, I wonder?' asked Christopher, and was poked in the back with a knife. He took the hint.

After about an hour they began to get the smell of woodsmoke, and a few minutes later they arrived at a hilltop clearing which contained a large collection of round, conical tents. Christopher looked around expectantly, but there were no old people, no children. *A war camp.*

Christopher and Joe were directed into the surprisingly roomy, smoke-filled interior of one of the tents. Inside, willow logs burned on a central hearth, with bread and meat roasting on pans. A number of burly men clad in leather jerkins sat on reindeer skins at the far side of the fire, eating from wooden platters and ignoring the newcomers. They had tattooed faces, and some wore odd, pointed felt caps. Christopher thought that perhaps he had at last met the men of the tribe – until he heard them talking among themselves, and then his body stiffened. *Sweet mother of God, we're dead,* he thought. *Hook, line and flipping sinker.* Joe heard them too and sent him a worried look. For once, Christopher could think of no way to reassure him. This did not look good.

The guards carried in the two large chests from *Paloma* and placed them on one side of the tent. One of them, who wore a black band on her forehead around her hennaed hair, handed Christopher and Joe a couple of small wooden dishes and pointed at the food. They ate, nervously but with some eager-ness, as they had had nothing since the previous day. When the guards left, a tall man came over, gave Christopher a wooden mug and gestured at a pail of water.

'*Tapadh leat*,' said Christopher. The man glanced at him in surprise and said something to his companions. They lowered the volume of their mumbling conversation.

Finally, the tent flap opened again and a figure in a hooded cloak entered, flanked by two warriors. The three sat down cross-legged by the fire, and the Albans ceased their talking at once.

The stranger chanted a few words of prayer or blessing in an alien tongue, then threw back the hood to reveal a striking young woman. She was darker in complexion than most of the tribe, with brown eyes that seemed almost black – beautiful but rather stern in appearance, with the expression of one accus-tomed to wielding power. Christopher had never seen a queen before, but he had no doubt at all that he was in the presence of one. She glanced at them quickly, then nodded to one of her companions, who got up and walked over to the chests, the locks of which had apparently been broken off. The warrior threw open the lids of each one in a theatrically casual manner. It was no surprise to see that they were full to the brim with silver coins; the final fruits of the Cooley mine, each one stamped with the cross of the Order of St Michael.

The Queen looked across at the Alban men.

'It is sufficient?' she asked, in Anglian.

'It is sufficient,' said the tall man.

'Then we have an agreement,' said the Queen.

There was a brief silence, but then Christopher spoke up.

'Way, way, hold on there now a minute, your queenness. That treasure was sent to you by the monks of the Rock. We brought it to you many leagues across the northern sea, through tests and travails, at great peril to our lives. Aren't we the ones you're supposed to have an agreement with?'

She turned and looked at the two monks, who resisted the urge to flinch under her gaze.

'You will get what you came for,' she said.

'*Whatever the heck that is,*' muttered Christopher to himself.

The Queen and her two companions left the tent. Most of the Albans got up and went over to examine the contents of the chests, but the tall man came over to Christopher and Joe. He was muscular and had blue symbols tattooed into one cheek. One side of his head had been shaved; the thick, wiry hair on the other side was plaited.

'You two lads led us a merry little dance,' he said in Anglian. 'We were hoping to cut out the middle man in this transaction.'

'Rob us along the way, you mean?' said Christopher with an ironic smile.

'Something like that. Well done on getting here. So you're the famous Brother Christopher, I presume? The explosives man? What happened to your secret weapon?'

'Well, what would be the point of having a secret weapon if you go and tell everyone all about it?'

The tall man smiled like a dog; his mouth simply opened and showed teeth.

'Fair enough. Is it true you boys have a boat that can disappear? '

'Maybe we do. And maybe we don't. Our vessel was designed by my colleague here.'

'We might be in the market for something like that. Just saying.'

'Call your dogs off the monks of the Rock and we can talk about it.'

The man looked the two monks over, sizing them up.

'We'll talk later. I'm Alistair, by the way.'

'Thought you might be.'

The man smiled again and went back to his companions.

'Who was that?' asked Joe.

'The Jarl,' said Christopher grimly.

As night began to fall, Christopher and Joe were shown to the Albans' tent, where animal skins had been laid on beds of willow twigs. Neither of them could sleep. Joe eventually went out to relieve himself, and when he returned Christopher was gone. He spotted him at the other side of the tent, in earnest conversation with the Jarl. After some time, he returned and lay down again beside Joe, smelling faintly of whiskey.

'So, did he offer you a big arms deal?'

'He tried.'

'What did you tell him?'

'I told him the truth. That we had a boat with a secret source of power that we learned about in the old books. That it had magic powers of invisibility, that it could disappear at will and skim across the waves like a seabird. That it could sink any ship by the power of magnets.'

'You'd want to watch yourself, playing that game with those fellas.'

'Well, it kept him interested. He wants to negotiate. He says he'll get the McCarthys off our backs if we'll share our technology with them.'

'But we haven't got anything like that!'

'OK, so I exaggerated a little. Every salesman does that. Listen, Joe: *Paloma* is a damn good boat, a clever and useful one, but it can be copied. The way I see it, we might as well sell them the technology now and get something in return, because in a few years' time they'll likely have one of their own.'

'I suppose so,' sighed Joe. 'And we have very little left to lose back at the Rock.'

'Exactly. That's what I'm saying. So we should get the best deal we can now. We can build a fleet of them if they give us the contract.'

'The McCarthys won't like that. '

'But the McCarthys are no friends of ours, are they? Not anymore. And the Albans could get us the silver mine back. And the brewery. It would be a big deal for the monks, Joe. And you could build your railway line from the mine.'

Joe pondered this.

'Well, I'm not learning fecking Alban.'

Christopher laughed.

'Don't worry. Keeping the Lord's language alive would be part of the deal. I told him that.'

'Any clues about why we're here yet?'

'He says he doesn't know anything about it. He's lying, I think. He told me something odd, though. He said they're here selling weapons technology, and that they're going to give a demonstration tomorrow. Said they were going to catch a whale.'

'A whale? How are they going to do that up here in the mountains?'

'Maybe some local monster. There's plenty of them around, so I hear. I'm looking forward to it.'

'Jaze, I'm not,' said Joe, and to Christopher's surprise, snuggled in under his arm.

'You know, you wouldn't be a bad old fella if you took a bit more care of yourself. I'm just saying, like.'

CHAPTER THIRTY-TWO

Next morning I was brought out of my cell and into a long, low-roofed hall in the castle cellar that I recognised as the former orchestra room. Hartwig the jailer was all solicitude.

'This is the concert venue, Mr Nielsen. If you'd like to take a seat, we'll be with you in a moment.'

I was placed in a wooden chair that had iron shackles on the arms and legs. The guards bolted them fast about my wrists and ankles.

'There is an upper throne in the castle, you see, and a lower one,' said Hartwig. 'This is the lower one. Now we just need to check the sound system.'

'The sound system?'

Hartwig gestured towards the ducts in the walls, which were designed to carry the sound of the orchestra up to the reception rooms above. He sent one of the guards up the spiral staircase, then handed a pair of pliers to the other one.

'Careful with his hands, he's a clockmaker. Just one of his fingernails for now.'

Hartwig took out a notebook and began to write in it.

Whoever boasts that they could withstand torture has never experienced it. In that moment of agony, you are no longer who you thought you were. You are simply pain, and nothing else. I howled like some kind of wild animal, alien even to myself.

The guard who had been above reappeared in the doorway.

'How was that?' Hartwig asked him.

'Fine. Loud and clear.'

'Excellent. That will be all for today, Mr Nielsen. We have already made good progress. You have given us some names, but you are still holding back information.'

'I have told you nothing!' I shouted furiously. And it was true, for he had not asked me anything.

'Oh, but I think you have, Mr Nielsen.' He consulted his notes. 'You told us that Lieutenant Tharup was involved, and Tillonsen your assistant, and Captain Johansson too, dear me, that's a shame. He will have to be arrested when he returns from the north. But we need more names, and you are holding out. We will continue tomorrow.'

'Are you mad?'

'It may seem like madness to you now, Mr Nielsen, but one day soon I warrant you might see the method in it. Are you a good actor?'

'What?'

'A good actor. I hope that you are, because we shall need you to scream rather loudly, you see. The louder you can scream, the less we will actually have to do to you.'

The following days I can only describe as surreal. When Hartwig was present we merely went through the motions of interrogation ('Louder, Mr Nielsen! You can do better than that!'), while on the occasions when Arkdur Andersson supervised the sessions, my screams were entirely genuine. By the end of the week I had lost most of my fingernails, while Hartwig had amassed a list of names and a catalogue of bizarre crimes that beggared the imagination. According to him, I had confessed that the plotters had been conspiring to put Ulrika Häkonsdotter on the throne and make devil worship the state religion. That was why I had arranged for the figure of Satan, rather than the King, to be carved for the planetarium clock. We had also conducted black masses in the Round Tower during which we rode around naked on goats. We had kidnapped urchin children from the street and sacrificed them in satanic rites, then scattered the ashes of their burned bodies from the top of the tower onto the populace, in order to bewitch them and turn them against their king. We had smuggled in lepers from other kingdoms and sent them out as preachers onto the streets of Kantarborg to spread disease among good Christian people. And so on. The list of supposed conspirators grew daily, and soon threatened to encompass every prominent merchant, cleric and officer in the city.

'But he's a stubborn one, my lord. His soul is hardened by the devil. He has more to tell us, I am sure of it.'

They spoke as though I were not present.

'The Queen is growing impatient. Do you think the remaining intelligence is of any value?'

'He has yet to reveal the name of the ringleader, sir. I think the Queen would be most interested in that.'

'Very well. But only until tomorrow at dawn. After that we will build a bonfire in the castle yard and dispose of him.'

'Not at Island Gate, then, my lord?'

'No. That is inaccessible to us for now.'

'Ah. The mobs, I suppose, sir?'

Andersson made no reply, but turned to me.

'You will be sentenced tomorrow, and then you will be put to death. Your confession has been more than adequate.'

'If you believe any of that nonsense, you're a fool!' I shouted.

Andersson looked into my face, and smiled.

'Well of course, Clockmaker. Information obtained under physical duress is useless, that has been common knowledge for centuries. The purpose of torture is not to extract information, but to get the accused to sentence himself to death. And that you have done most excellently.'

He left the room, and Hartwig came over to unbolt my irons.

'I'm sorry Mr Nielsen, I can no longer stay their hand,' he murmured. 'We must hope that things go swiftly.'

At the time, I thought he was referring to my death.

CHAPTER THIRTY-THREE

Christopher woke before dawn when he heard the Albans moving around in the tent, muttering to each other. He elbowed Joe awake.

'Whale hunting time, I think,' he whispered.

The two monks followed the Albans out into the cold grey morning. There had been a light fall of snow in the night. They were surprised to see people everywhere, moving silently, cooks handing out steaming porridge in wooden bowls, warriors assembling their weapons. They had heard nothing in the tent.

Jarl Alistair beckoned to them.

'Come on over here, lads, I'll show you something I bet you've never seen before.'

Inside a tent, his men were putting together a complicated-looking device with a long metal tube and a large spool of wire.

'That's our whale hunter,' he said. 'Spring-loaded harpoon gun, Kantish design. We have four of them here today.'

'And you're going to catch a whale with that? Here?'

The Jarl smiled his doglike smile.

'Aye, that's what we're planning on doing. You boys coming along to watch?'

'Friendly type, isn't he?' said Joe as the Jarl strode away.

'Isn't he just, Joe? Horn of a bull, hoof of a horse, smile of an Alban.'

Once assembled, the heavy devices were loaded onto sleds and dragged down the muddy slopes, two Alban men pulling in front and one behind to brake the sled on the inclines. The hunting party consisted of around fifty warriors, about half of them Albans, moving in single file through the forest, the head of the line occasionally visible between the trees as they descended into the valley. After about an hour the path levelled out and they emerged into a large clearing.

The Jarl addressed his men in their own language and directed them around the site. They deployed two of the harpoon guns among the trees on one side of the clearing, and two on the other. Each had another complicated-looking weapon set up beside it, with an array of rotating tubes.

'That's a Hansen gun,' said the Jarl. 'Also spring-powered. Ever seen them before?'

'We've seen their results,' said Christopher grimly.

'Ah, right. Well, hopefully we won't have to use them today. It's just a back-up.'

Some of the warriors had lit a bonfire in the middle of the area. It gave off heavy black smoke.

'You know how you go fishing,' said the Jarl. 'You bait the hook. And then you wait.'

After that, nothing happened. The morning wore slowly on, the sun occasionally fighting to appear through the clouds. The clearing, too, was covered in a thin layer of snow. Christopher and Joe were feeling the cold and retreated into their cowls with their hoods pulled up. The Albans, bare-armed and sometimes bare-chested in their leather jerkins, seemed not to notice.

'God, it's freezing. How does anybody *live* around here?'

'Maybe they don't, Joe. Maybe they just come here to hunt whales.'

'And then they export the meat on the railway, I suppose?'

'Yeah, you'd have a whole industry going there,' laughed Christopher. 'I think we have it all figured out.'

In the late afternoon, the sound, when it finally came, was at first like a buzzing insect. But there was a regular beat to it. Man-made. Then, from out of the clouds, an impossibly large airship slowly made its appearance.

'Jaze, look at the size of it!' gasped Joe.

Christopher appraised the vessel with a professional eye.

'Well-armed, too, by the look of her.'

The ship circled the area several times, its clockwork motors clattering, before hovering over the landing site and slowly descending. As all could see, she was indeed the epitome of modern weaponry. Hansen guns fore and aft, conventional light gunpowder cannons amidships, maybe a hundred men or more on board armed with muskets and incendiaries. Prepared, it seemed, for anything.

Prepared for anything except what actually happened. With a quite prosaic thock-thock-thock sound, Alban harpoons snaked out across the clearing and pierced the ship's wooden hull from four different points. Then the lines were wound back, tautened and made fast. In a single move, *Freya* was immobilised.

'They'll just cut them off,' said Joe.

'Metal cables,' said Christopher. 'It'll take them a while.'

There was a silence. There was no answering fire from the airship – all around, nothing would have been visible from the ship's deck save the dense pine forest.

Then something shot out of the woods with a crackling hiss and landed in the airship's rigging. The distant figures of *Freya*'s crewmen could be seen scurrying up the shrouds to extinguish it.

'What was that?' asked Joe.

'A message to the crew,' said the Jarl.

'Now they know what their options are,' murmured Christopher. 'Surrender or burn.'

At first, nothing happened. The Jarl's men made ready to fire a second incendiary, but then a ladder was lowered down the side of the vessel, and the figure of a tall man could be seen descending and walking towards the woods. He wore a brown cloak and what looked like a velvet hat, and was carrying a large white sheet, which he waved as he walked.

The Jarl observed his progress through his spyglass.

'*Sin am fear*,' he said. 'That's our man.'

The figure paused a short distance from the forest edge. Then his voice rang out, distantly echoing among the trees.

'Norbert, by the grace of God King of Kantarborg, the

243

Wends and the Goths, wishes to parley with Ulrika, Queen of the North.'

'Who's the Wends and the Goths?' whispered Joe.

'Ancient nomadic tribes,' said Christopher. 'Used to wear black and build cathedrals.'

The tall man resumed his progress towards the trees, stumbling a little in the snow.

'Doesn't look much like a king in those clothes, does he?'

'Oh, that fellow's not the King,' said the Jarl. 'He's much more important than that.'

CHAPTER THIRTY-FOUR

You do not sleep on the night before your execution. I watched the full moon rise into the sky outside, above the King's Garden, and found myself wondering if the Garden of Eden really was up there, and whether mankind would ever return to it. Perhaps I might see it myself after my death, if what Erik Kramer said was true. But the absurdity of the idea made me smile. I had no clear idea in my head of a God or an afterlife, but I prayed to whatever might be there, as condemned men do. I thought of Marieke, and wondered how she would receive the news. She knew that I was taking a chance, coming here. A life at court is a life spent on a knife edge. She would grieve for me – but she was a young and attractive woman, so she would surely not remain alone for long. That was some comfort to me. And I was glad I would not be leaving children behind.

As the night wore on, I saw the moon gradually turn a deep crimson in colour, and I realised that this was the night of the lunar eclipse. A blood moon, they call it. But if this was an omen, it had come a little late for me.

The night seemed to be full of noises, but perhaps my hearing had been magnified by my fear. A constant drumming seemed to be coming from the direction of the gardens, along with the shouts of men and women. It was long after curfew. My mind playing tricks? In such a state of consciousness, you see and hear all kinds of strange things. I was cold and tired, and still in pain after my interrogations – but some part of me, the rational part, was standing aside and observing all this quite dispassionately, even as I grieved and suffered in my heart.

By morning I must have looked like a wild man from the woods, though I tried to retain my composure when Hartwig came for me.

'All ready, Mr Nielsen? It won't be so bad, I'll make sure of that.'

I nodded at him, unable to speak. In his own strange way he had done his best to save my life, for whatever reason. Perhaps he had hoped that the King would return and intervene. But if what Erika had said were true, the King would doubtless be gone for a very long time yet.

I was brought up to the throne room. The Queen, who was the acting monarch and my judge in this 'trial', was seated on her throne in her full regalia, her remaining wolfhound at her feet. What a masquerade. I almost laughed when I saw her.

The noise outside seemed to be increasing. The drumming was continuing, and several times I thought I heard shots and what sounded like screaming. The Queen raised her voice above the din.

'Clockmaker Nielsen, you have confessed to crimes against God, your king and your country. Do you have anything to say before you are sentenced?'

I opened my mouth to speak, but before I could say anything there was a sound like an explosion, and more shouts. Then sustained and continued cheering.

'Tell the captain of the guard to shut that rabble up!' shouted the Queen angrily. 'We have court business to conduct here.'

Hartwig nodded and left the room.

A volley of shots was heard, followed by screams. Something struck one of the castle windows, shattering it. Several of the court personnel in the throne room abandoned their posts to look outside. A commotion could be heard in the castle corridors. The Queen was about to resume speaking when, to my amazement, Captain Johansson walked in, holding his sword.

'Your Majesty, I apologise for interrupting the proceedings,' he said, 'but it seems a critical situation has developed.'

In the next second a strangely assorted group of people pushed their way into the throne room, armed with muskets and bows and arrows. One of them stepped forward, and threw back her hood.

'Hello, cousin,' said Ulrika.

'What the devil are you doing here?' the Queen demanded.

'Saving your life, it would appear. Johansson - get them up onto the roof.'

From the roof of the Rose Castle, the reality of our situation was instantly clear. Thousands of people, drumming, roaring and jeering, thronged the King's Garden and the surrounding streets. They had not yet been able to breach the moat and gain access to the castle itself, but it could only be a matter of time. The few guards who still faced them looked woefully under-armed and were falling back. The royal airship *Freya*, flying a flag I had not seen before, had been made fast to the mooring masts on the towers, and a precarious-looking ladder had been lowered from it to the castle roof. Johansson and I organised the evacuation, aided by the Alban crew.

'The Queen goes, and her immediate retinue,' shouted Johansson to me. 'That's the deal. But what about Andersson? It's up to you.'

'Let me talk to him,' I shouted back.

We went below and found him standing among the Queen's personal servants. He stiffened when he saw me. We separated him from the rest, and waited until the others had gone up to board.

'Arkdur Andersson,' I said. 'You accused and tortured an innocent man, and you must be punished for it. Your punishment will be this: you will be allowed to live, and for the rest of your days, you will know that it was my mercy that saved your miserable life. Let that make you humble. Now run!'

'That was generous of you,' said Johansson as we watched him disappear up the stairs.

'It was worth it,' I replied with a grin. 'I surprised him.'

We went back up to the roof. The noise of the mob, now

scenting victory, had intensified.

'What about you? You're a known associate of the King.'

I shook my head. Johansson waved the signal, and the ladder was drawn up. We untied the lines and *Freya* drew rapidly away, her clockwork motors almost inaudible above the drumming and shouts of the crowd.

Back below in the castle, it felt as though we were standing on the deck of a rapidly sinking ship. Some servants were crying and wailing, others looting whatever they could find, stuffing ornaments into sacks. The Queen's wolfhound was galloping up and down, barking at everything and everyone. In a corridor I saw Hartwig, my former jailer, hurrying towards me, carrying my jacket and a small bag. With a shock, I recognised my final salary payment.

'Keep it, Hartwig, for God's sake.'

'Can't do that, Mr Nielsen, sir. All possessions to be returned to prisoners on their release. It's the law.'

He handed me the items and turned away. Outside, the pandemonium was near at hand now. We could hear window glass smashing. They must have got across the moat bridge.

'Only one way out,' I said to Johansson. 'Let's find a lantern.'

Johansson and I clambered up from the tunnel and onto the platform of the ancient underground station at Northgate. Johansson put the lantern down.

'I think we should probably stay here for a while,' he said. 'Let the mob rage until they tire. When it gets dark we can try and get to the Round Tower.'

'This is what the ancients knew,' I remarked. 'If you stay underground, you're safe. No Kantarborgan will dare follow you.'

'Something must have got them, though, just the same. We've found hundreds of skeletons down here.'

'Maybe some demon from the Irrational Layer?'

'Maybe. We'll probably never know.'

We sat down against one wall and rested. It had been a somewhat trying day, to say the least.

'Thank you. For saving me.'

'My pleasure. But to be honest, that was not the reason we returned.'

'I know. But still.'

We sat for a while without speaking.

'Ulrika rescued her. Why?'

Johansson was silent a moment.

'Ingeborg's family will pay a hefty ransom for her release, and the Northlanders will have to recognise Ulrika as queen. But I don't think she's finished. She's playing some long game we don't yet understand.'

There we sat, like two men waiting for a train that would never come. Or at least, I hoped so. You never could be sure with the Irrational Layer. There was always the possibility that a train of the dead might come screaming up from the underground.

Eventually, I must have dozed off. A long time later, in the darkness, I suddenly heard Johansson's voice again.

'She always loved you more than me, you know.'

'Who did?'

'Erika. She loved you more than me. I was just her key. Her way in.'

I sat and took this in. Remembering some of the things she had said.

'You were engaged to her?'

'The plan was that we would marry when all this was over. But we quarrelled about the way forward. She was a diehard. She thought courage alone was enough. She was wrong.'

'But you were with the rebels?'

'I am a loyal officer of the King's men, Karl, I've always said that. But if I must choose between the kingdom and the King, my duty is to choose the kingdom.'

'It must have taken a lot. You were always one of his most trusted officers.'

'Well at first I was just in love with Erika. Like half the city. I believed we could have an assembly and keep the King. But he betrayed the Irdai, who worshipped him. And he tried to make a slaver of me. I delivered one consignment to Alba, and I swore I would never do it again. The poor wretches thought they were going to the promised land. That is no proper business for a military man. So I talked to the Albans. We discussed the possibilities.'

'Why didn't you just kill him?'

'That's what Erika said. Get rid of the whole pack, replace them with an elected president. But if we'd assassinated the King some cousin or other of the royal house would have started a rebellion, and then we'd have had a civil war on our hands. Ulrika's child is a chance to keep the continuity. As someone once said to me, the people want someone to worship. They want glory and flags. They want magic, not everyday life. So I arranged the swap.'

'But now things have got out of control.'

'I have recalled the navy from the north in the name of the King. They will be here in a couple of days. By then people will be tired of anarchy, so we can step in and restore order. Then we bring Valdemar down from the north.'

'That's the child?'

'One of them.'

'*One* of them?'

'His twin sister will remain in the north.'

'An heir and a spare?'

'Quite. We'll get the King's uncle to act as regent until the boy is old enough to assume the crown.'

'Won't he miss his mother?'

'He's an aristocrat, Karl. He hardly knew Ulrika. His nurse will come with him from the north.'

That prompted a painful memory of my last encounter with *Tanta.*

'But will Kantarborgans accept him as king?'

'Crown Prince, to begin with. Well, his legitimacy is not in question. His parents' wedding was witnessed by a very senior churchman, who of course is bound by his vows to tell the truth. Clever.'

'And then we hold elections for an assembly,' he continued. 'A constitutional monarchy. With the boy as a figurehead monarch with no real power. That way, we get the best of both worlds, and we can keep the nobles quiet.'

Elections, like the ancients used to have. It was hard to imagine in Kantarborg.

'Who do you think will win? The League for Democracy?'

'I doubt it.'

'Really? Why not? They were the ones responsible for this… upheaval.'

'Yes, but all they want to talk about is politics. Politics isn't about politics, Karl. It's about pageantry. Right now, my money would be on Erik Kramer.'

'Good grief.'

'We have to be realistic. He's popular, and he offers people dreams. They like that sort of thing, you know.'

'He promises them the moon.'

'Well, exactly.'

'So what will you do now?'

'First of all, I'm going back to the north. I have to negotiate the King's release from the Ice Palace.'

'The Ice Palace! They're keeping him there?'

'Yes, they've just rebuilt it for the winter. The price of his release is his abdication in favour of his son. He has no real ransom value anymore.'

I thought of the King surrounded by those walls of ice.

'Would you take him something? From me?'

CHAPTER THIRTY-FIVE

Christopher and Jarl Alistair stood in intense conversation outside the Alban tent, while the tribe packed up the war camp around them.

'So, do we have a deal, then?' asked Christopher.

'You give me your word, as a man of God?'

'I do.'

'Then we have a deal. You share your boat technology with us, and we'll place the Rock under our protection.'

'And the silver mine. And the brewery.'

The Jarl laughed.

'One step at a time. But the whole peninsula will be ours soon enough.'

'I want it in writing. The property of the order to be returned. And we get to speak our own language at the end of the peninsula.'

'That's a lot to ask for a flipping boat.'

'It is. Mind you, I bet the McCarthys would be interested in it, too.'

The Jarl considered.

'Exclusive rights? You share your technology with us, no-one else?'

'Renewable every five years.'

'Ah fer...all right, all right, give me your hand on it man! I'll get my lawyers to draw it up.'

They shook hands, and the Jarl produced a hip flask. The two men celebrated with a swig each.

'So did you lads get what you came for, afterwards?'

'Today, they say. They're bringing him up from the valley now.'

'Him?'

'Yeah, I think I've finally worked it out. I mean, who else

would be worth that much to the Church?'

The Jarl winked and strode back to his men, who were lashing the harpoon guns to sleds. A commotion of reindeer was being marshalled into place at one end of the clearing.

'Any chance of lighting a fire?' asked Joe. 'I'm fecking freezing.'

'We'd better wait, Joe, they don't want smoke in the daytime. They said they'll take us back down today, soon as he gets here. Speaking of which, that might be your man now.'

A reindeer led by a warrior emerged from the trees, dragging a wooden sled. It stopped in the middle of the clearing and the warrior helped what looked like an elderly, rather frail man to dismount. He had a long white beard and was dressed in a white robe, now rather muddy, with a red, fur-lined cape and hood.

'Jaze, is that who I think it is?' asked Joe in wonder.

'I think it might be, Joe. I think it just might.'

The two monks hurried over to the sled and knelt in the snow.

'Holy Father, welcome,' said Joe, with a beatific smile.

The old man stood and stared at them, looking confused and afraid.

'I have seen terrible things,' he muttered at last. 'Terrible things.'

Christopher got up and took the man's arm.

'That's all right now, your popeness, don't you worry about that. We'll have you back home again in no time.'

'Terrible things,' said Pope Nicholas of Birmingham distractedly, as they walked towards the tent.

CHAPTER THIRTY-SIX

A week later, when life in Kantarborg had almost been restored to normal, I made ready to leave the kingdom. But there was one thing I had to do first. In the early morning I took a walk in the rain, across the bridge to Foundry Street and along the canal to what was left of my old childhood home, and knocked on the cellar door.

Tanta made me welcome, almost as though she'd been expecting me. Old Rolf was confined to his armchair now and could not get up to greet the visitor, but waved and smiled at me warmly. I drank their tea and talked with them for a while. *Tanta* told me tales of when I was a child, things I didn't remember. It seems I had been something of a handful. Water occasionally dripped onto my lap. The ground floor above leaked, they apologised, though they tried to cover bits of the wreckage with tarpaulins. They rented out one room in the cellar to an apprentice ferryman, which was their only source of income, now that they had sold whatever they could salvage from the old house. I had thought of offering to buy their clock, the one I had repaired as a child, but that was gone, now, too.

I knew they would not accept the bag of gold coins as a mere gift, so I hid it under my chair and 'forgot' it on my way out. It was far from a fortune, but it would help them to get through the cold season. Then I walked back to the Round Tower, packed my things, locked the door for the last time, and pushed the big key under the door. The planetarium clock was about to chime for noon, so I stood in the wet street with my suitcase to watch the automata perform their little piece of theatre. It did look rather fine. The figure of the King would no doubt shortly be replaced. I had heard St Christopher Columbus mentioned as a possibility. Tattoos and all.

On the wall of the tower, someone had painted fresh white

graffiti: *Erika lives!* Well, who could say? I doubted it, but I had not seen a body, after all. Rumour had it that she was buried in an unmarked grave somewhere in the King's Garden. If the League for Democracy came to power, they planned to rename it Erika Thorne Park.

I was going to hire a carriage, but I found the clockwork train service was running again, so I paid the fare and it took me to the quay at the south-eastern corner of Agaholm, where I caught the afternoon steam packet back across the Sound. Despite the season the sea was, thankfully, a little calmer than it had been on my way over the first time. There were few passengers. I got talking to the captain, who told me that times were not looking good for the service.

'Timber's expensive now, sir, so we've had to put up the ticket prices. And if Kantarborg brings back the Sound Dues, we're finished. No-one will be able to afford the crossing. The Northlanders will be angry, and before we know it, we'll be at war again. When will they ever learn, eh?'

When indeed.

To my surprise and delight, Marieke was at the quay to meet me, waving as the boat pulled in, wearing her Sunday dress and holding a dark green umbrella. I had written to her to tell her when I was coming, but with all the unrest I did not know whether she had received the letter. Thankfully, she had not heard of my arrest until after my release. Her embrace was warm and we both shed a few tears. She fussed over my still-bruised fingers, where the nails were gradually growing back. Then she took my suitcase and we made our way up the cobbled street towards the shop.

'A lot has happened,' I said.

'Yes. Here, too.'

She gave me a sly smile as we drew close to the shop, and took out some keys.

'For one thing, we don't live in the shop anymore. We live upstairs.'

'We…what?'

'Svensson died, so I bought his apartment.'

'But…how? With what?'

'With all the money you've been sending me, of course, Karl!'

'But what about the debts?'

'You mean Hapgaard? You don't have to worry about him.'

She opened the door to the apartment and showed me in.

'So…what do you think?'

The apartment was small, but it was a palace compared to what we had been used to. There was a dining-room, and a bedroom, and a generously-proportioned kitchen. Everything was freshly painted. She had decorated it tastefully with locally-made furniture and a few pictures and ornaments. Outside the back windows, the chaos of what had been Svensson's garden had been cleared, the ground dug and ready for spring.

'It's wonderful, Marieke, but…what about Hapgaard? What happened?'

'At first my father kept him away. But then one day he saw me at the market and followed me. He threatened me like he threatened you. I wept a little and told him we had no money, but that I could offer him the favours of a woman.'

'My God. And did he accept?'

Marieke gave me a look.

'No, I mean, yes, of course he did…,' I stuttered. 'So what happened?'

'I took him down to the waterside and distracted him a little, and then I cut his throat and threw his body into the canal.'

I stared at her in shock.

'But…was it not discovered?'

'Of course it was. But he was a Kantarborgan, Karl. He has no family here.'

'But he has dangerous friends!'

'Hapgaard was a small-time loan shark. He had no friends.'

'But the letters…'

'He wrote them himself. Anyone can spell badly, if they try.'

She paused for a moment.

'Well, he may have had one friend, but he is gone now, too.'

'Who?'

'Karl Nielsen, you are an educated man, but sometimes I think you have no sense at all. Who benefited most from you getting into debt?'

I looked blankly at her.

'Your royal friend! Who else?'

I sat down on a chair by the dining table. This was a lot to take in.

'So next time you have a problem, you tell me! All right?'

I nodded. It certainly seemed like the wisest policy.

'And the money…?'

'Half went on the apartment. The rest is under the bed. We can live on it for a while, until business picks up.'

I considered that for a moment.

'Marieke, I was meaning to talk to you about that. I don't honestly know if the clock-making business will ever be much good around here. But maybe I could try something else as well. As a sideline.'

'Something else like what?'

'Well, there's an idea I'd like to discuss with you…if you think we should invest in it, that is. It's for a new kind of music box.'

'Music box? You mean like my mother's sewing cabinet?'

'No, this is different. Machines that can play discs. I know how to build them, and I have a feeling it might catch on. If I can find out how to make the discs, that is. But I think I can.'

She smiled at me indulgently. Men and their dreams. I smiled back. Life is good, when you have plans.

CHAPTER THIRTY-SEVEN

[From the correspondence archives of Cooley Abbey. Undated.]

Dear Father Abbot –

I hope that this finds you well. As you probably know by now the mission went very well. We had a few adventures along the way, but we managed to deliver our passenger in the end to the Mercians, who were delighted to have the Holy Father back again. Well, maybe all except Cardinal Dexter, who as acting pope was very surprised to see him as you can probably imagine.

The ransom money was paid over to the queen of the Northern tribe. The rumour is that she commissioned the Albans to abduct the Pope so that he might be a witness at a wedding ceremony – though why a heathen tribe would want the Pope for this purpose, I have no idea. The Holy Father himself has refused to talk about it.

Speaking of the Albans, you've no doubt heard that we ran into Jarl Alistair while we were up north. I enclose the first draft of an agreement I managed to hammer out with him. I know it will probably stick in your craw to contemplate negotiating with them, and I wouldn't blame you for that at all, but seeing as we had more or less lost everything I think it might be the best deal we can get under the circumstances. It gives us back the mine and the brewery, and it also allows us to freely speak the language of the Lord at our end of the peninsula, which I'm sure you will agree is a good thing as the way things are going it might otherwise be in danger of dying out in our land altogether. In return they want our technology, especially Joe's underwater vessel design, and the question is whether they will use it for good or evil. Anyway, there is of course no obligation on you to sign it, so you can see what you think.

Now to another matter. You said to me once that if I met someone I couldn't live without, that I would have to leave the order. Well I'm afraid I think that's what's happened. Now I must emphasise that no sin has been committed, but we came close to it a couple of times if you know what I mean. In fact, if it wasn't for the presence of the Holy Father on the trip home the situation might have been a great deal worse by now. So I would like to formally ask you to release Joe and me from our vows, and if you could see your way to loosening up again what was tightened in heaven and turn Joe back into a woman that would be great, as I think it would be the most convenient for all concerned. In a way I kind of feel now that I've done what the Lord called me to the order to do, and so if I give up the monking life He will probably forgive me. He might even be relieved.

As for the future, I'll probably do a bit of fishing to tide us over, but Joe is all set on becoming a railway engineer like they had in the old days. He wants to know if he could get a scholarship to study at Kilkiernan, and I said I'd ask you about the possibilities. He's talking about getting the Albans to build a railway line down along the peninsula, all wind-powered clockwork, so not sinful. It all sounds a bit mad but Joe is highly capable as you know, so who can tell what he might come up with?

Anyway, I think that's all for now.

Yours in Christ,
Brother Christopher Columba

CHAPTER THIRTY-EIGHT

Far away in the snowy northern forests, on the very edge of the known world, lies the great crystal edifice of the Ice Palace, entombed in the indigo twilight of the Arctic winter. No footprints lie in the snow outside; no guards pace or dogs bark at the entrance, with its Doric columns of ice and wide wooden door. If you were to visit, you would probably find no sign of life at all in the Great Hall, save for the ticking of an old brass clock. But along an empty, slightly misty corridor with a snow floor, lined with carved ice statues of mythical beasts, you might just catch, floating in the frigid air, the faint sound of tinny, scratchy music:

> *You say it's only a paper moon*
> *Sailing over a cardboard sea*
> *But it wouldn't be make-believe if you believed in me.*

Acknowledgements

My grateful thanks are once again due to my translator colleagues for help with all kinds of things in the production of this book, particularly beta readers Liz Cencetti, Dagmara Meijers-Troller, Margaret Schroeder and Titia Schuurman for their very helpful comments and criticisms. Thanks also to Andrey Dorozhko (andreydrz.com) for the great cover picture, to Tam McTurk for help with Scots Gaelic, and to clockwork expert James Pekarek for useful comments on clockwork mechanisms.

There are many references in this novel to works by other writers, but it would be remiss of me not to mention my debt to *A Canticle For Leibowitz* by Walter M. Miller Jr., which I recommend to the reader.

Finally, thanks to my son Christopher for help with the cover design and for his promotional animations in Oculus Rift, to my daughter Catriona for marketing advice, and to my daughter Ciara for the moon.

About the author

Originally from Ireland, Billy O'Shea was educated at Trinity College Dublin and the University of Copenhagen. He has so far failed at being a grape-picker, a dishwasher, a dock worker, a TV sound technician, a diamond sorter, a pirate radio DJ, a musician, a translator and a writer. He lives in Copenhagen, Denmark, with his wife and three children.

If you have enjoyed *It's Only A Clockwork Moon* (or even if you haven't!), please consider leaving a review of the book on Amazon or Goodreads.

It's Only A Clockwork Moon is the second book in the *Kingdom of Clockwork* series. The paperback and audio versions of the books are available at the Round Tower of Copenhagen and from www.blackswan.dk. Kindle versions are available from Amazon.

Facebook community: facebook.com/KingdomOfClockwork